Polyphony

VOLUME 1

"*Polyphony* is like a box of fine chocolates. I devoured them all in one sitting—all the nutty caramels, the chewy nougats, and the ones with the tang of sweet orange in their centers. It's a rich collection indeed, with new work by, for instance, Andy Duncan, Carol Emshwiller, Leslie What, and absolutely fresh flavors from new writers such as Vandana Singh and Victoria Elisabeth Garcia. Every piece is a delight. Truly, you can open this book anywhere and know you'll be biting into a toothsome morsel. Impossible to say which are my favorites, but thankfully I don't have to choose. Just open the box of chocolates and dive in."

Molly Gloss
Author of *Wild Life*, *The Jump-Off Creek*, and *The Dazzle of Day*

"Face it: for the most part, SF, Fantasy and Horror—the genres of the ostensibly fantastic—have long ago hit the snooze button and rolled back over for a long lazy hibernation, while the world outside their bedchamber ferments and explodes in ways almost too bizarre to imagine. But now comes an irresistible wake-up call. The stellar new original anthology series *Polyphony* is a fizzy bottle of champagne sprayed across the sleepers' faces. Old hands—Shepard and Emshwiller—consort with newer writers—Duncan and McHugh—and first-timers—Singh and Garcia—to produce a slipstream banquet that is truly a many-voiced paean to the inexhaustible possibilities of the literature of the marvelous."

Paul Di Filippo
Author of *A Mouthful of Tongues*

"So far, most of the remarkable slipstream fiction being published today has been falling into the chasm between genre and literary fiction. Genre science fiction and fantasy magazines seem designed to put such stories only into the hands of people guaranteed to be disappointed by them; mainstream literary publications are uncomfortable with anything that carries the whiff of genre. *Polyphony* is the promised land for readers of the strange, miraculous, and speculative. Cross the river and enter."

John Kessel
Author of *Corrupting Dr. Nice*, *The Pure Product*, and *Good News from Outer Space*

(more)

"Polyphony means "many voices." Or "two or more independent melodic parts sounded together." This first volume of *Polyphony* lives up to both definitions. It offers an array of strong voices and arranges them so as to showcase not only their harmonies but also their distinctions. Established voices like Lucius Shepard's, Andy Duncan's, Carol Emshwiller's, and Maureen McHugh's chime provocatively with the haunting new voices of Victoria Elizabeth Garcia and Vandana Singh. The reader also hears terrific solos by Leslie What, Ray Vukcevich, Carrie Vaugh, Douglas Lain, and James Van Pelt, and a stunning 11-part recitative by Bruce Holland Rogers, a whole concert in itself.

"*Polyphony* is a stirring venture. Anyone attuned to first-rate storytelling will applaud its debut and eagerly await performances to come."

Michael Bishop
Author of *Brittle Innings, Blue Kansas Sky,* and the forthcoming *Brighten to Incandescence: 17 Stories*

"Leslie [What's] comic stories are indeed fun to read, but I've noticed quite often that there is a serious aftertaste when the bubbles and froth have disappeared. That's very nice. 'Blind Date With the Invisible Man' is one of those stories that linger afterward."

Kate Wilhelm

"Philip K. Dick would have admired Douglas Lain's 'The Sea Monkey Conspiracy,' and would have been unsettled by it, for the same reason—he would have seen himself in the alienated young narrator/protagonist. He might have argued that it's a sequel to—and perhaps better than—his 1979 story 'The Exit Door Leads in.'"

Paul Williams
Author of *Only Apparently Real: The World of Philip K. Dick*

Polyphony

VOLUME 1

DEBORAH LAYNE
PUBLISHER, EDITOR

JAY LAKE
ASSOCIATE EDITOR

 Wheatland Press
http://www.wheatlandpress.com

Polyphony

Published by

Wheatland Press

http://www.wheatlandpress.com

P. O. Box 1818
Wilsonville, OR 97070

Anthology copyright © 2002 by Wheatland Press
Introduction and headnotes copyright © 2002 by Wheatland Press
The Holy Bright Number (A Charlie Poole Story) by Andy Duncan © 2002 by Andy Duncan
How Lonesome Heartbreak Changed His Life by Lucius Shepard © 2002
        by Lucius Shepard and Electric Story
Blind Date With the Invisible Man by Leslie What © 2002 by Leslie What
Love Story by Ray Vukcevich © 2002 by Ray Vukcevich
Anthropology by Victoria Elisabeth Garcia © 2002 by Victoria Elisabeth Garcia
The Heroic Death of Lieutenant Michkov by Carrie Vaughn © 2002 by Carrie Vaughn
The Doctor by Carol Emshwiller © 2002 by Carol Emshwiller
The Sea Monkey Conspiracy by Douglas Lain © 2002 by Douglas Lain
The Room on the Roof by Vandana Singh © 2002 by Vandana Singh
Do Good by James Van Pelt © 2002 by James Van Pelt
Laika Comes Back Safe by Maureen McHugh © 2002 by Maureen McHugh
The Main Design That Shines Through Sky and Earth by Bruce Holland Rogers © 2002
        by Bruce Holland Rogers

Library of Congress Cataloging-in-Publication data is available upon request.
ISBN 0-9720547-0-7

Printed in the United States of America

Layout and cover design by John Elliott

CONTENTS

FOREWORD

We love short fiction—science fiction, fantasy, horror, mainstream, literary, humor and all the multiplying subgenres and offshoots that have spawned repeatedly since the *Epic of Gilgamesh* was first cut into wet clay along the banks of the Euphrates by some harried scribe with a too-dull stylus. We love the unusual stories that strike the reader a glancing blow and shoot off into the darkness of the cracks between literary categories. We love to find new venues that publish these cutting edge stories—what some people call "slipstream."

The bad news in publishing today is that the midlist has collapsed and the periodical market is contracting. The good news is that the electronic markets and advances in small press publishing and print on demand are widening opportunities for new and established writers. It seemed to be time to try an old idea yet again. Thus *Polyphony* was born in the dashboard lights along I-5 between Eugene and Portland, Oregon, out of a weekly writers' carpool discussion about markets, style and genre.

Some periodicals are friendly to slipstream fiction: electronic publishers *SCI FICTION* and *Strange Horizons*, commercial titles *The Magazine of Fantasy and Science Fiction* and *Asimov's Science Fiction*, and *Talebones*, as well as *Century* and *New Genre* among small press ventures. While we count all these publications among our aesthetic kin, none of them are exclusively dedicated to the sort of fiction we have in mind. Taking as our example Damon Knight's *Orbit* series from the 1970s, as well as contemporary series, *Starlight* and *Leviathan*, we decided to try to use the advances in small press publishing to produce a serial anthology that was self-consciously dedicated to the between-categories fiction we love so much.

While we wanted to publish stories that might not fit neatly into literary categories, we also wanted to react against the notion that writers of literary short fiction needn't be paid for their work. University-sponsored quarterlies and small-press literary magazines are under-marketed, hard to find, and parsimonious. Generally, they pay only in copies or nominal honoraria. This, we believe, is wrong. We went into this endeavor with a vow to pay word rates that would qualify as professional.

Armed with a commitment to pay professional rates and to find genre-jumping stories with strong literary values, we started issuing invitations to writers whose work we believed exemplified our editorial vision. The response was, to say the least, gratifying. Besides the established professional writers (including some of our personal favorites), the table of contents of this first volume also includes two previously unpublished writers, Victoria Elisabeth Garcia and Vandana Singh. We intend to continue to search for new writers in future volumes. While Volumes 1 and 2 are filled with invited stories, beginning with Volume 3 we will accept open submissions. We know there are plenty of good writers out there breaking genre boundaries and we are eager to meet them.

In assembling this volume, we were privileged to read an astonishing array of fiction. Some of it went further afield than our original vision. Some of it fell closer to the core of genre than we expected. All of it thrilled us. *Polyphony* has been a protean project, wrestled bodily from the tides of fiction.

Great and humbling assistance has been rendered by an array of writers, editors and just plain opinionated people. That fateful carpool was the one which takes us weekly to the meetings of the Wordos Professional Writers Workshop in Eugene, Oregon. We owe the Wordos a debt of gratitude for much more than their distant location. In particular, Bruce Holland Rogers has been a source of wisdom and encouragement from the beginning. Indeed, he was the first author to commit to writing a story for *Polyphony*. He has continued to offer advice and counsel with patience and wit. We were honored early on to receive the What!Lunch? Seal of Approval and we thank Leslie What for her faith and support. In fact, the support of all our authors has been invaluable. Other publishers and editors have also been quite willing to share their experience and to offer moral support along the way, especially Patrick and Honna Swenson of Fairwood Press.

Deborah's advice to anyone who wants to start a publishing venture is to be married to a web and design wizard. Her husband, John Elliott, did all the design work—from our web site to the book you are now holding in your hands—and made it look easy. Finally, our families have lived with this volume without complaining, and for that we are truly grateful. Jay thanks Susan and Bronwyn. Deborah thanks John and Nicholas.

Look for *Polyphony 2* in the spring of 2003, and *Polyphony 3* to follow in the fall of 2003. Visit us at `http://www.wheatlandpress.com`.

Literature has come a long way from the first dip of a willow stylus in the muddy river, but Enkidu still shambles through the shadows of imagination. Come with us to see where imagination leads us next.

Deborah Layne
Publisher, Editor

Jay Lake
Associate Editor

August, 2002
Portland, Oregon

INTRODUCTION TO

THE HOLY BRIGHT NUMBER
(A CHARLIE POOLE STORY)

ANDY DUNCAN

Andy Duncan's collection *Beluthahatchie and Other Stories* won the World Fantasy Award, as did his story "The Pottawatomie Giant." His stories have appeared in *Asimov's*, *Realms of Fantasy*, *SCI FICTION*, *Weird Tales*, *Starlight 1*, and *Starlight 3*. In 1998, Duncan was a finalist for the John W. Campbell Award for Best New Writer. Since then, a number of his stories have been honored: "Beluthahatchie" was a Hugo finalist; "The Map to the Homes of the Stars" was reprinted in *Best New Horror*; "The Executioners' Guild" was a Nebula and International Horror Guild finalist; "Fortitude" was a Nebula finalist; "Lincoln in Frogmore" was a World Fantasy Award finalist; "The Pottawatomie Giant" was a Nebula finalist and was reprinted in *The Year's Best Fantasy & Horror*; "The Chief Designer" was reprinted in *The Year's Best Science Fiction*; and "Senator Bilbo" was reprinted in *The Year's Best Fantasy*.

Charlie Poole was a legendary bluegrass banjo player who traveled through the Carolinas. Artists as diverse as Bill Monroe and Steve Earle count him among their influences. It's said that anyone who ever met Charlie Poole, even just to shake hands, came away with a story.

THE HOLY BRIGHT NUMBER
(A CHARLIE POOLE STORY)

ANDY DUNCAN

Once a high-yellow business girl named Clarissa lived in a dead cropper's place at the head of a trail in a hollow up Tobaccoville way. The trail was made by deer and widened by men and narrowed again by the mountain itself in the years after the last cropper died and burley leaf dropped cheaper than souse meat and the bank let the fields go to laurel and huckleberries, so as she picked her way up the hollow the first time, she must have been walking on faith that the way led anywhere at all. Or maybe instead she had no faith, and walked into the woods for that reason instead, which is another kind of faith and one often borne out in the hills. But walk she did, and was surprised or not by the one-room cabin she found at the head, and that very evening the folks on the other side of the ridge saw smoke pluming up from the dead cropper's chimney and resolved to coon-hunt elsewhere for a spell, for the dead have been known to kindle a fire. Soon the trail started widening up again, as fear of the dead lessened or grew, either way leading men all over the county to tramp the trail to pay their respects to Clarissa. On a chestnut stump at the edge of the clearing she set an unopened box of Red Devil Lye: on its side meant please abide; standing straight, no need to wait. Those who waited stood several trees apart, smoking, not speaking, each imagining himself alone between the great black woods and the lighted window.

One new-moon night when only a granddaddy coon could have found his way from the turnpike to the head of the hollow, a stranger named Charlie Poole sauntered up the trail whistling, banjo in one hand and bottle in the other. As he passed the Red Devil he kicked it over. When he reached the front door he kicked it open. "Whoa, now," said Clarissa as he plucked her up dripping and kicked the washtub a-slosh across the floor. Her wet cat shot onto the stove, snarling.

Later Clarissa said, "I got a good notion to gate that trail. How'd you find me in the pitch black dark?"

He fought free of the friendship quilt, grabbed the back of her head and said, "This dowsing rod here."

Later she said, "I purely hate a banjo."

"For the rest of your life on this round Earth," he said, "whenever you hear a banjo, that'll be me, talking."

Still later Clarissa padded naked as a jaybird through the dewy gray grass, snatched up the Red Devil box and carried it back to the porch. A groundhog watched her from the garden patch.

"Look, then," she told it, and went inside, slamming the door.

Months passed. Visitors got no farther than the stump, where, confused, they turned back. No one entered, no one left the hollow.

(Many years later, a young woman writing notes by hand amid a stack of books and records at a little desk in the college library in Chapel Hill asked herself what Charlie Poole could possibly have been doing for four and a half months in the spring and summer of 1924. The answer occurred to her even before she set pen to paper to record the question, and she snorted with laughter at herself, a sound that so emboldened the young stranger at the adjoining little desk that he peered over the partition and spoke to her. Whatever he said wasn't much, but it was enough.)

One afternoon in the cabin in the hollow, Charlie Poole was laughing fit to bust. Clarissa's tabby had decided his bouncing pecker was a play-pretty and was trying to jump up and bat it as Charlie galloped from one end of the cabin to the other, daylight breaking through the floorboards each time he landed, Clarissa's arms around his neck and her legs around his waist and her lips against his ear murmuring giddyup. But Charlie's laughter faltered and died as he slowed to a canter and then to a walk. Clarissa had to lick him to get his attention.

"Charlie! I said, let's fetch that tick and straw from the yard and get this bed back together. It's aired enough, and there's thunder coming."

"You hear it, too?" Charlie said, standing still.

When his pecker quit bobbing, the cat lost interest and went to wash itself under the stove. Clarissa slipped off Charlie's back and knelt beside the water bucket, drank deep from the dipper. "God damn, it's hot in here," she said. "Wish that storm would come on. Might break the weather a little."

"Ain't no storm," Charlie said. The way he said it made her look at him.

Another *boom boom boom* sounded, closer now, as if just the other side of the ridge. The canning jars rattled.

The cat yowled as Charlie trod its tail in getting to his clothes. The rocker righted itself a little at a time as Charlie relieved it of britches, brogans, shirt.

"Charlie," Clarissa said. "Charlie?"

The *booms* were in the hollow now, continuous and evenly spaced, like a heartbeat or a funeral march.

Charlie's gaze met hers for a second as he slipped on his braces. "You ain't dressed yet?" he asked.

One more deafening *boom*, then a silence painful to the ears.

A voice rumbled from the front yard.

"Charlie Poole, come out and be known to the Lord."

Clarissa stood, mouth open, arms at her side, staring at the door, heedless of her nakedness, of the dress Charlie was trying to thrust into her hands. He finally draped it over her shoulders like a shawl.

"Charlie Poole, come out."

A heavy *thump* like a body flung down made the porch boards groan and jumbled the knickknack shelf. A souvenir dish from the Natural Bridge fell to the hearth and smashed. Another *thump*, then another, coming closer. With each one a bit more daylight appeared beneath the door.

Clarissa was trying to put on the dress, really she was, but in her terror and her focus on the door her arms were leaden, and her fingers wouldn't work. It was like trying to button when she was a girl, while watching the contrary Clarissa in the head-to-toe mirror at the Federated store in

Winston.

Behind her, someone pounded on the sash, but she didn't look around. The whole floor of the house now sloped toward the door. Off balance, fearing she would pitch into the arms of whoever was now turning the handle, she instead fell backward onto the sagging ropes of the bed frame, where she clawed for purchase like a spider as the dress slithered to the floor.

The sudden breeze as the door swung open smelled of summer mud and honeysuckle. Filling the doorway, stooping to peer inside with deep-set ice-blue eyes, was the largest man Clarissa had ever seen.

He wore a bluish-white seersucker suit, jacket buttoned, pants creased as sharp as the ridge line, shirt collar hooked tight but no tie. His neck was as thick as Clarissa's waist, his jaw ponderous, his mouth wide and crooked like the glancing blow of an axe, his rectangular head made more so by his terrible haircut, razored so close that he was patchily bald. His nose and brow were lumpy, too much in them. Meeting his steady, shadowed gaze, Clarissa thought of two miners' headlamps deep down in the seam.

The well-dressed giant bared his teeth and said, "Evening," so loudly she flinched and so low in pitch that her bones vibrated.

The giant stepped inside, massive shoulders hunched, buzz-cut head sweeping dust from the ceiling. The little cabin rocked like a cradle as he moved about, gazed at the dimestore gifts that cluttered the shelves, the few dresses huddled in the chiffarobe, the stove battered as if clenched in a fist and unfolded again. Clarissa suddenly hated her whore's nest, and all it contained, and herself.

"No, you don't," the giant rumbled, his back to her. She gasped, the answer to her unspoken thought more invasive than this uninvited hulking presence among the scraps of her life.

The giant knelt and began picking up the shards of the Natural Bridge, piling them in a calloused palm. They clicked together like a cricket's legs. "You don't *hate* nothing, Clarissa," the giant said. "You're just *ashamed* of a right smart of it." He drew one last shard from between two floorboards, topped off the pile, then cupped his palms together and rocked them. "Afraid this plate here has been to breakfast," he said, looking mournful, but in his hands the bits looked less like fragments of something broken, a ripped jumper, the insides of a jack-o'-lantern, and more like fragments of something yet to be made, the squares of a quilt, kindling. The cat twined around the giant's ankle, purring, and rolled onto her back to present her belly.

"He lay down as a lion, and as a great lion," the giant recited. "Who shall stir him up?"

He closed his eyes, brought his cupped hands to his mouth and blew into them, his cheeks inflated like a child puffing out a candle. "Restore unto Clarissa this geegaw, O Lord," the giant said, and blew again, then opened his eyes and his hands. The smashed bits of plate were unchanged. The giant's whole face wrinkled as he beamed at Clarissa. "Indeed, the Lord's work is ever marvelous to behold," he said. "You got any glue?"

Sitting on the edge of the bed frame now, a rope burn streaking across her thigh, she shook her head.

The giant grunted and stood, shoved double handfuls of plate into his jacket pockets like a bashful suitor. "My name's Ralph Poole," he said. His smile faltered on "Poole."

Since the giant entered, Clarissa had not been studying about Charlie. But now, with a pang of guilt, she looked for him. She, the cat and the giant were alone in the room. The tatty curtains in the open window billowed in the rising breeze.

"Gone, of course," said the giant Poole, shaking his head just as she realized, with something like nausea, that Charlie Poole was never coming back. "No matter," the giant continued. "He ain't no harder to find than cigarettes and beer." He reached for the dipper, one huge hand enfolding the battered tin handle all the way to the bowl. He peered into the bucket as he stirred, the dipper clanking against the sides. "I reckon you know, Clarissa, that my little brother stinks like blinky milk. He is a varmint and a rakehell and a hard, hard man."

"I know him," Clarissa said, enraged — *I could have gone with him but you stopped me, somehow you stopped me* — and blinking back tears. "But I don't know you."

The giant Poole lifted the streaming dipper, swung it toward her. "Drink," he said.

The dipper rasped across her cheek once, twice, leaving a damp trail.

Still furious and sick at heart, she also was suddenly thirsty. She parted her lips. She drank the hot, metallic well water that had come to taste like home, looking into the giant's eyes as he gauged her throat movements and tipped the dipper steadily, unerringly, as if his arm were hers.

When she was done he dipped more water and poured it onto her upturned face, onto her shoulders, her chest, and somehow she felt calmer and less naked, not more. The water was colder now and she shivered, her body awakening despite herself, as the rivulets coursed down her arms and back and backside and legs. Empty dipper still in hand, the giant Poole regarded her nipples without expression, a look Clarissa knew well.

She weaved a bit as she stood. Wanting to hurt him, she spread her feet a bit farther apart for balance, put her hands on her hips and said, "It'll cost you."

The giant Poole's high-pitched chortle made Clarissa flinch and sent the cat streaking beneath the bed. "You think I don't know that?" the giant asked.

He scooped her dress off the floor one-handed and tossed it at her. She tried to snatch it from the air but her body caught most of it, the fabric plastering to her damp skin. She had no trouble putting it on. Then the giant handed her the cat. It lay draped across his hand, purring.

"Where are we going?" she asked.

"To get some glue."

Outside, the sun was past the ridge line, and a cloud was rolling through the hollow, spattering rain as it brushed the tops of the chestnuts and poplars. On the porch, leaning against the woodpile, were a gnarled walking stick and a double-headed, leather-handled drum. The giant reclaimed these as he passed. Clarissa held the cat close for warmth as she stepped from the porch onto the flat, mossy, rain-hollowed rock that served as a step, a puddle already collecting at its green center, and then onto the clover that long since had taken the grass. Splintered locust wood, then water and stone, a damp cushion of green — she stood for a moment on each, her bare feet digging imaginary toeholds to mark the place as hers forever, and then walked forward, following the mist-enshrouded figure of the giant along the path.

Entering the woods, the giant began to beat the drum one-handed with the stick, the steady *boom boom boom* flushing quail and squirrels and larger creatures, too, that crashed and slid and plopped out of sight as he advanced. Clarissa quickly saw that however she hurried, inviting stumbles over roots and thrashes among clinging, clammy leaves, the gap of twenty feet between her and the giant never closed, so instead she took her time, content with the drumbeat and the purring mass against her chest and the familiar underfoot treacheries of the trail. She tasted the rain and filled herself with the bullfrog-scented air.

In the thickest woods, just as Clarissa could only hear, not see, the giant before her, she heard another, more distant music: a banjo.

The drumbeats stopped, and Clarissa knew the march had stopped, too. She stood, swaying amid a copse of honeysuckle. She had not been lying when she told Charlie she purely hated the banjo and all the tunes he and Satan could commit with it, but he *would* play them, so she couldn't help but recognize this one – "Budded Rose," Charlie had called it.

"Too damn many notes flying out of this thing," he once said, sitting drunk on her porch wearing only his bowtie and picking the evening away. "Better catch 'em, now. Hear that? Here they come. That's *one* for your pocket, and *one* for your stove, and *one* for when you wake up hungry at night."

At first she thought this "Budded Rose" was coming from that very porch, but then it was ahead of her, and then off to the side toward the rock fall, and then downslope and sharing a laugh with the water in the branch. It was everywhere; it was nowhere. Nowhere. Hungry at night, indeed. She wept into the cat's fur, feeling as if she had awakened from the saddest of dreams.

Up ahead, the drumbeat resumed, and Clarissa walked forward again, though she was no longer following the giant but coincidentally walking along behind him. Clarissa was done following Pooles. The second had broken the spell of the first; now the first had broken the spell of the second. One day Clarissa would cast a third spell herself, and not on any damn Poole. Now if only Charlie's banjo would hush.

To her relief, the giant, with more volume than skill, at this point began to sing. The words matched the drumbeat exactly, as if they had been in his head all the time.

I want to join that holy bright number
I want to join that holy bright number
I want to join that holy bright number
And turn some ransomed one home.

They number one hundred and forty-four thousand
They number one hundred and forty-four thousand
They number one hundred and forty-four thousand
Oh, turn some ransomed one home.

The song was easily learned, and Clarissa sang along as she trudged down the hollow. Her voice grew louder, the giant's, fainter. By the time she reached the turnpike, a rutted silver scar leading into a gloom only deepened by the distant lights of Tobaccoville, the giant and his drum and his voice had melted away as if they had never been, and any stray fluttering notes of "Budding Rose" (*One for your pocket, and one for your stove*) were temporarily lost in the rattle and snarl of a pulpwood truck laboring up the grade. Clarissa held the squirming cat tighter as she stepped forward and stood, proud and ready, in the middle of the road. Standing straight, no need to wait. She forced herself to listen to nothing, squinted into the glow of the headlamps cresting the hill.

INTRODUCTION TO

HOW LONESOME HEARTBREAK CHANGED HIS LIFE

LUCIUS SHEPARD

Since 1985, when he won the John W. Campbell Award for Best New Writer, Lucius Shepard has been one of the most honored writers in science fiction, fantasy, horror and beyond. He won the World Fantasy Award for his collections *The Jaguar Hunter* (1987) and *The Ends of the Earth* (1991). In 1986 his novella "R & R" won the Nebula Award.

In the past year he has published two novels, *Colonel Rutherford's Colt* (an Ebook from Electric Story) and *Valentine*, as well as several novellas at *SCI FICTION*, the *SCIFI.COM* fiction project, including "AZTECHS," "Over Yonder" and "Emerald Street Expansions."

Shepard also writes a regular film (and film industry) review column for Electric Story; his reviews are online at www.electricstory.com.

Upcoming in 2003, Shepard has a mini collection of articles and stories about hobos called *Two Trains Running*, a short novel from Golden Griffin called *Louisiana Breakdown*, and a novel entitled *The Iron Shore*. Born in Virginia and raised in Florida, Shepard has lived in the Midwest, New England, New York and most recently the West Coast. His travels throughout the world are reflected in the exotic settings of much of his work, especially Latin America. He currently lives near a strip mall in Vancouver, Washington, but says he, "not for long..."

An earlier version of this story appeared in the *Electric Story* edition of Shepard's collection, *The Jaguar Hunter*.

HOW LONESOME HEARTBREAK CHANGED HIS LIFE

LUCIUS SHEPARD

"Jesus and the moneylenders," the journalist said to Mizell. "You know the story. Jesus tries that clear-out-the-temple shit here in Vietnam, they'll co-opt his Christian ass. They'll sit him down and say, 'Man, we don't care you preach, you prophesy, change puppy chow into peanut oil. If it feels good, do it. But if you're gonna take ten percent from the flock, we gotta have twenty percent off the top.' What choice does he have? These bastards are relentless. They'll break down anyone's moral fiber. So he agrees. Pretty soon they want a bigger percentage. Jesus has to increase the tithe to keep his operation going. And the flock, they gotta start hustling so they can pony up their end. Before you know it the Man From Galilee is running smack in from Laos and pimping Chinese girls just so he can get his message across."

"It's not that bad," Mizell said absently. He reminded himself to check on Anna — she'd been in the ladies room a long time.

"You're used to it is all." The journalist shifted in his chair, studying Mizell with what seemed wry conjecture. "Me, I'm still in a state of amazement."

Mizell couldn't tell if he was being fucked with, whether the journalist was doing real attitude or simply trying out new material. He had a dark, Mediterranean face that was difficult to read. Curly black hair and a bushy, graying mustache and an old livid scar along the jaw line under one ear. The face of someone, Mizell imagined, who might in weak moments consider himself a romantic figure. He was dressed for low-end travel — jeans, an olive T-shirt — and carried a leather shoulder bag.

"There's this cop I ran into, okay," he said. "I mean, this is the essence of the situation right here...this cop. He stands out front the New World Hotel from dawn till, y'know, nine, ten o'clock at night. Every day. His entire job is to hand out tickets to people who run red lights, and to extort extra money. One day the power goes out, the traffic lights stop working. No red lights, no bribes. No job. He doesn't give a thought to unsnarling the traffic jams and shit, he just goes home. That's the end of his responsibility. It's the Vietnamese way. You can't fucking escape it."

He asked if Mizell wanted another beer. Mizell said No, and tried once again to remember the journalist's name. He'd forgotten it the instant he heard it, because he hadn't expected they would be spending much time together.

They had met an hour before outside Zee Bar in Saigon, a yuppie spawning ground where no one did any serious drinking. They had taken a table amid potted palms and aqua lighting and piped-in lounge music in a dim corner of the place, which was almost deserted at that hour of the afternoon. When the journalist learned they were driving to Vung Thao, he had begged a ride. Mizell did favors for a living; he took the occupation seriously, carried cards with his fax and phone numbers, and cultivated a casual, approachable look, kind of an aging surfer thing, so as to encourage business. The thought of doing a favor for free — even such a small one — caused him to hesitate; but he decided that having the journalist along would help pass time on the drive. It was for sure Anna wouldn't be up to conversation.

"What are you looking for in Vung Thao?" he asked, and the journalist said he wanted to find the rave — someone had told him there was going to be a rave out that way.

"I heard about this guy calls himself Lonesome Heartbreak," he said. "Crazy fucker dresses up like Roy Rogers and plays guitar."

"Oh, yeah," said Mizell. "He'll be around. The DJs always give him a slot. Everybody loves a freak."

"You know him?"

"I did business with him once. They screwed up his visa and I helped him get an extension. He seemed like an interesting guy. I was still curious about him, so I broke into his van and checked him out."

The journalist had turned his attention to the bar, where a couple of thirtyish occidentals with gelled hair were talking into cell phones; now he cut his eyes toward Mizell. "Wow," he said mildly. "You must have been extremely curious."

"Just keeping up to date." Mizell took a swig of beer.

"So what was in the van?"

"Relics of his dead wife. Photographs. A bronze urn full of ashes. A clipping from the *London Times*. She was killed crossing a street in Highsmith. Hit by a car. The stuff was arranged on this sort of altar. I got the idea he's completing the around-the-world trip they were on. Their honeymoon. Like it's this ceremonial deal."

Mizell examined the check. "The Japanese kids who hang out at Vung Thao tend to disavow him. They consider him an embarrassment."

The journalist mulled this over, then asked if he'd ever been to Japan.

"The consensus society." Mizell made a sour face. "Not for me."

A new song from the speakers. Green jungle noises, bird calls, vibraphone notes simulating rain, and a girl singing whispery and frail, complaining to whoever would listen that love was transitory, the world in disarray, everything was so very, very sad. One of the yuppies at the bar said something in a loud voice; the other laughed. The bartender, scarcely more than a silhouette against a neon-lit mirror, held a glass up to the light for inspection. And as if central to this little movement, Anna stepped out of the bathroom, walking with exaggerated languor, the way she always did when she was trying to hold it together, gliding past the yuppies, presenting her slim, cool, silvery blond, astrally disengaged Nordic princess self for their review. The zipper of her jeans was open, spoiling the effect.

She sat down next to Mizell. Lowered herself deliberately, cautiously, as if expecting something to go wrong, the chair to lurch, hit her in the ass and send her floating head over heels into nowhere. The air conditioning was full-on crispy, but a sweat had broken on her brow. Mizell asked if she was okay. She gave him an unsteady smile and crossed her legs, still cautious in her movements, exploring her space. Her eyelids drooped, but he could see the green irises, pupils reduced to BBs.

The journalist was giving her his X-Ray look—to distract him, Mizell asked what he was writing about.

"Fuck, I dunno. I was going to write what it's like to come here, this place with all the evil history, y'know, from the viewpoint of someone who missed the big event of his generation 'cause he was running around Greenwich Village with a peace sign on his back, trying to get laid." He shot a dubious look at Mizell, as though anticipating disapproval.

"It seems kind of impure," Mizell told him.

"Impure...yeah." The journalist laughed. "It's turning into a goddamn self-flagellation tour. I don't know what I'm doing in this fucking place."

Two fat, sunburned, bearded men in jeans and T-shirts nosed through the Zee's front door, letting in gas fumes and traffic noise. They wore baseball caps on which the names of Marine units were embroidered. After a brief look round, they about-faced and tried to wedge through the door at the same time, shouldering one another off-balance in their haste to leave.

"You don't see too many black vets around," the journalist said. "Ever notice that?"

Mizell shrugged. "Must be the black guys have better things to do."

A degree of energy had returned to Anna's face, but she wasn't yet capable of speech. She made a weak noise in her throat and then appeared to have difficulty swallowing. The journalist was studying her. That pissed Mizell off, that he would catalogue her, turn her into an anecdote. "We should go," he said.

"When this guy suggested I look you up," said the journalist, "I wasn't going to do it. I like to find my own way. But I'm glad I did."

"Because I'm giving you a ride?"

"I'm impressed with your level of involvement...the quality of your information. You are as advertised."

"Shouldn't we go?" Anna's eyes were fixed on her right forefinger, watching it go tap tap tap on the tabletop, as if amazed by her control. "I want to drive, Bobby. Is it all right if I drive?"

"Maybe the second leg," said Mizell.

The journalist dug out his wallet, selected a couple of bills. "Yeah, the guy told some stories about you, man. Made you out to be this miscreant superhero. Mister Connected. The Man Of A Thousand Phone Numbers."

"I'm okay to drive," Anna said.

Mizell's curiosity was piqued; he asked the journalist who had described him so.

"I drive better than you," Anna said petulantly. "You always drive too slow."

"I don't know," said the journalist. "Some guy...I forget his name."

In the days following the war, Vung Thao had served as a resort for Russian bureaucrats and their wives. They had stayed at a hotel constructed for their exclusive use, a pink stucco cake of a building that would not have been out of place in 1930s California, three stories of white balconies and French doors, and a red tile roof set on the beach among landscaped palms and hibiscus, fronted by an outdoor cafe. The cafe was lit by necklaces of colored light bulbs strung on bamboo poles, and at the tables, each sprouting a pink and white umbrella from a hole at its center, pale men in ill-fitting suits had sweated and sipped vodka in the company of diminutive cadres with red stars on their caps, plotting the course of the new Marxist Wonderland.

Mizell wished he had lived in that Vietnam; he believed that in the rawness of victory there had been a spirit that would have nourished him. Not of hope, certainly. The Vietnamese were too unsentimental to buy into hope. Perhaps an elated defiance that made hope unnecessary. A feeling that would provide momentum. Which was what Mizell needed. His life had evolved into a series of lazy orbits, like that of a fly circling a sweet spoilage, landing now and again to take sustenance, rising up to mate and buzz, eventually confronted by menace, then darting away to the next rotten treat. Ten years of this. Goa to Indonesia to Vietnam. Growing expert in the hierarchies of minor officialdom and lesser criminals, trading in the currency of information, of knowing who to bribe in whatever contingency, who had the best drugs, the most beautiful girls, their weaknesses, the extent of their power. It was something he'd fallen into, something he'd learned he had a talent for. Doing a favor for a friend in Goa had turned a college graduation trip into a decade of dissolute commerce. Though he took pride in his ability to negotiate, to manipulate, it dismayed him to realize that he had become a creature appropriate to the current incarnation of the hotel: its balconies crumbling; umbrellas faded; catering to young travelers such as filled the cafe that night. Overweight British girls with fanny packs, sober Swedish youth, French guys with wispy beards and wire-rimmed glasses, insufferably cheerful, beer-swilling Aussies, American dopers, post-teen Greenpeaceniks out to earn a merit badge in reality by hiking the Ho Chi Minh Trail. Like them, Mizell was part of the new invasion flowing into Vietnam, wielding the ultimate weapon of a bland, brightly-colored, alluring culture to smash all resistance, winning the final battle of the war with hardly a casualty. Unlike the rest, he had no plans for withdrawal, no degree program to which he might return, no job prospects or career track, just a few vague designs concerning the immediate future — a new apartment, detox for Anna, and the recognition that a plan might be necessary.

It was full dark by the time they reached the hotel. They grabbed a table at the cafe, the only one available, on the edge of the beach, where flagstones gave out into mucky yellow sand. A poor location if you were thirsty or hungry: The Vietnamese waiters were not highly motivated, spending most of their time smoking beneath the paper lanterns that overhung the entrance to the hotel, and rarely did they respond to signals from patrons sitting far from their station. At the adjoining table — two tables pulled together, actually — were a dozen or so twenty-somethings, cleancut boys and girls who were given to hugging one another and jabbered away madly, eagerly. Happy animals at play. Given their uniform age and appearance, Mizell thought that they must be members of a group, some church- or university-sponsored excursion. The journalist cast a disconsolate eye on them and with a gesture that included the entire cafe, all the motley assemblage, said, "Everywhere I go I wind up falling in with these people. I guess I don't spend enough money on hotels."

"You could do worse." Anna looked annoyed and Mizell could relate — the journalist's habit of editorializing his negativity had become grating.

"Hell, yes," said the journalist. "This place is so sad and fucked up, you can always do worse. It's different up north, but once you drop below the Seventeenth Parallel, it's a theme park of defeat. Everybody tells the same goddamn story. Re-education camp. Lost their wife or their brother, and now they're living in a dormitory. One of their kids blown up by an old land mine. And then you've got all the bonehead ex-pats and their business. The Vietnamese form of hideous business. Even the expats you meet, the ones who're not boneheads...like this couple I met in Hue. This twenty-seven year old Yalie and his perfect girlfriend. Getting rich from booking Filipino bands all over Asia and tootling around on their motorbikes. I mean there was nothing wrong with them, they were nice people. They were just somehow horrifying. The war wasn't even on their radar screen."

Anna sniffed, disgusted. "We must be horrifying, then. The war's not on our radar screen, either."

"All that perspective you've got happening must be a pain in the ass," said Mizell. "You should relax. Go with the moment."

The journalist said, "That's your secret, is it?"

Mizell thought it best not to respond.

Out over the water, a bloated bone-china moon was sailing among low clouds, and there was a heavy brine smell. From behind the hotel came a blast of techno that veered into distortion, followed by an amplified voice giving instructions: a sound check in progress. The clicks and pops from the PA seemed connected to fluctuations in the heat. Sweat trickled down Mizell's neck, soaked the back of his shirt.

Anna touched his arm, pointed to a slender middle-aged man in a suit of beige linen standing off among the tables, his hair trimmed to stubble. Tanned; sharp-featured; with a prissy set to his mouth. "David!" she called. The man spotted her, hurried toward them.

"Don't get pushy. All right?" Mizell said to her. "Just let it happen."

"I'll be fine." She said this airily and that worried Mizell. He thought he detected a looseness in her, evidence of some new unraveling.

"Remember what we know about this bastard," he said.

"I'll be *fine!*" She poisoned him with a stare, then smiled at the man as he came up, stood and embraced him.

"Mistuh Mizell!" The man draped an arm about Anna's shoulder and beamed. "I 'preciate you givin' Anna a ride. I would have sent my car, but I had so much to deal with heah."

Mizell told him it wasn't a problem.

The man gave the journalist a cursory glance, then favored Mizell with an oily, good buddy smile. "Well, I 'preciate it anyway. I hope we'll get a chance to chat later. In fact, let's make a point of it." He looked to Anna.

"Shall we?"

The journalist watched them walk away. "That's a seriously attractive woman." Then, after a pause: "What's up with you two? I started out thinking she's your girlfriend, but now I don't get it."

"She works for me. Guys tell her things. Sometimes they tell her things I can use."

"But she sleeps with you, too."

"When she feels like it. When we both feel like it."

"She works for you, sleeps with you, and" — the journalist held up three fingers — "you keep her high."

"She keeps herself high," Mizell said testily. "I know her head's not right. I can't do much except try to protect her."

The journalist gave a rueful shake of his head. "The amount of brain damage in this country is fucking unbelievable," he said.

Mizell tended to agree, but doubted they were thinking about the same thing. He tapped a passing waiter on the arm, asked for a beer. The waiter — a man with a face so crumpled by age, it was impossible to discern his expression — recoiled. As he scuttled away, Mizell realized that he had touched an old napalm scar on the man's arm, the skin bubbled, mottled, like pink plastic and crispy bacon melted together.

"Where'd you meet her?" asked the journalist. "Saigon?"

"Djakarta. She had trouble with the police. I put the police captain together with a Malaysian businessman who helped him with a project. Afterward, Anna and I hooked up and came here."

"So what you do now, your business, you were doing it back then, huh? Why'd you leave Djakarta?"

"The more you learn about a place, the deeper the shit you're stepping in. Things get too heavy, it's best to move on. Find some place less complicated."

"Like Vietnam?"

"Like Vietnam used to be five, six years ago."

"That's when you came here?"

"I got in on the ground floor." Mizell said this with relish, knowing it would irritate the journalist.

The group at the adjoining table, who had also been having trouble getting a waiter's attention, began to sing an old Bob Dylan song, "You

Gotta Serve Somebody," linking their arms, swaying to the tune. The journalist hunched his shoulders, as if preparing to absorb a blow. "How's Vietnam different now?" he asked.

"Things are starting to get deep. Like this guy Anna's checking out. The side of grits she left with. Guy's name is David Moskowitz. He's the new breed of hustler. We used to just get con artists and drug dealers. Moskowitz marks an evolution. He was under suspicion for counterfeiting tickets and a couple of murders back in the States. Now he's into concert promotion over here."

The singers brayed out the chorus, and two of the women hugged one another, as if enlivened by the notion of service. A gust of wind blew in off the water, setting the colored light bulbs to bobbing. Glass broke close by, a girl shrieked, and Mizell caught a sweet scent on the wind, like incense curling in from a blackness that reached to China. He tipped back his head, closed his eyes, and tried to find its end.

"You went to college, right?" said the journalist. "What'd you major in?"

"Jesus!" said Mizell. "You doing my biography?"

"It's how I get to know people! I ask questions."

"I was raised in Denver by a single-parent mom. Turn-offs? Prison rape and yappy little dogs. When I'm feeling blue, I jerk off and read Flaubert. I don't have a favorite color."

"If that's how you want to come across, it's cool with me."

"I don't want to 'come across' at all, man. I don't want to be in your fucking article!"

"Don't get paranoid! I'll change the details. No one'll know it's you. Anyway, chances are you'll be cut out of the piece. Editors love to cut my shit."

Mizell decided that he really needed that beer. He waved at the idling waiters, but they continued to ignore him. "I majored in theatrical arts. Film," he said, turning back to the journalist. "I was planning to direct."

The journalist smiled. "Who can guess the purposes of fate?"

"Exactly!" said Mizell.

"So when you got into all this, the business stuff, it's like you asked yourself, What's better than making movies?"

"And what was my answer?"

"Being in the movies."

Mizell refused to embrace the notion that he might be a role player, but could not entirely reject it. "I don't know...maybe."

"Sure you did. It's the height of slacker romance. Playing games on the dark side, lost in the mystic Orient."

"Now I'm a slacker, huh?"

"Beats me," said the journalist, and for the first time in a long while, he smiled. "Could be you're just faking."

A stage had been erected in the jungle behind the hotel, supporting a battery of speakers that in the confusion of strobes and colored spotlights resembled black doorways leading off into the dense vegetation behind them. The DJ was a shadowy figure at his boards, and the crowd — several hundred strong — staggered and hopped, crawled, danced, and perpetrated sexual assault beneath a canopy of palms, amid scents of opium, ganja, perfume, and delirium. Early in the proceeding, Mizell caught sight of Anna. Watching her charm Moskowitz, he remembered when things had been different, not just business and the occasional fuck. They'd never had any big problems. Their addictions, her dope and his extra-legal games, had served both as defenses against real intimacy and a reason to stay together. The relationship had not taken much effort to maintain; in fact, it had always been the easiest thing to do, a loose undemanding partnership. Without ever crossing each other's borders, traveling on needles and adrenaline, they had co-depended their way across Asia. Yet there had once been a feeling of bright quiet involved in their closeness that might have transformed them. He doubted it was accessible any longer; if it was, something drastic would be needed in order to salvage it.

About an hour into the set, Lonesome Heartbreak walked on stage and plugged in his Telecaster. Short and muscular; his black hair was trimmed into bangs, hanging down over his neck, and this, along with his air of defiance and disdain, lent his broad face a trollish aspect. He wore a white silk cowboy shirt with red fringe along the sleeves, red slacks, and white cowboy boots, and was outfitted with a headset mike. He strummed a chord pulsing with reverb and began to sing a Buddy Holly song, "Heartbeat", in an easy tenor with barely a trace of accent. He sang each successive verse with increased fervor, rolling his eyes up to the palm crowns, moving with crabby quickness about the stage, a clownish figure, yet touching for his intensity, his commitment to the song. Then as he laid into the final verse his performance came unraveled. Discords shattered the progressions. His voice rasped, cracked, rose into a scream, and he hunched over the guitar, face contorted with effort. The crowd pressed close, pumping their fists and shouting as he screamed the word "heartbeat" over and over. Throat-tearing screams so genuine in their grief, they generated in Mizell the desire to join in, to vent some blood emotion that had been hibernating inside him and now, though there was no article of despair to which it attached—no obvious one, at any rate—was stimulated to waking by this powerful influence.

Lonesome Heartbreak unstrapped his guitar and tossed it into a speaker, producing a squall of feedback. He fell to his knees, fists clenched on his thighs. Sweat trickled down his face, pasting his bangs to his forehead, and he continued to scream. Such vicious insults to the larynx, Mizell half-expected to see blood jet from his mouth. At length the screams grew weak; the DJ brought his own music up under them, making them danceable. The journalist pulled Mizell away from the stage to a spot where normal speech was possible. "I should talk to this guy," he said. "Wanta introduce me?"

"Okay...sure," said Mizell, thinking it might be interesting to see how the journalist would handle the assignment. "But I might leave you alone with him. I want to check on Anna."

They made their way through the fringes of the crowd, clumps of giggling stoners, couples dry-humping against palm trunks, and walked along the beach toward the spot where Lonesome Heartbreak usually parked his van, slogging through sand still wet from an afternoon rain. The journalist, as he did whenever there was a void to fill, went back to talking in disparaging terms about Vietnam, recounting a conversation with the owner of a ceramic tile company he'd met in the pool at the Hotel Rex, yet another tale of graft and corruption.

"What did you expect?" Mizell asked. "A happy marriage between Walt Disney and the Workers' Paradise?"

"I expected something vital. But this place...it's the sort of karmically endangered place where bad things are supposed to happen. Terrible things. And they did. But that's over now. The moving finger has moved on. All that's left is leftovers. Another broken anthill where nothing important will ever happen again."

They walked a minute in silence.

"Know the worst thing I've heard since I've been here?" said the journalist. "I mean it's not actually the worst, but it's a hell of a symptom. Don Johnson...you know Don Johnson? The guy from Miami Vice? He bought an island off the coast. Just off Saigon. He's building his fucking dream house."

"Yeah...so?"

The journalist looked at him with consternation. "What is it with you people?"

"'You people?'"

"Generation Yeah...So?, or whatever the fuck you're calling yourselves. It's like history began for you at puberty. You have no sense of impropriety. Everything is everything else."

"I have to admit," Mizell said, "we lack an emotional center."

"Don't you worry. Something'll come along."

The moon had risen higher, clearing the clouds, and in its light the van, an ancient VW showing pale gray, standing at the base of a dune topped by tall grasses, looked as idiosyncratic as its owner. Speckled with decals from dozens of countries, dinged, battered, the windows blacked out. The words LONESOME HEARTBREAK'S WORLD TOUR were painted in fat cartoonish letters on the side. As they waited the journalist broke out a joint and offered it to Mizell, who declined. The journalist lit up, coughed and hacked and said "Aw, shit!" Then, once his coughing had subsided: "This is fucking mutant weed. No wonder we got our asses kicked." Wind rushed through the grasses atop the dune; the journalist tipped his head to the side, listening to it sigh. "I hear choppers," he said and laughed softly. On a whim Mizell changed his mind and begged a hit off the joint, drew the smoke deep. Seconds elapsed and he heard no choppers. If they were ghosts they were non-mechanical, liquid and slithery. Vietnamese. He did a couple more hits. The journalist was right. It was mutant weed.

Ten minutes drained away before Lonesome Heartbreak came trudging along the beach with his head down. His shirt was flung over one shoulder, guitar in hand. When he spotted them his step faltered, then came forward again, passing by without a word. He unlocked the van and slid back the side door. He was more heavily muscled than Mizell had thought, his upper body developed like a weightlifter's. After watching him on stage, it was strange to be this close. Mizell imagined he could feel all that suppressed emotion, a vibration, an almost impalpable radiation.

"Remember me?" Mizell asked. "I helped you out with that visa problem?"

"I remember." The words were half-grunted, the tone used by movie samurai to rebuke subordinates or confess an egregious sin.

"I've got this guy here wants to write something about you for a magazine."

Lonesome Heartbreak struggled into a T-shirt, one imprinted with his image and an announcement of the World Tour, and stared gravely at the journalist. "American magazine?"

"*The New Yorker*," said the journalist.

Lonesome Heartbreak pursed his lips and nodded slowly, thoughtfully. "Sure...write what you want."

"I need to ask you some questions." The journalist moved a step closer. "From what I hear, your performances...they're a kind of tribute to your fiancée. She died in an accident, I believe?"

Lonesome Heartbreak made a guttural noise, a noise of animal perturbation. "You the asshole break into my van?"

"No!" The journalist cast an anxious look at Mizell. "It's just what I heard. Some guy told me I met in a bar."

"Same motherfucker break into my van, I bet." Lonesome Heartbreak rested his guitar in the sand, the neck leaning against the passenger door.

"Her name Mayumi Ishida. We go drinking in London. Very drunk. Too drunk. On the way home..." He performed a quick movement of his right hand, lifting it above his head with a flourish, the gesture an actor might choose to signal a dramatic impatience. "I was big fool. I know love. Not death. Not grief. Only love. Now I understand these things." He sat in the open door of the van and rested his hands on his knees, looking down at the sand. "Now I understand," he repeated in a dull voice. "So I must change my life. I travel, I play. Sometime"—he glanced not at the journalist, but at Mizell, and spoke more assertively—"sometime she with me. Not far. I touch her. I know her like she is alive." His voice lost energy again. "But she not there."

Mizell was embarrassed to see him so exposed. It was even more complete an exposure, he thought, than he had managed on stage. The journalist seemed unaffected. "When you say you've changed your life," he said, "do you mean when you return home, you're going to take up some new occupation?"

Lonesome Heartbreak glared at him, but said nothing.

"Going by the decals on your van, I figure you're on the last leg of your trip. When you get home, what are you planning to do?"

Lonesome Heartbreak got to his feet and addressed him with a curt bow. "I piss," he said, and stalked off behind the van.

Once he had passed out of sight, the journalist said, "It's like grief's a choice for him. You get that, man? The old bushido thing. Yukio Mishima. The son of a bitch is on a death trip. He gets duded up like Hank Williams and goes around doing this self-abnegation shit. When he's had enough, he does the deed...he offs himself."

"Naw, I'm not getting it," said Mizell. "Seems like a leap."

"It's pretty damn clear to me."

"Why don't you ask him about it?"

"I just did, man! But I'm not gonna push it. I don't want to torture the guy."

"His English sucks. You don't know what he's thinking."

The moon brightened, as if a film had been washed from its surface, and the candy pink hotel, its top floor visible above the palms, glowed like a fairy castle. A succession of wavelets, little black surges edged with foam and furtive light, slopped onto the shore. Lonesome Heartbreak came out from behind the van and sat back down, hands on knees. Mizell, stirred by a boost of curiosity similar to the one that had inspired him to break into the van, hunkered down beside him. "My friend has a theory," he said. "He thinks when you get home you're going to commit suicide. He thinks your trip is a prelude to that."

"Pre...lude." Lonesome Heartbreak apparently did not know the word.

"Something you have to do before you die."

Stiffly, like an idol coming to life, Lonesome Heartbreak turned a scowling face to him. Mizell recalled a Diane Fossey documentary he'd seen, Diane sitting beside the alpha male, displaying submissive behavior, while the gorilla peered intently at her, perhaps attempting to understand their differences. He imagined he detected a charred residue in the darks of the man's eyes, the old shocks of disaster, and the thought of death, a shadow standing among ebony pillars, waiting to step into conscious light, real yet not real, like the wind in tall grasses.

"Why you want to know?" asked Lonesome Heartbreak, the words enunciated haltingly.

Mizell tried to manufacture an answer that would not be an outright lie. "Maybe I need to know." Saying this, he felt spooked, oddly sensitized, as if what he'd said was true.

Lonesome Heartbreak came abruptly to his feet, went to the rear of the van and flung the doors open. He beckoned to Mizell, but the journalist responded more quickly and Mizell was forced to peer over his shoulder into the van. The bronze urn, the newspaper clipping and the photographs set within an antique wooden cabinet—it was all the same as before; but whereas on his first visit to the van he had been clinical in his observations, this time he saw in the relics the shape of a life, the vital absence they sustained by the magic of their arrangement, like a pentagram enclosing a trapped spirit. His eye went to a photograph of Mayumi Ishida in a schoolgirl uniform, possibly a graduation picture, then to another showing her posed coquettishly in a miniskirt. A third displayed her holding a drink, laughing wildly, three other laughing, apparently drunken girls with their faces pressed closed to hers. Though she was tiny—this demonstrated by a fourth photograph that depicted her standing next to Lonesome Heartbreak—her features were not typically Japanese, but Eurasian. High delicate cheekbones. Dark lustrous eyes. Fey and sexy. She was here, Mizell thought. Gathered somehow.

"You see?" Lonesome Heartbreak asked him.

Mizell said, "Yeah," but he didn't see, not really. Nor was he sure whether the man was asking for validation or advice. His head was clogged by a weird despondency. It seemed to stem from no internal source; it was as if he had stumbled into a poisonous cloud, or maybe a cloud that had cleared his head of poison and made him aware of a heretofore undetected misery.

"I no see," Lonesome Heartbreak said. "Soon, maybe. But now..." He shook his head glumly.

Advice, then. He might want to know if Mizell could help him see what

he could not. He must be desperate, Mizell thought. Or else he perceived
the procurement of a visa extension to be an existential dilemma equivalent
to the question of self-destruction. Which maybe it was. The moon
dimmed, and the photographs and the urn and the clipping appeared to be
floating, trembling against the darkness. Mizell expected a voice to
manifest. A sign. Any second now.

"What *do* you see?" the journalist asked in what Mizell took for an
inappropriately light-hearted manner. Annoyed, he started to say, Nothing,
but checked himself, fearing this might have a bad effect on Lonesome
Heartbreak. "Life," he said in a tone that to his own ears sounded terribly
unconvincing.

"Yeah, she was a beautiful woman." The journalist made an operatic
gesture and with what seemed genuine sincerity, said to Lonesome
heartbreak, "Mayumi, man. She's beautiful."

Lonesome Heartbreak grunted and closed the van doors. Relieved,
Mizell said, "I have to check on Anna."

The journalist glanced at him anxiously. "You going back to Saigon
tonight?"

"I doubt it."

"Can I catch a ride in the morning?"

"Yeah, I guess...if we're still around. I mean, you better have a back-up
plan. I can't promise what Anna wants to do."

"Hey, if it's too much trouble..."

Mizell snapped at him. "I'm not sure what's going on, okay?"

"Whatever."

The journalist shouldered his bag and gazed off toward the hotel. The
pot had made Mizell feel uncertain, incompetent to act. He was still annoyed
at the journalist, yet ashamed at having given in to annoyance. He watched
Lonesome Heartbreak lock the doors, stuck in the place and moment.

"Hey," The journalist nudged Mizell. "There's your woman now."

David Moskowitz, his suit jacket flapping in the breeze, was hustling
toward them along the beach; he was hauling Anna by the wrist. Bringing
up the rear was a long-haired Vietnamese kid wearing an orange T-shirt
and cream-colored slacks. As they came near, Moskowitz gave Anna's arm
a tug and sent her sprawling into the sand. He stepped close to Mizell, so
close that only his eyes were in focus.

"You wanna know my business?" he shouted. "Fuck you! You wanna know *my* business?" He shoved Mizell back against the van.

"The hell's your problem?" Mizell started toward Anna, who lay where she had fallen, staring vacantly at them — it was plain that she had done up again. Moscowitz gave him another shove. The Vietnamese kid had taken a stand about ten feet away; in his right hand was something black and snub-nosed. The journalist edged toward the slope of the dune. Lonesome Heartbreak folded his arms and looked on without expression.

"Man, you need to employ a more accomplished actress," said Moskowitz. "Your bitch is way too smacked out to do good work." He pitched his voice high and sugary. "'David, do you have any contacts in Laos? David, can you get me some heroin?'" He let out a brittle laugh that seemed to rekindle his anger. "Fuckin' amateurs! Fuck were you thinkin', messin' with me?"

Mizell calculated his chances of taking the gun. Judging by his rapid shifts in mood, Moskowitz's heart was probably playing hip-hop beats, fueled by a potpourri of stimulants; but the Vietnamese kid looked solid.

Moskowitz adjusted the hang of his jacket and pointed to Anna. "Meryl Streep heah informs me you're a fountain of knowledge concernin' Saigon. You're a conduit. You perform a service. Izzat right?"

"I like to know where I live."

"Do you now? Wellsir, I intend to be a blank spot on your map. One of those mysterious Abandon All Hope Ye Who Enter places. You unnerstand?"

"That's what you want..."

"That is most definitely what I want. Don't you fuckin' forget it!" Moskowitz paced toward the water, glanced back to Mizell.

"Know what else I want? I can use a smart young fella like yourself. Somebody knows all the back doors and the bear traps."

Maybe, Mizell thought, what had been unthinkable in Djakarta and Goa was do-able in Vietnam. Maybe he was ready to step up to the next level.

"You still theah, ol' son?" Moskowitz peered at him, his lean face washed pale by the moonlight. "We didn't lose you, did we?"

"I was wondering if it would be possible to work for you."

Moskowitz's expression was one of mock incredulity. "Did I lead you to believe I was offerin' you a job? No way, chico! You're being shanghaied."

"If it gives you a kick," Mizell said, "I can swear eternal fealty. But I thought you might appreciate a measured response. Y'know, one based on an estimate as to whether I can keep both you and my contacts happy."

Moskowitz studied him a moment, chuckled. "Am I gon' wind up likin' you? I'd purely hate that."

"Life's funny that way."

After a pause Moskowitz nodded as if to affirm an unspoken conviction. "Theah are so many threads here, I'm not sure I can deal with them all. I'm not sure it's worth it." He cut his eyes toward the Vietnamese kid, then back to Mizell. "Let me have a sample."

Mizell didn't understand.

"A sample of your expertise. A taste," Moskowitz said. "So I can determine your value. It's common practice among drug dealers."

"I'm not a drug dealer."

"Yes, but *I* am. So humor me."

He was being offered, Mizell realized, an opportunity to fuck Moskowitz up. It was a test, but no matter how slick Moskowitz believed himself to be, he was a new guy, out of his depth, and if Mizell was careful, he could set him up for some real tragedy. There would be risk, though.

"I'm waiting," Moskowitz said.

Mizell grew suddenly tired of Moskowitz, more tired of himself, of his games, his folly, and it was an impulse sparked by this last recognition that prompted him to say uncaringly, "Sure...okay. How about this. 'The pellet with the poison's in the flagon with the dragon.'"

"You think I'm jokin' with ya?"

"'The chalice with the palace holds the brew that is true.'"

Moskowitz slapped him hard. Mizell's cheek stung, but he resisted the impulse to rub it. Frustration and anger tightened his neck.

"Hey, take it easy!" said the journalist.

Moskowitz looked at him coolly. "Now who might you be?" The journalist made to answer, but Moskowitz interrupted "I believe you must be what's sometimes referred to as 'an innocent bystander'. Someone who comes to harm as a result of sticking his nose in."

"I'm just trying to calm things down, man," the journalist said.

"It's not required...*man!*" Moskowitz addressed himself to Mizell. "I understand your reticence. Honestly, I do. But..." He shook his head "I simply *can't* understand why you think you can thwart me. I mean your Anna's a fine piece of ass, but she's purely expendable."

Lonesome Heartbreak gave an exasperated sigh. "I go," he said; he picked up his guitar by the neck and turned to the van.

"Whoa there, Hiroshi!" Moskowitz said. "Don't be rushin' off now."

Lonesome Heartbreak paid him no mind.

Moskowitz signaled the Vietnamese kid to handle this spot of bother. The kid approached the van, stepping over Anna's legs; as he planted his left foot, Mizell saw Lonesome Heartbreak tense, saw what was coming, and started moving forward at the same instant Lonesome Heartbreak swung his guitar by the neck, bringing it in a short windy arc to smash into the kid's jaw. It made a much softer sound than Mizell would have anticipated, almost a plush sound, like a two-by-four whacking a pillow. The kid dropped, his legs twisting beneath him: the gun fell to Anna, half-burying itself in the sand. She stared at it dazedly, reached out a hand. But Mizell snatched it up and trained it on Moskowitz. Its cold compacted power unnerved him, set his thoughts flurrying, and he backed away, needing to get the picture in frame. On an illuminated patch of sand, Lonesome Heartbreak holding his busted guitar neck; the Vietnamese kid, face dark with blood; Anna struggling to her knees, breathing shallowly; the journalist stepping into view from behind Mizell; Moskowitz in a half-crouch, mouth open, arms out, palms down, like a surfer whose wave and board had vanished and left him sailing through the air; and beyond, shining them all into being, the lunatic bonehead moon riding above silver-edged peaks of cloud, like a painting on black lacquer.

The journalist said something and Mizell told him to hang on, he was thinking. He could call Eddie Pang in Cholon. Let him take care of Moskowitz. Eddie would be no bargain. The cost would be high. Lots of favors. But it might be the way to fly. Less messy than pulling the trigger himself. Someone had to do it. Moskowitz wouldn't go away on his own.

"You gonna shoot me, Mistuh Mizell?" There was a touch of curiosity in Moskowitz's voice, as if this were something he wanted to know, and not what it truly was—the beginning of a negotiation.

"I want it to be a surprise," said Mizell.

"If you're gonna shoot him," said the journalist, "I'm outa here. Not that I think it's such a bad idea."

Contrary urges were scooting about in Mizell's head, the pressures within his skull squeezing thought into new alignments.

"We got us some wiggle room heah," Moskowitz said. "We have choices available."

He was regaining his confidence and this infuriated Mizell—he took a shooting position, legs apart, elbows braced. Something hot spiked down through his body, a unity of anger and intent nailing him to the moment. In the moonlight, the stubble on Moskowitz's scalp resembled dirty residue left in a tub.

"This isn't wise, Mistuh Mizell," he said. "I want you to think it over. Theah must be a way you can establish some guarantees."

"What sort of guarantees?"

"You require a defense against recriminations. And rightly so. I believe we can work somethin' out. Theah's a big pie to cut up in Vietnam. A very big pie. Just ease back a little and we can all pig out."

It was not going to happen. Mizell was not ready for the next level and he thought that most likely he never would be. The problem, however, still existed.

"Let me put this on the table..." Moskowitz began, but was interrupted by Lonesome Heartbreak, who made a growly noise and got to his feet; his cowboy shirt was draped over one shoulder. He held up a hand to Mizell, staying him, and crossed to Moskowitz. He grabbed Moskowitz by the neck with his left hand, controlling him like an adult with an unruly child, and before the man could let out a yelp, he delivered two short punches to the forehead with his right. He let Moskowitz fall, unconscious, then began ripping the cowboy shirt into strips, moving with a stolid efficiency that seemed quite unreal to Mizell.

"Nice!" said the journalist, moving up beside him, peering at Moskowitz. "That was like some Bolo Yeung shit, man. You know Bolo Yeung? The action guy?"

"Jet Li better." Lonesome Heartbreak finished securing Moskowitz's hands and feet. Then he stood and grabbed the gun from Mizell. "He shoot me," he said, waggling the gun toward Moskowitz. "Afterward"—he tapped Mizell's chest—"you put..." He waggled the tips of his fingers, grimaced; then he brightened. "Fingerprints! Fingerprints on gun. His fingerprints. Call police."

"He's not gonna shoot you," said the journalist. "Man's not gonna be shooting anybody for a while."

"I shoot myself!" said Lonesome Heartbreak, he grinned and tapped his head with the barrel, as if announcing a brilliant idea. "Then fingerprints. Call police." He appeared to be inspecting his torso for a good place to park a bullet.

"Bullshit!" said the journalist, and Mizell reached for the gun. Lonesome Heartbreak fended him off.

"Look," said Mizell anxiously. "You don't have to kill yourself! There's another way! Just let me figure it out."

Lonesome Heartbreak frowned in perplexity. "I shoot myself in arm!"

Mizell gave the situation a couple of spins. "Shit! You know, maybe this'll work!"

"Naw, man. This is not at all cool," said the journalist. "Call the cops, why don'tcha?"

"Oh, cops will be called. I have to figure out which ones."

"Why don't you just shoot him?"

"You want to do it?" Mizell asked, and the journalist said, "Naw...not my thing."

"I thought you understood the Vietnamese way," said Mizell, beginning to feel ordered, on top of the situation. There were interesting symmetries here. Ironies. "If I shoot him, I'll be paying off the cops the rest of my goddamn life. But this way...and this *is* the Vietnamese way, man. They're going to love Moskowitz. They'll squeeze him til he shits pennies. Then they'll throw his bones to whoever barks the loudest. But I have to be the one who shoots himself."

Lonesome Heartbreak offered an objection, but Mizell—startled to hear himself arguing for the right to bleed—said, "No, listen. I know some important guys. I've done favors for them. There's a cop here in Vung Thao. Colonel Vinh. He'll take care of this. But if you do it...they don't know you, so they don't care if you get justice. Maybe asshole here can buy his way out. If I do it he's history, because they don't want those favors to stop."

Lonesome Heartbreak did not understand, so Mizell explained it again. More carefully. Nailing down each point. Lonesome Heartbreak's face arranged itself into stubborn lines, as if the opportunity to hurt himself were a longstanding dream and he was reluctant to give up on it. But maybe, Mizell thought, the journalist was wrong about him. Maybe his intentions were, for want of a better word, inscrutable to Western eyes. To any eyes. What he had done to the Vietnamese kid might be interpreted either as courageous or a suicide attempt, and it could be, as he'd suggested, that he did not know what he intended to do. Perhaps his actions now were defining that decision. The funny thing, though, was that he, Mizell, was concerned about Lonesome Heartbreak. And not just because the man had saved his ass. It seemed the cynical barrier he had erected against such involvements had been dissolved. The dead girl, he told himself. Mayumi. That must have done it. The apprehension that something similar might be in his future. That he was a fool. That he knew love—albeit love stunted by denial, by disuse—and not loss.

At last Lonesome Heartbreak clicked his tongue against his teeth and nodded. "Okay." He handed the gun to Mizell. "You shoot yourself."

"I don't know about this shit," said the journalist.

"You're going to back us up, right?" Mizell asked him. "You're going to tell the same story?"

"Yeah. Yeah! I just find it bizarre."

Mizell glanced at Anna. She had curled up on her side in the sand. Asleep. Dreaming. Do it quickly, he told himself; don't think about it. He pushed the muzzle against the fleshy part of his upper arm, trying for an angle that would merely crease. He drew a deep breath, exhaled, closed his eyes. His finger tightened on the trigger. He stayed in this position for quite some time. "Fuck!" he said. He drew another breath, tried to prepare. "Fuck!"

"I help." Lonesome Heartbreak took the gun, gripped Mizell's left shoulder. Mizell closed his eyes, felt the muzzle press firmly into his bicep. He jerked his arm away. "Not like that!" he said. "Just graze me!"

Lonesome Heartbreak's brow creased with bewilderment.

"Don't shoot me straight on. Make it a flesh wound." Mizell illustrated the concept by flicking his shirtsleeve with a finger.

"I understand!"

Mizell dropped to the sand, stretched out his legs, propped himself on his right arm. "Give me a minute."

Lonesome Heartbreak kneeled beside him. His wide face was calm, like that of a doctor with a needle. "Look at water," he said, pointing with the gun.

Mizell could have used some of Anna's stash, but the water would have to do. The sky. This was so fucked. But what the hell, he had a tattoo. Now he'd have a scar to go with it. A vaccination against the Moskowitz disease.

"Now?" Lonesome Heartbreak asked.

The lopsided moon seemed to be rolling along the edge of a cloud that was passing beneath it. Above and to the right of the moon, a single star winked bluely, big diamond rays from an atom heart blowing out to be somebody's angel, some diviner's fire. It was all pretty cool if you kept your eye on the sky and never looked down. All black velvet and pointy Christmas stars and a pink hotel ablaze with party lights. Look at it long enough and you could let the light straight into your brain. Anna knew that.

"I'm ready," Mizell said.

On hearing the shot Moskowitz began shouting for help and Lonesome Heartbreak was forced to gag him. Then he bandaged Mizell's arm with a remnant of his cowboy shirt. That done, he and the journalist helped Mizell to sit with his back against the van, next to Anna who was still sleeping. The Vietnamese kid moaned, but it was apparent that he was no threat.

"Hurts like hell, huh?" The journalist sat down cross-legged beside Mizell; with his face in shadow, he might have been a Stalinist ghost. "I got shot once. A rubber bullet. Still hurt like hell."

Mizell said, Fucking A it hurt, but he was amazed how quickly the worst of the pain had subsided. Partly due, he supposed, to the tightness of the bandage. His arm was almost numb.

"Made me sick to my stomach, it hurt so much. I puked all over myself." The journalist appeared to be assessing Mizell's condition. "Maybe when you're prepared it's not so bad."

There was a ringing in Mizell's ears. He felt distant, frail, and though the journalist had stood up for him with Moskowitz, the bond was not sufficient to make him want to chat, to compare old injuries and new.

Lonesome Heartbreak slung the Vietnamese kid up onto his shoulder in a fireman's lift. "Doctor," he said, and shook his head vigorously, as if in assurance that a doctor would fix the kid right up. "I go now."

"Bring me back a beer, okay?" said the journalist humorlessly, and Mizell had the suspicion that he was feeling left out.

"Don't forget the name," Mizell said. "You need to talk with Colonel Vinh. Whatever they say, insist on talking to Vinh."

Lonesome Heartbreak tapped his forehead. "No problems."

Mizell would have liked to understand exactly what had happened on the beach. He wanted to know how the World Tour was going to end, and more than that, though they were just two people working an angle together, unmindful of each other's purposes, perhaps even somewhat at cross-purposes...he felt there was a synchronicity between them that deserved acknowledgment. Yet he couldn't think how to say what was necessary, or what he would say even if they could communicate subtleties. Language was not the only barrier here. No real conclusions were possible. Except it seemed there were some occasions when it was not so bad to shoot yourself, and other occasions that you were born not to understand.

"Okay," said Lonesome Heartbreak, gazing at him solemnly; he gave the thumbs-up sign. "Okay." He set off along the beach with his burden.

"That guy," said the journalist. "What the hell is going on with him? First he's on the high road to hara kiri , y'know...then he turns into Captain Japan."

Mizell had nothing to add.

The wind blew harder, stinging his skin with sand grains, and as it dropped off, tattering into gusts, he could have sworn he heard ghosts whispering in the grasses atop the dune. Phantom soldiers plotting an attack. The lost souls of sappers. Watching Anna sleep, he remembered Djakarta, all the years between. An old mildewed emotion, itself a ghost, began to materialize inside him, fogging his thoughts, reminding him of passion and its shadows — sadness and desire. They were all there for him, he realized. He could breathe them in; take a hit and they would go back to dancing in his brain. It could be that easy. A simple choice and there he'd be again, on the edge of totally fucked-up, falling in love with a junkie. He saw now the accommodation he had made, the tactic he had employed in order to keep her close and yet not close, attaining the object of his desire without shouldering the attendant risks. Self-manipulation taken to the level of a deal, a favor done by himself and for himself.

Anna sat up, rubbing her eyes. She caught sight of him and came crawling over, collapsed against his wounded arm, causing him to cry out. When she saw the bandage she asked with blinky concern what had happened.

"It's no big thing," he told her.

Like magic, the words seemed to absolve her of the need to worry. She settled happily beside him, avoiding the arm. "Let's go back soon. I'm sleepy."

He couldn't believe she had no further questions. It was doper logic. Denial and modern chemistry twisting events into an acceptable shape. She might be farther gone than he'd assumed. Without his marking the change, she might have passed another landmark on the road to dissolution, stepped closer to Halidol and long afternoons in a quiet room with a shaft of golden sunlight striking through a high window and dark blue shadows sitting in dim corners with their heads down, muttering to God. And yet she looked beautiful, a bit mussed but essentially untouched by the sorry rituals that had played out on the beach. That had been playing out for years. It was time, he knew, for their world tour to end. He needed to make a decisive move and he wondered if he had it in him. Given his natural indecisiveness and the size of her habit, it was a long shot. Even if he saved her he could wind up losing her to rehab evangelists and their born-again psychology, to the prejudices of the newly purified. Fearing that eventuality was probably part of the reason he hadn't acted before now. He was tempted to make a promise to himself, but recognized it would be too easy a moral satisfaction.

"You all right?" he asked; the throbbing in his arm intensified and he tried to calm his heart.

"Uh-huh. I've been thinking."

"What about?"

Anna sighed, a little girl noise, a half-voiced musical note. "We could go to Hong Kong. See what it's like now. We haven't been to Hong Kong since before the handover."

She shifted, pushing her breast against his arm. It didn't hurt as much this time. Her pulse was so unsteady—a couple of firm beats, then a flutter. To be this noddy for so long, she must have cooked up more than usual.

"That'd be fun...Hong Kong," she said. "Don'tcha think?"

"Fun!" said the journalist gloomily. "There's not enough fun in the world. That's the whole problem."

The wind came hard again, lifting scatters of bright foam from the wave crests. The lights were still blazing at the pink hotel, and though Mizell did not like to admit it, he thought the man might have a point. Ant-sized black shapes scurried about on the sand in front of the hotel, carrying off crumbs and bottles from the party, running into the sea to laugh and drown one another under the deathshead moon in the opium water between China and the end of time. It looked like lots of fun. Anna said something too softly to hear, like a prayer spoken in a dream, and Mizell's chest tightened.

"Yeah," he said, trying for conviction. "Forget this mess."

INTRODUCTION TO

BLIND DATE WITH THE INVISIBLE MAN

LESLIE WHAT

Leslie What has sold some fifty short stories since making her debut in 1992 in Isaac Asimov's Science Fiction Magazine. She also writes nonfiction and poetry. She has been a nurse, a performance artist, a maskmaker, and Jello artist—(or, as she says, "imagine George Sand / Martha Stewart / Ernie Kovacs, with attitude").

Leslie attended the Clarion Writing Workshop after nursing school. When Clarion ended, she moved her stethoscope, typewriter, and tap shoes to Oregon, where she worked as a nurse, performed as a tap-dancing gorilla, and studied writing with her Clarion mentors Damon Knight and Kate Wilhelm.

In the past ten years or so, she has managed a low-income food program, volunteered as a Campfire Youth group leader, written for an alternative weekly, written confessions, written documentary scripts—one of which was produced on PBS—written manuals on aging and caregiving, and edited a book of poetry by at-risk youth. She has been an Artist-in-Schools and has taught writing at several conferences. She currently volunteers with a religious burial society and another social service organization. She works at home as an antiques dealer and freelance writer, and was a writer-in-residence at Clarion in Summer 2002.

About "Blind Date With The Invisible Man" Leslie says, "[This story] explores how people move around in and attempt to influence the world: some work quietly behind the scenes, unseen but effective; some believe their actions insignificant and unnoticed; some attempt to change everything and everyone through any means available; some are so involved with the personal that they are blind to the problems of the outside world. The story is an excerpt from a novel in progress by the same title."

BLIND DATE WITH THE INVISIBLE MAN

LESLIE WHAT

Friday the Thirteenth progressed like any other day until early evening, when Jaclyn began to feel spooked. She was about to meet the invisible man for a blind date; until now, they knew each other only from the Internet. Jaclyn hoped the encounter would go well, perhaps lead to an extramarital affair. While her husband Barry had had numerous affairs, if it happened, this would be her first. Unlike Barry, she would not confess her sins, knowing all too well that bragging didn't absolve one of wrongdoing.

Max had recommended the restaurant, "Africaux", a trendy Ethiopian place with bad lighting and finger food, a combination that created an atmosphere in which he felt less conspicuous. She arrived early, gave her name to the hostess, then staked out the perfect stool in the bar. She was perspiring, not enough to leave a stain, but enough to be embarrassed if he shook her hand.

Max and she had been corresponding for three months. The two had originally met in a chatroom, with the relationship quickly progressing into private mode. The two had instant messaged, flirted, lied, exaggerated, shared, bonded, and lusted, not in any given order. They had played out their keyboard affair; it was time for the relationship to either deepen or end.

Jaclyn was dressed in an attractive but not-too-sexy black jersey dress, one that hid all flaws yet allowed for the possibility of perfection. The dress was her favorite because it symbolized hope.

Two weeks ago, the invisible man had suggested they follow netiquette by trading pixel pictures, but, since he was invisible, Max's picture hadn't provided a clue as to what he looked like. His picture had revealed only a gray and wavy background; in the center was a crease that could have been the outline of a man's head, or just her imagination connecting the dots.

She had photographed herself and doctored the image, smoothed away the suggestion of wrinkles, choosing to blur reality, not erase it. People always looked better when you couldn't quite see everything.

The small television perched atop a shelf in the corner interrupted a baseball game for a special announcement. A news guy moved his lips; the picture broke away to scenes of a riot-in-progress in downtown Seattle.

Her interest piqued. Barry, her husband, and his anarchist friends were there protesting the WTO summit. She watched a building burn and watched a man jump from a window and a crowd roll him over the ground to put out the flames.

She squinted, trying to see if anyone in the background looked familiar. "I don't believe in fire," Jaclyn whispered. Fire wasn't solid—it had no substance. A thing could not be real without those qualities.

"Excuse me," she said, trying to get the bartender's attention. He was preoccupied crushing ice for margaritas, and did not hear her request above the blender. She wanted to be the kind of woman who could make more noise than a small machine. If Barry were there, they would already have been seated at a table. "Excuse me," she said again, and this time, the bartender gave her a *wait a second* signal.

Jaclyn stared into the mirror and watched newcomers check their reservations with the hostess. The hostess used a penlight to see the register. The mirror distorted the reflection. She guessed the glass was coming unglued from the wall because the center was clear and the edges increasingly fuzzy.

She shared the usual doubts about revealing herself to a stranger; her fears alternated between picturing an escaped serial killer, a compulsive liar, a gentleman rapist, or the kind of man who would be called a dog if he were a woman.

The bartender finally walked her way. "What's your pleasure?" he asked. He was a young man, good looking enough to be either gay or already taken.

"I'd like a glass of California chardonnay," Jaclyn told him. Chardonnay was the white bread of wine, an invisible wine that didn't call attention to itself. She preferred the reds, a burgundy or merlot, but it seemed unwise to make a statement with the wine this early in the relationship.

"Good choice," said the bartender with a practiced smile that let her know it was his standard line. He made a great show of teasing out the wine cork and twisting the bottle to pour without spilling a drop. "Cheers," he said.

"Thank you," Jaclyn answered. She sipped from the goblet. A little sweet, but all things considered, a pretty good five-dollar wine.

She watched her reflection in the mirror as her lips closed around the delicate goblet. The tip of her tongue lingered like a shadow on the rim. There was something arousing about watching herself drink, but then nearly every action had sexual connotations when observed by a woman in desperate straits.

At this moment, the invisible man might well be checking her out. He might be watching, undetected, deciding if he wanted to go through with this or not, while all she could do was wait at the bar, nursing a Napa chardonnay and trying to look as if she felt laissez-faire about what she hoped would be her first adulterous affair.

If Max didn't like her, she'd be back at square one. Unless the bartender was available. Unless Max was the type of guy willing to sleep with someone he didn't like, not because of compassion for her situation, but because he'd already blocked out the time, and what the hell?

At this stage in the game, there were plenty of things that could go wrong. She wasn't sure what to expect; she envisioned the scene from *The Invisible Man*, the one in which Claude Rains wound a bandage tightly around his face to prove to Gloria Stuart that he was a man of substance.

Her standards, this early into the night, were high enough to hope for a man of substance. She knew that after a couple of drinks and a little more time spent in anxious waiting, she would be happy with a good lay, but would settle for a bad one, which was usually the case anyway.

She wanted to leave Barry and needed the pretense of an excuse. If you didn't tell the lawyers something, they made you go through mediation. She was afraid to tell the truth for fear Barry would go to jail. She hated him, just not enough to lock him away.

"All alone?" asked the bartender. He refilled her goblet, waving away her hand when she reached for her wallet.

"I'm meeting someone," she said and the bartender nodded.

It turned out that the invisible man was easy to spot in a crowd, but only because he must have recognized Jaclyn from her photograph and sneaked up to sit on her lap.

"Oh," she said, excited, and secretly pleased that he had seen through her disguise. His clothing rustled and he was wearing after-shave with the sweet scent of purple grape juice. "I'm Jaclyn—how do you do," she said in haste.

Apparently he felt no need for introductions. The invisible man whispered, "I do fine," in her ear, which might have, given another scenario, turned her off. But she had no experience beginning an affair, and an invisible man seemed like a safe bet, and she wasn't about to let a slight faux pas turn her off when she had come this far. She hoped he wasn't too unattractive, not that she would ever find out, but just, well, because she deserved that.

"Shall I order a drink or might I have a sip of yours?" Max whispered.

His icy breath against her earlobe triggered a shudder. "Be my guest," she said. She gestured toward the bar.

On his way to the glass, some part of him brushed one of her nipples. That caused a slight tremor. Butterflies, she remembered. The excitement of a new relationship, when lust was so powerful that nothing else mattered.

The invisible man had mentioned in passing that he wrote speeches for politicians. It pleased her, knowing he had deep and important thoughts. She had always been attracted to intelligent men. She wanted this to work into more than a one night stand.

She felt Max's lips explore her neck. It had been a long time since she had been seduced; one forgot the excitement of the game. "Wow," Jaclyn said. "Nice."

The invisible man whispered, "Thanks," and used his tongue like a feather to tickle her ear.

She drained the glass and signaled for another.

"Is it your habit to sit in your date's lap and whisper?" Jaclyn asked him.

"Don't like to draw attention," he said.

"I understand," she told him.

So, he wasn't exactly a brilliant conversationalist. That made sense, in a way, that he saved the important words for speeches. The spoken word was probably too ephemeral for a guy like him. In any event, his discretion was a plus, just one more reason to go for an invisible man. If any of the truth about her life came to light, especially Barry's illegal activities, she might have to find another job. Which would be difficult, as Barry had recently pissed off the guy who had manufactured her technical school diploma.

Max slid his arms around her waist. He seemed to be about the same size as she, a good quality for a lover. She dreaded the thought of sleeping with a man with a smaller butt. Trying not to be too obvious, she ran her fingers through his hair, to see if he had hair, which he did.

"*Like* that," he said, so she tried it once more.

What a relief! Thank God he wasn't bald or covered with keratinous skin growths. Max was clean-shaven, another plus. Her husband grew hairier by the year. She ran her fingers along his chin and tried to imagine his face. When she touched his mouth his lips parted and he circled her knuckles with his tongue.

Ohmygod! she thought. This is really going to happen!

The hostess signaled that their table was ready.

The bartender worked his way over to refill her goblet. "Enjoy your evening," he said.

"Thanks," Jaclyn answered.

"Allow me," Max whispered as he slipped from her lap to stand behind her. He slid one hand beneath her buttocks and gave it a little squeeze.

Not being invisible, Jaclyn blushed, certain that despite the dim light, the bartender had noticed her rising color. She picked up her wine and took a hasty sip. They followed the hostess to a low table near the back; Jaclyn's walk veered toward a wobble. They removed their shoes; Max took his seat on the cushions facing her as she took hers. She hoped her descent to the floor was not without grace. Wildly ethnic fabric so bright it glowed in the dark hung like mosquito netting around each table and provided privacy screens. It was very romantic.

The hostess lit a floating candle that smelled like pine-scented Sterno, yet gave off no perceptible light, then handed Jaclyn a menu. Jaclyn was embarrassed to ask for another. After the hostess left, Jaclyn pushed the menu across the table and said, "Just tell me what's good."

"Everything," said Max. "It's that kind of restaurant, as long as you like spicy."

"Great," she said. She disliked spicy food, which always seemed like it was trying to cover up something rotten with an unnatural heat.

"How's your job?" Max asked.

"Okay," she said. "Nothing special. She was a medical transcriptionist and had just transcribed the notes on three barium enemas. She didn't want to talk about it. "How about you?"

"You know," he said. "Politics." Max had once owned a seat on the Chicago stock exchange, trading futures. He gave the air of being independently wealthy, something difficult to confirm just by looking at him. He could have been wearing a Timex and claimed it was a Movado. His accessories could have been Mexican, not Italian, and she would never know.

She tried to keep her suspicious inclinations from getting the better of her, easier to do when she felt his barefoot toes curl around her calves. She twitched, excited. He was like electro-shock therapy, but nice.

She saw the oddest vision pass by on its way to another table. It looked like a time-release photograph of a city of night, but was probably some flaming dish or another about to be served. The scent of chili peppers made her eyes itch. She pushed back the crushing feeling that this was all wrong with a gulp of wine. She was counting on herself not to screw things up. It was too late to get cold feet.

"It's nice, taking off your shoes," she said.

"Mine are slip-ons," Max said. "Bruno Magli."

"Italian," she said.

The waiter poked his head through the curtain to ask, "Are you ready to order, or do you need another minute?"

"Another minute," Jaclyn said.

The waiter said, "Of course." With a great flourish, he handed Jaclyn an oversized multi-colored napkin and instructed her to tuck it into her neckline.

"Thanks," Jaclyn said, thankful he did not appreciate the awkwardness of her situation. Max ignored his napkin, and why not? Who would know if he wiped his hands on his shirt?

When the waiter had left them alone, she whispered across the table, "I don't know what to do. Should we order two dinners? Or do you want to split?"

"The portions are huge," Max said. "We can split and leave room for dessert."

She looked at the menu and hoped her disgust didn't show. All the desserts were made from warm cottage cheese.

"Order a Number Three and a side of flat bread. It comes with salad," Max said.

It had been a long time since she gone on a date and she wondered if the prevailing mores still prevailed. They hadn't made clear beforehand who would pay for dinner. What if his money was invisible? This was all so new, so strange.

No one had bought her dinner in years. Barry couldn't hold a steady job, so her income not only paid for all household expenses, but the bomb supplies. Stop, she told herself – I'm fixating. She was here to have fun, not to feel bad about her life.

"Give me your hand," Max said.

She reached across the table and accidentally knocked over his water glass.

"Oh God! I'm sorry," she said.

"Don't worry," Max said. "Happens all the time."

She righted the glass and dabbed at the tablecloth with her napkin. "Did I. . .? Are you wet?"

"I could ask you the very same thing," said Max.

She could feel heat again flood her cheeks. Were all invisible men this brazen? A stranger had felt up her ass and was working his foot up her calves toward her inner thighs. She had passed the point of no return. Barry was gone and the house was empty. She was a bowl-of-cottage-cheese away from bringing Max home and fucking the pants off of him, assuming he kept his pants on until then. For all she knew, he had left them on the barstool.

So why did it all feel so wrong?

The waiter brought out a new table cover and expertly replaced things.

"We're ready to order," Jaclyn said.

"What would you like?" he asked.

"We'll have a Number Three and an order of the flat bread," she said.

"Excellent choice," said the waiter. "It comes with salad."

"Could we have some extra napkins?" Jaclyn asked, and the waiter nodded. Given better light, grease stains would show, and she might need to use this dress again, just in case things didn't work out tonight. The napkin fabric was the kind of pattern that would hide all stains, a thoughtful touch. The waiter returned with napkins and a salad and hovered over her with the pepper mill.

"Please," she said, followed by a quick, "Thank you," which he ignored. It was dark enough here that he couldn't possibly see how much pepper he was grinding, but she didn't want to make a scene or look like she was a whiner. A waiter holding a pepper mill was nothing if not about control. He asked you what you wanted then decided on his own how much spice you needed. The feeling that she lived in a world not under her control was sometimes so overwhelming.

The waiter grinned and said, "I think that's enough."

"How do you know?" she asked, more annoyed than ever.

He left them alone.

She pushed the plate toward Max. "I'm not very hungry," she said.

"I don't eat vegetables," said Max. "Or red meat."

"Oh," she said. She stared at the small mound of solid food that swam like an exclamation point in black sauce. It was a drumstick. They must have ordered chicken.

"You're very attractive," Max said.

She thought, "Really?" but managed to sputter, "Thank you."

A minute of uncomfortable silence followed.

"How did it happen?" she asked. "I hope I'm not prying."

"No. It's fine," he said, and sighed. "It was so weird. One day, I was at the Exchange, just like always. I was working the floor, placing orders. I had my hand up and was screaming for attention but nobody took my orders. At first it was just a feeling, you know, the kind everyone gets where they are imagine they are anonymous. Then I looked down, and I couldn't see my feet. Or my legs. Or anything else." He laughed self-consciously. "I don't know why, but I grabbed my penis. It was slightly reassuring that my dick hadn't disappeared, even if it was invisible like the rest of me. At least I knew I wasn't dead."

His story made no sense to her. "Are there others like you?" she asked.

"I don't know," he said. "I haven't heard. It's only been a few months, you know."

She nodded. "I guess it takes a while to find your element," she said.

"Some never do," said Max.

Now was when she wished she could read his facial expressions, to see if he was ribbing her. Instead, she forced her mouth into a weak smile, like she understood yet was above all jokes. She was used to playing this role; she'd had lots of practice around Barry's snotty intellectual anarchist friends.

Dinner was uneventful, if not highly spiced and difficult to wipe from her hands. Everything, except the cottage cheese side dishes, looked like it was covered in sauces made from tar.

The waiter popped into the curtain to ask, "Dessert?"

Jaclyn waited for Max's cue and when he volunteered nothing, said, "No thanks."

The waiter cleared away their stained napkins and dishes and left a bill.

"Let me get this," Max said.

Her relief was an audible sigh.

She finished her third glass of wine. "Will you excuse me for a moment?" she asked. "I've got to go 'straighten my seams'."

"Of course," said Max. "I'm ready for some fresh air. Shall we meet right out front?"

"Sure," she said. It took a bit of maneuvering to get up from the table. She used the facilities and fluffed her hair with a little bit of water, hair gel, and the electric hand dryer. She retouched her lips and stared down every other woman in the bathroom to build up her confidence. There were at least four who were uglier, and/or fatter than she.

Finally, she left. As she strode toward the door, Jaclyn had a fleeting fear that Max hadn't really paid the bill, that any second the waiter would run after her and drag her back to settle accounts. She rushed out and looked around. "Max?" she called, wishing so she could count on him.

"Looking for someone?" Max asked, sweeping his arm through hers.

Thank god he hadn't dumped her.

Max bent down to nibble on her neck. "What's your pleasure?" he asked.

That was the second time a man had asked that very thing.

What was her pleasure? Wasn't it obvious? A light evening rain had left a thin coating on the sidewalk, capturing shadows and reflections like a runny watercolor. She cleared her throat. "Would you like to come over for a drink?" she said, noticing her words were slurred.

"I'd love that," he said. "Are you sure you're ready?"

Her voice came high and tight. "Sure!" she said, Mickey on helium.

"Do you have your car?" Max asked.

She nodded and led him toward the lot behind the restaurant.

"I don't mean to pry, but you seem a little tipsy," said Max. "Would you like me to drive?"

She tried to imagine the scene and sobered up quite quickly. "I'm okay," she said. "Really."

"I believe you," he said. "But I'm here if you need me to take over."

She managed to get them home and park with only a small scrape to the side of the garage.

She unlocked the door.

Because of Barry's paranoia, the house looked like she lived alone. Worried about the FBI finding incriminating evidence, Barry had long ago destroyed all photographs and official records. He only owned one change of clothes, which he carried in his backpack. He wasn't an easy man to love.

Max was all over her the second they walked across the threshold. His soft hands swept across her shoulders and unzipped her dress. The fabric fell like a water puddle to her feet and she kicked it out of the way. They tumbled to the couch. He unhooked her bra like a pro and lunged for her breasts.

"Ohmygod," she said. This was it. This was sex, the way she remembered from her years in the cult. This next part felt uncomfortable. "Um, do you have a condom?" Having planned this out, she did. In her wallet beside her fake ID.

"It's okay," he said. "I'm safe."

She didn't know him well enough to trust this. "I have one right here," she said, and grabbed for her purse.

"No," he said with a hint of a snarl. "I've had a vasectomy and I've tested negative. It's okay."

She tried another tactic. "What about me?" she said. "How do you know I'm safe?"

He laughed. "I'll take my chances. It's just that I hate using a rubber," he said.

She'd heard this trope so many times before and still didn't believe it. "I have some ultra-thins," she said. "Cherry flavored."

His hand parted her thighs and he breathed in her ear. "No," he said, begging. "I couldn't feel a thing. I'm already invisible—how much punishment do I deserve?" He touched her like he knew what he was doing.

Ah well, she thought. It was early enough in her cycle and she had always been reliable. She had suggested safe sex; clearly her obligation had ended. The way she felt, what difference did it make if she got AIDS? At least there would be drugs and sympathy, and maybe, especially if Barry ended up killing anyone during the protest, she could write a book.

She heard a metal sound as he unzipped his pants.

She slid her hands down his belly and fondled his glass-smooth erection. "Oh my," she said. He felt…different!

Sex was marvelous, incredible, and unreal. She enjoyed doing things to Max that she'd stopped doing to Barry after he became an anarchist who never washed.

They were at it for an hour.

After, Max asked, "Was it okay?"

Jaclyn gasped. "Well, yeah!"

Max felt warm as a breath, soft as a puppy's belly, crisis line-sensitive, wrestler strong, and so very thorough, the way an accountant might be if there were any accounting for sex. He was the perfect lover. She couldn't find any words to say and simply hugged him tight.

Contentment felt nice for a change.

"The bedroom's upstairs," she said after a while. "I can loan you a toothbrush."

"Great," he said, and followed her up.

She washed and brushed and wound herself into a black silk negligee that was mostly shiny string. They slipped into bed and were soon at it again. They had S-E-X, with all the hyphens, and in ALL CAPS, at least twice more that night, an experience she had thought was all but over for her.

Unlike Barry who always turned away once he was finished, Max spooned against her back and gently set his hand upon her rump.

She slept, dreaming of smiles and more sex and more smiles. She dreamt of feeling excited at the thought of seeing her lover's face for the first time each day.

In the morning she woke up and turned to ask Max what he wanted for breakfast. "Max," she called, thinking him in the bathroom. "Max!" she called, a little louder. She trudged downstairs and started the coffee. She turned on the radio to listen to the news.

"...riot in Seattle," said the announcer, and she hurried into the living room to turn on the television. Every channel showed another face of the riot, all footage from the previous day.

"It isn't real," Jaclyn said. She closed her eyes and lifted up her hands as if warming them over the television set—they never used their fireplace, which Barry thought was too polluting.

From the TV speaker, sirens blared, people screamed, static buzzed. She shivered. "If fire was real," Jaclyn said, "I could feel its burn all the way from there to here."

She flipped off the television and listened as the house quieted down and the coffeemaker stopped dripping. "Ma-ax!" she called out. "Want some coffee?"

She realized, then, that he was gone. Next, she saw the note. It wasn't exactly a note, just a piece of blank white paper taped to the front door. She looked closer. Silly man, she thought. He must have used invisible ink.

Lemon juice, she thought. Or vinegar. That was how you read invisible notes. She recalled Barry using up all their acidic liquids to make explosives; hadn't he reminded her to buy more vinegar?

Typical, she thought, folding the note into fourths and thinking of Max as her fingers closed around the edges. A sudden pain gripped her tummy and her first thought was appendicitis, but she immediately grasped that this was not the case.

Jaclyn was ovulating. Miss Regularity was being irregular. How unlike her. She touched her belly and worried she was going to have Max's child. Would she even be able to see it? If not, how would she prevent it from running into the street and being run over by a car?

Stop! she told herself. I'm fixating about a baby who was not even born. And just because she'd had unprotected sex more times than she could count with an invisible man and was unexpectedly ovulating didn't mean that she'd get pregnant with an invisible baby.

Or did it?

"What's your pleasure?" Max had asked. She unclenched her palm, smoothed out the paper, and tried to imagine what Max had written. Maybe it was better, just imagining. Maybe it was better, never being disappointed by truth.

She stared at eight by eleven-inch whiteness. I've got it! she told herself. She closed her eyes and traced invisible lines, as if she were reading Braille.

"I'll call you," it said. Or something simpler, in his voice, more like, "Call you."

After a cup of herbal tea, she logged in to check for messages from Max. After all, that was the real test of affection: whether a man you had slept with still liked you enough to talk to you by email.

There were three new letters from him, all from this morning, all sweet variations of Thinking of You.

He was online now, so she instant messaged him. There seemed no point in beating around the bush. "I'm pregnant," she wrote; his response came quickly.

"What do you want to do?" he asked.

"I want to keep it," she answered.

"I'm glad," he said.

They arranged to meet for coffee.

"Maybe you should move in with me," he said.

"We'll talk," she said, but decided to bring her suitcase, just in case.

Motherhood was an occupation for which she felt utterly unprepared. Being pregnant was like watching something on television: you knew it was happening but it didn't seem quite real. She imagined an invisible infant and pictured him—of course it would be a boy—without shape, rather like beach sand. Her role as its mother would be to drip water over the sand, use a spoon to sculpt a form, create a substantial and ornate castle that would inspire others to imitate her style.

No, Jaclyn thought, that's not right, for the next time the tide came in, the wash of the waves would dent the fortress and the moat would flood, or else some thoughtless bully would step on the tower, and everything she'd worked so hard to create would collapse.

She patted her belly. Not so much like sand, she decided, but sculpted of something hard, like marble. The Venus de Milo—capable of withstanding all ravages of time, waves, bullies. She could hardly wait to see Barry's expression when he came home from his weekend of in-your-face demonstrations, his weekend of tormenting others who got in his way. "What's up?" he would ask, in his I'm-so-much-more-aware-than-you tone of voice.

"My pleasure," she would answer, leading him to suspect her of engaging in activities while he was away. Maybe he'd worry. His opinion of her no longer mattered. She was happy enough not to care if he even noticed everything had changed.

INTRODUCTION TO

LOVE STORY

RAY VUKCEVICH

Ray Vukcevich's first novel, *The Man of Maybe Half-a-Dozen Faces* introduced his detective Skylight Howells to surrealism-starved Douglas Adams and Terry Jones fans everywhere.

His first collection of stories, *Meet Me in the Moon Room*, was nominated for the Philip K. Dick and the Bram Stoker Awards. Originally from Arizona, he is now very happily living in Eugene, Oregon.

LOVE STORY

RAY VUKCEVICH

We were doing it like dogs. Or, if you want to get picky about it, we were doing it like everyone imagines dogs do it. Real dogs pump away for a while and then the male twists around and gets off and the two of them share a contemplative moment facing in opposite directions. Private. You take the low road. Pensive. Are you still back there? Such a thing, if not impossible, probably would have been pointless for Lucille and me, but it reminded me of my grandmother and long lazy summers in the Arizona mountains. Grandma had a couple of dogs named Chuck and Muffy who were fully functional pit bulls but no one thought much about pit bulls in those days and most dogs just did what came naturally. What my grandmother liked about Chuck and Muffy was they could and would kill anything that got into the yard.

When I told Lucy I was thinking about the first time I saw the way dogs do it in the summertime at Grandma's place, she said, "So this is your idea of romantic pillow talk?"

My grandmother had a few misconceptions about the way dogs do it, I told Lucy. She never understood why the dogs would choose to ignore her warnings and continue with their nasty ways. They would be fine for months, and then bang! she'd come around the corner of the house and there they'd be — Chuck in the middle of his twisting routine, and she'd shout, "They're stuck!"

Because that's what's liable to happen to us, Lucy, when we do sneaky, nasty things. We get stuck. Grandma turned the hose on the dogs. Stop it! Stop it right now, you dirty dogs! They always persevered and finished and then sat hangdog and dripping and endured their lecture and then shook the water off grinning and went on with their business. Nothing got them down for long.

Except when you called the guy dog "Chuckles."

Chuck hated that, and he would curl his lip at you like he was saying the old lady seems to like you, so unlike other things that get into the yard, I'm not going to kill you, but you'd better knock off that Chuckles crap or you're going to be in for it!

Once I found out Chuck was short for Charles, I wondered if Grandma had named the dog after me. When I asked her about it, she said, "What an idea!"

Years later when I told Lucy that story I could see the light go on even though she made heroic efforts to hide it, little smiles going on and off, sideways glances. Here's something I can use! After we were married when she wanted to get my goat she would hit me with it like "I don't know about that boat, Chuckles."

Growling at her was totally ineffective.

Now we're grandparents ourselves, but we have no dogs.

"How come we never had dogs when Jenny was growing up?" I asked Lucy.

Jenny (call me Jennifer) is our straightlaced daughter. It's like personality traits skip generations. My granddaughter Amy is a very wacky kid. She drives her mother crazy but in a good way, I think, and that makes me happy. I remember one time Jenny was trying to get me to baby-sit, and being so indirect about it. On the one hand she needed to be somewhere in a hurry, but on the other hand she didn't want to appear to need anything from the likes of Lucy and me or just me in this case since Lucy was off playing her viola with the community band. My theory is that Jenny's brain was infested with some conservative virus she picked up from that husband of hers who you have to wonder how he can bend at the waist what with the stick he's got lodged up his wazoo.

"Sure, leave her with me," I told her. "We'll spend the afternoon smoking big cigars and watching inappropriate movies."

"Dad!"

"Eating foods with lots of saturated fat."

Amy was grinning ear to ear, and I could see she enjoyed seeing her mother scandalized. Since it was so easy to scandalize Jennifer, Amy was in for years of laughs.

"Picking our noses and playing with matches!"

"It's like you don't want her," Jenny said. "It's like you're trying to make me take her to a day care center or something."

"What! Not want her?" I pulled Amy into the protection of my arms and she looked back up at me still grinning. "You better watch out. Chances are I'll just adopt her. You two will come back and we'll all pretend we don't even know you."

"Dad!"

But now is now, and oh, look they've all just banged into the kitchen, and Amy asks, "Can I have a cookie?"

"Not now, sweetie," Lucy says. "Grandma's busy."

Busy having her neck nibbled by Grandpa while the Republican son-in-law looks like he's just walked in on some kind of lowlife, sneaky and nasty activity that proper dogs wouldn't be caught dead doing.

"Will somebody hose those two off?" he says.

"Oh, be nice," Lucy says.

"Do we have to stand here and watch this?" the uptight, okay his name is Robert, son-in-law says. I've known his name from the very first night she brought him home to meet us. I just don't like to use it.

Jenny is speechless.

"Come on, you guys," I say. "Hold up your scorecards."

"You want points for this!" Jenny is scandalized again.

I'm about to give up altogether on Robert, but then I have to hand it to him. He does, in the end, flip through his cards and give us a ten.

A soft smile threatens the lips of our lovely daughter, Jennifer.

Amy claps her hands together.

A marching band comes in one door and out the other and you have to wonder how they all fit in there since that second door leads to the bathroom.

And pipers piping.

And waves of mice singing show tunes in little squeaky voices sweep Lucy and me up and wash us back into the bedroom where we really belong.

It's like someone somewhere has planned the whole thing.

"So, you can come clean now, Lucy, and admit you've really been a CIA operative under deep cover all these years we've been married."

"We have ways to make you bark," she says.

"I know Robert's big secret," I whisper.

"Oh?"

"Amy told me."

"Oh?"

"He has an Hawaiian shirt."

"Don't you dare say a word about it, Charles!"

"Someday we'll be doing it like dogs," I say, "and my heart will explode and I want it to be just like this, Lucy."

"In your dreams, Chuckles," she says. "Do you think I want some dead guy collapsing on me?"

"Some dead guy? Like I could be just any old dead guy?"

Is she even thinking about it?

"I don't think I'll be able to help it, Lucy."

"No, only you," she says, "you're my dead guy."

INTRODUCTION TO

ANTHROPOLOGY

VICTORIA ELISABETH GARCIA

Victoria Elisabeth Garcia was born in the San Luis Valley, the descendant of gunslingers and German aristocrats. She attended Simon's Rock College and the University of California at Irvine. Sometime during that part of her education, she may have managed to be hip for as many as thirty-six hours. In law school, at the University of Colorado, she was paid to summarize both the tort law of Papua, New Guinea, and Madonna's unauthorized biography.

Now a resident of Portland, Oregon, she works as an AmeriCorps member-attorney, representing Native American survivors of domestic violence. In her off time, she crafts incendiary tracts with the Portland Surrealist Group, and fusses over other people's dogs with her husband, author John Aegard. This is her first published story.

ANTHROPOLOGY

VICTORIA ELISABETH GARCIA

My Dearest Maribel:

I was absolutely delighted to receive your last letter. Engaged! And to Mr. Cattersly, no less! You can be sure, lovely Maribel, that I will spare no effort or expense to be at Bramley for the ceremonies. If there is anything *at all* that I can do to assist you in preparing, please wire me *immediately*. You know that I have no dearer friend than you.

I must say that I might have felt (secretly!) a little despondent at the news of your romantic good luck had certain happy events not recently occurred. But as it happens, I have a surprise for you, Maribel darling. I too have an admirer. I'm sure that you have met him: It is Dr. Hechenbach, the cultural anthropologist. Surely, your husband-to-be heard at least one of the lectures he delivered during his stay at Crowsdon Bog! And just as surely, you have heard his name mentioned in the halls of the Human Sciences Society. He is as brilliant as they say, Maribel, as well as dashing, divinely handsome, and, dare I say, quite well to do.

I met him quite by accident. I had gone to visit my dressmaker down on Bentmonkey Street and, having reduced my waist measurement by two inches, I stopped at Swopfort's to treat myself to a small slice of muffin-bread with lime sauce. I had just sat down, sugared pastry-spoon in hand, when who should come in but the famous fellow!

You certainly could never have known his fame for the way he looked at Swopfort's that day. His buggy had broken an axle out near the Pimping Hollow Bridge, two miles from town. Fearing to leave his books and important papers in the wrecked conveyance, Dr. Hechenbach had fashioned a harness from the horses' tack, and had lugged his two library cases into town on his back. By the time he made Swopfort's, the poor darling looked ready to expire. His hair was nearly black with sweat. His face was red as a cooked lobster. Panting, he writhed out of his makeshift harness, and the cases thudded down on the polished floor. Thus freed, he wasted no time in slumping to the floor beside them, his chest heaving.

Lidalia Swopfort came out from behind the counter immediately, her red pin curls looking ready to explode.

"Now see here, you!" she cried, brass ice cream scoop flashing dangerously in one hand.

Dr. Hechenbach, still panting, craned his neck to look up at her. He gasped a little, seeming unable to form even a single word. Heedless of his distress, Lidalia advanced.

"I simply cannot have you sweating rivers onto my floor, sir!" Lidalia's face looked feverish, and she planted her feet in a broad stance, as though readying herself for a fight. I tell you, Maribel, the lovely creature looked absolutely murderous! I knew that unless I intervened, there would be trouble indeed, so I rose from my perch at the sauce bar and strode over to them.

"Excuse me, Lidalia dear!" I exclaimed. "Lidalia, Lidalia, please don't be upset! This is my cousin Theodore, come to see me from Lipscree! Theodore, do get up. You know what the doctor says." It was a complete fabrication, of course. I hope you won't think the less of me for having misled poor Lidalia. Truly my only thought was to prevent the excitable darling from flying into a rage and removing the man's innards like so many scoops of Strawberry Swirl.

The human lump on the floor, to whom I had not been introduced, regarded me with a bloodshot eye. I nodded encouragingly to him and gave him a wink. He came to his feet with a "harrumph." His legs trembled a little.

"Come along, Theodore," I said. "Get in the carriage. Your Winona will see about your cases!"

At the time, I thought the man on the floor was a drifter; a tinker, perhaps, or an itinerant bookseller. It had been my intention to deliver him to Issa Lungrave at the Inn of Waves and Tangles, so that she could give him soup, clean clothes, and a safe, dry place to sleep for the night. Imagine my surprise when he asked my driver to take him to Thrimcut Gardens! Imagine my further surprise when, alighting my coach at the Gardens, he was greeted heartily, dare I say a little desperately, by Elphaz and Delilah Thrimcut themselves! A quartet of bandy-legged servants in quilted satin uniforms removed my passenger's library cases and, woofing, struggled up the driveway toward the Gardens. The manse's chrome-work leaves and spires glittered in the sun.

As I sat, puzzled, in my carriage, Elphaz Thrimcut broke away from his wife and guest. Under Delilah's arch and questioning eye, Elphaz produced a long, thin piece of onion-skin paper printed in curling blue letters. A ticket, Maribel! And it bore my erstwhile cousin Theodore's face, along with the legend, "Devoted Voyages—An Anthropological Lecture by Dr. Hugo Hechenbach." Elphaz gave me a queer, twisting smile and a heavy wink, and I tell you, Maribel, I was too flabbergasted even to thank him!

The next night, I went to the Coal Hall with my diaphanous ticket in hand. I had thought to invite Perlita or perhaps Jane Grass to accompany me, but try as I might I could not secure another ticket. The lecture was ridiculously exclusive.

A million candles blazed in the red glass chandeliers. I had arrived early, and took a seat in the middle of the third row, just behind Elphaz Thrimcut. As the Hall filled, I came to feel a certain anxiety, for it became increasingly clear that I was the only woman present. All of the wealthiest men of the town were there, in top hats and velvet vests. Each favored me with a mackerel-eyed look of contempt. At first, I thought to slip away, but my curiosity was inflamed. I held my ground and sat, wearing my bright flamingo tulle, and with legs crossed, I waited the lecture to begin.

A much-transformed Dr. Hechenbach soon took the stage. In his newly pressed suit and stovepipe hat, I could see that his limbs were long and manly; that he had a charmingly froggish and self-satisfied pot-belly; and that his feet were tantalizingly large. The houselights dimmed. Behind me I heard the clang and whir of the Coal Hall orrery coming to life. Someone had outfitted the orrery with a series of photographic slides. As each star in the mechanism grew bright, it projected an image on the wall behind the good Doctor.

The first of these was the nude figure of a woman, supine, with glossy plums for eyes and a body apparently rendered from Swiss cheese. It was a shocking sight, Maribel. Once again, I thought to leave, but there was something almost too succulent about the image. I licked my lips, nearly able to smell the richness of the cheese. Shifting in my seat, I resolved to stay. Dr. Hechenbach arranged his pages, gazed out into the crowd, and began.

"For the Inglendussen Villagers of Lapland, rennet is considered a powerful aphrodisiac." The orrery whirred again, and we were next treated to the sight of a black-streaked wash tub with a goat inside. A golden-haired man knelt beside the tub, laving the goat with a bar of soap. The man bore the kindest expression I have ever seen.

"Among these villagers, there is a caste of gigolo goatherds, whose duty is to care for the erotic life of the villagers." Again, the orrery whirred. The next image was that of a very large, very ripe pumpkin. Dr. Hechenbach shuffled his papers. He turned his back on the crowd briefly and regarded the pumpkin. When he turned back he wore an easy smile on his face, much like that of the goatherd in question. In that moment I resolved to make him mine.

After the lecture, I waited in line to shake his hand.

I expected him to be quite pleased to see me, but he seemed instead to be rather distracted. I removed one bright fuchsia glove and offered my hand. His lip curled when he saw my bare wrist, and he extended his hand only half way. I stood, perplexed for a moment. Then he jerked his head in the direction of my other hand; the hand that held the glove. Puzzled, I offered him the empty scrap of velvet. He grasped it firmly and gave it a few brisk tugs. He then smiled the thinnest of all smiles, and turned away.

His distraction, rather then quenching my fervor, only served to whet it. I chanced a look over my shoulder as I walked toward the exit. During the course of the lecture, his hair had become disheveled in a most appealing way.

The next day, after helping Issa to serve the breakfasts at the Inn of

Waves and Tangles, I went to Chickilickit's Bookstall and purchased two introductory texts on anthropology. These I took home, along with a box of urchin crackers and a large round of *fromage*.

I passed the afternoon lovelily, Maribel. Even though it was summer, I had Tabitha lay a fire in the study. I filled my father's old meerschaum pipe with basil and settled in my leather armchair to read. After I had sat for only a few minutes, my face began to perspire. I removed all of my outer garments and recomposed myself, in corset and knickers, and became quite lost in the world of the Trobriand Islanders.

As the dinner hour drew nigh I grew ravenous. That morning, I had ordered broccoli, steamed with sugar cane, for my dinner. Now I called Tabitha and asked that she cook several chickens with bacon in addition. I also requested a second wheel of *fromage*. At the thought of curls of fat baking on the tender breasts of my chickens, I became so hungry that I thought I might gnaw the upholstery right off the furniture. Starvation made me daring. In a half-swoon, I penned a quick note to Dr. Hechenbach.

"Isn't it interesting," I wrote, "that the Trobriand Islanders' nuptial yam-huts are often largest during times of absolute famine?" This, I placed on a silver tray and gave to Humphrey, my driver, to deliver to Thrimcut Gardens.

Dr. Hechenbach arrived just as the chickens were being removed from the oven. He wore two jackets, both rust-colored and both quite dirty. He still had his library cases with him, borne by a quartet of the Thrimcuts' bandy-legged servants.

"Good evening, Dr. Hechenbach! So *very* glad that you could make it!"

"Harrumph," he replied. I lead him into the dining room, where he seated himself at the head of the table.

It might seem to you, dear Maribel, that it was somewhat unseemly for an unmarried woman like myself to dine alone with an adventurer from so far away. Do not think that your Winona is so silly a thing that she forgot all such concerns. For a moment, I thought of summoning my driver to act as a chaperone, but after a few moments' contemplation of the charming curve of Dr. Hechenbach's sweet, fleshy ears, I abandoned the thought. I was convinced, Maribel, that there was nothing he might do that might compromise me in any way. It seemed that in some abstract manner, he and I were already of a flesh, and that he could no more besmirch me than one finger could taint another finger of the same hand. I took a seat at the end of the table.

Soon, Tabitha arrived with the broccoli, chicken, and *fromage*. I directed her, with a hand signal, to serve Dr. Hechenbach first. He declined all food, and instead, removed a large tome from one of his library cases and with a thud and a clink, spread it across his place-setting.

Tabitha arranged the chickens before me. I whispered to her to bring me skewers. These I used to impale each chicken in turn, so that I could eat them like ears of corn.

"Tell me, dear Dr. Hechenbach," I said between bites, "do you have any family?" He regarded me balefully and returned to his work.

I slurped the last of the meat from the first chicken, beginning to feel uncomfortable. After taking a swallow of water and picking up a stalk of broccoli, I began again.

"You must have traveled to so many beautiful places. Tell me, Dr. Hechenbach, which of them has the mildest weather?"

"Hrmpft," he said.

As I gulped down my third stalk of broccoli, I began to feel a bit desperate. I dabbed at my mouth with a napkin and excused myself. As I passed through the door of the dining room, I broke into a run. I'm afraid it must have sounded like a stampede of elephants, Maribel, but I felt that I could spare no time. I flew up the steps and yanked open the door to my library. The books were still there, atop a pile of my discarded clothing. I snatched one up and flipped through it, the text dancing on the page. There had to be something there. Burial customs I saw, and agriculture, and warfare, and finally, ah, there it was, yes, love. I read over the three magical lines that at least four times to make sure I had them exactly right.

I then ran back to the table. Dr. Hechenbach seemed to have finished his book, and had a packet of papers in front of him. I straightened my dress and smiled my most appealing smile.

"Tell me, Dear Dr. Hechenbach, is it not fascinating that the Yanomamo creation myth begins with the violent rape of the mother goddess?" He looked up then, and there was warmth in his face. I continued.

"The birth of the goddess from a piece of fur-covered fruit seems terribly," here, in my anxiety, I began to lose track of the sentence. "I mean, from a purely theoretical perspective it would seem to invoke the work of Clifford and of Tambiah in that it, it. . . ."

His eyes flashed. He hopped down from his chair — really, he is rather short, Maribel — and he opened the second of his library chests. From that, he extracted a thin book, bound in red. He riffled through its pages, then smiled, looked up at me, and began:

"The fur-covered mother-fruit, of course, is a trope that appears frequently in South and Mesoamerican mythology. For instance, the *Cattacoyon* people of alpine Chile revere a particular vermiform fruit-mold which grows on the bottoms of the berries of the chicle tree. The mold, according to legend, was generated by the goddess's afterbirth. Pregnant *Cattacoyon* women rub their bellies with this mold so as to assure the birth of strong infants."

"Why, how incredible, Dr. Hechenbach!" I exclaimed. Surely, you have met some of these women during your travels. What was the result of the rubbings? Did they really have nice, fat babies?"

As I said this, Dr. Hechenbach's eyes grew cold. He placed the book once again in his library case and, with a single gesture to the Thrimcuts' quilted servants, he departed, leaving me alone with my chicken bones.

As you can imagine, Maribel, I was not able to sleep at all that night. You would think that after such a repast I would never want to eat a thing again. You would, however, be wrong, dear. Something deep inside me had snapped into devouring wakefulness. At three a.m. I crept down to the servants' quarters and woke Tabitha. "Meat loaf," I whispered to her. "And mushrooms. And marshmallows." She stood, stretched and wrapped her eyelet robe about herself. I followed her down the stairs. "Eggs and peas. Corn vinegar. Quail eggs with mustard and chicory."

I brought my anthropology books down to the kitchen and, while Tabitha chopped, I learned about Inuit song-dueling, and about the drum courts of Sierra Leone. It was enchanting, but still, I felt restless.

The crack of dawn found me back at the door to Chickilikit's Bookstall. I darted to the Human Sciences section as soon as Elba Chickilickit had the door unlocked. There had to be a book somewhere about anthropology and love, love, love and anthropology. Something. There had to be a book with which I could fill myself, in order to gain the love that Dr. Hechenbach was surely capable of giving.

There were books about anthropology and horse care. There was a book about anthropology and refrigeration. On the subject of anthropology and the planning of children's parties, there seemed to be countless volumes. I was about to complain to Elba about the inadequacy of her stock, when I was seized with a rather foxy idea.

"Dear, dear Dr. Hechenbach," I wrote on the endpaper of a book of poems. "I am so terribly interested in the subjects we discussed. Please, please, can you recommend a good survey that might cover these topics?" I bought the poetry book, tore out the endpaper, and gave it to Humphrey, my driver.

"Please see that this gets to Thrimcut Gardens," I told him.

The next day, Dr. Hechenbach did not return, but eight of the Thrimcuts' servants did, in their most formal uniforms with the varnished beetle-wings and the extra arms at the sides. The team carried with them an intricately carved mahogany chest, smaller than Dr. Hechenbach's but seemingly just as heavy. They also carried a cheese-dome larger than any I had ever seen, along with a large quantity of lumber.

The tallest of the servants, in a yellow uniform and a monocle, approached me. He held a lace-edged card in his hand. Reading from the card, he said.

"At Madame's request, a high-ceilinged room is to be converted for use in anthropological inquiry." He looked at me sheepishly through the monocle.

I directed them up the stairs to the library. The servants brought in all of their tools and supplies, then, after chasing me out, they closed the door.

All morning, I heard shouting, sawing and hammering. I bade Tabitha make me a plate of spinach-and-game hen sandwiches with feta and arranged myself in the hall outside the door. Near lunchtime, the door came open and the Thrimcut servants, their wings bent and their satin stained, streamed out.

Inside, the servants had disassembled a desk, four tables, a lamp and my armchair in order to create a pedestal, fifteen feet high at least, on which the great cheese dome was perched. There was also a ladder of sorts: a zigzagging pathway with rungs only as wide as my hand. This stretched nearly to the top of the pedestal. A rope seemed to be attached to the apex of the cheese dome. This rope ran to up to a pulley set into the ceiling, then descended, to hang near the top of the ladder. I couldn't contain myself. I swallowed a pair of sandwiches and, hiking my skirt up, mounted the ladder.

There was a large black-bound book under the cheese dome. When I pulled the rope, the dome rose, slowly and wobblingly, and I was able to touch the book. "Anthropology in its Entirety" read the cover in gilt. I ran my fingers over the letters and noticed that they seemed to have a pulse.

I opened the book at random and began to read.

On page 9,878 I found something direly important.

In 1874, Brancusi and Bellmer embarked on an epic study of the mating habits of the anthropologists of Ohio. In that study, they found that pair bonding, far from being the breezy and casual thing it is among local civil engineers and government officials, is a profoundly intricate affair for this population. It seems that, at some point during the immediate post-diluvian era, neighboring populations of librarians, librettists and luthiers suffered a massive die-off of males. These groups then turned to the local anthropologist community. The females of these groups, particularly the luthiers, secrete highly powerful pheromones, and were able to lure away most of the male anthropologists. This was the beginning of disaster for both groups.

Male anthropologists are not able to sire fertile offspring with luthiers, and are not able to sire offspring at all with librarians or librettists. Librarian, luthier, and librettist numbers plunged. Meanwhile, the thwarted anthropologist females became violent, forming bands that raided luthier-librettist-librarian villages and wreaked wholesale destruction. Anthropologist males who were caught in these villages with the smell of the local women on them were captured and eaten alive.

Though these events seem to have happened over two

hundred years ago, anthropologist males of Ohio are still quite skittish around females of any species other than their own. Most are not able to achieve tumescence without hearing at least one previously unknown scrap of anthropologist lore.

So that was it. One previously unknown scrap of anthropological lore. One tidbit of knowledge, and beautiful Dr. Hechenbach would be mine.

Certain that Dr. Hechenbach knew every bit of material in the large black book, I bribed my way into the university museum and plunged into the anthropology collection. In the tallowy dimness of the library caves, I filled note card after note card.

"The sea-dwelling people of the Acadelian islands fashion their feasting garb from sheets of isinglass," I wrote. My driver Humphrey brought me a leg of mutton in snail-egg sauce, and I handed him the card. Two hours later, he returned with a corresponding card.

"At the first feast of the year, called P'l'rdoiun, they capture a sea-cow which they slaughter. After eviscerating the sea-cow, they insert the youngest child who is able to walk into the chest cavity and stitch it shut. When they open it the next day, the child, if it has survived, is said to be capable of prophecy."

Dammit!

I tried again. "In Madagascar, a ship full of financiers was stranded two hundred years ago during a bitter storm. They were never rescued, and eventually bred with the local population—"

The card had not been gone from my hand for one hour before I received another card in return:

"Eventually, amortization became a form of sacred mathematics," began the response.

This was stupefyingly difficult.

I decided to make something up. Glancing up at the reference desk, I noticed that one of the librarians had a pet frog in a cage. I picked up my pen and began to write.

"In California, it has long been customary for local females, once incarcerated, to assume the name and identity of a famous fictional character—" I finished the last of my mutton and, after handing the note to Humphrey, I waited. Gradually, the candles dimmed. One agile librarian shinnied up a rope that hung from the middle of a chandelier and plucked out the burned-out candle ends. She gave me a knowing look.

"Keep your pheromones to yourself," I muttered. I pray, dear Maribel, that she didn't hear me.

It was quite dark when Humphrey returned. He bore yet another card, which he handed to me.

"Occasionally, a prison will come to be home to more than one Chaucerian cook. This produces a horribly unstable situation in which bloodshed is often the result—"

I sat, befuddled with longing. How could he know?

I had Humphrey gather up my dishes and take me home.

As soon as we arrived, I dashed through the door and up the stairs into the library. I almost fell several times as I scrambled up the zigzagging ladder. With a deep exhalation, I yanked on the cord. It took nearly all my strength, but I was able to heft the book and turn it on its face. Then I looked in the index. Prisons—United States—California—Costuming, and—*see also* Supporation, Culinary.

This was impossible.

My stomach growled loudly. I nearly fell off of the ladder. I thought back to the muffin-bread in lime sauce I'd been having when I first met my beloved Dr. Hechenbach.

I closed my eyes. Hunger. Lidalia and her ice cream scoop. Rickety ladders. What if a village of little girls made ladders out of ice cream?

I leafed through the index again. Nothing under ladders. What about ice cream? I looked there too, but saw nothing. A smile crept across my face. I felt my entire body start to flush. I was about to hurry down the ladder, but at the last moment I decided to err on the side of caution and look in the book under "girls."

And there it was. The letters of the listing were fainter than the others, but clearly visible. I stared at them, despondent. Then I noticed that the letters were darkening.

"HAH!" I yelled. The page number was just becoming visible- 6,102. I flipped madly through the pages until I got to the right page and, yes, it was true. The words were only beginning to resolve themselves. When I touched the type it felt warm and a little sticky.

So that was his game.

Maribel, I have never yelled so loud in my life. I put both hands on the spine of that book and shoved it off its pedestal. It landed with an ear-splitting "crack!" Then I hurried down the ladder after it.

I made myself a harness of straps and thongs and I bound the book to my chest. Thus accoutered, I bade Humphrey drive me to Thrimcut Gardens.

The wheels crunched lightly over the oyster shell driveway. Humphrey helped me out of the carriage, and then I waved him away. And then I was alone.

The moon seemed waterlogged that night; it cast pale damp light over the glass spires of Thrimcut Gardens. The chrome ivy that covered the brickwork looked dim and cold. I could hear the wind singing in the telegraph wires. My feet crunched on the shells as I stepped up to the door.

I rang the bell. After a few minutes, the door was opened by a Thrimcut servant whose satin uniform glowed like the behind of a firefly.

The snail-egg mutton had stirred my guts. I belched loudly. "HECHENBACH!" I yelled. The firefly-servant turned and ran.

I followed him, struggling under the book's weight. Up a slippery spiral staircase I charged. "HECHENBACH!" I yelled again. Glassware rattled. The firefly servant reached the top of the stairs and bolted down a hall and around a corner, where I lost him.

I fell against the wall, my cheek rubbing against a tapestry of tulips and lady-birds. My breath came in sharp bursts. I felt as though I might cry.

Then the firefly man was back, leading Dr. Hechenbach by the hand.

Hechenbach's eyebrows raised when he saw the book attached to my chest. I undid two buckles and it fell with a crack to the floor. I knelt beside it, and riffled quickly to the index page. Looking him in the eye, I began to improvise.

"To promote fertility, members of the upper castes of Paris are given to burning film stock under the Eiffel Tower on the first day of the new moon." I quickly found the entry under "Eiffel Tower," and I watched as the letters shifted.

Dr. Hechenbach closed his eyes. "The tradition is actually older than the Eiffel Tower," he said, haltingly. When the page number had formed, I leafed quickly to the proper one and, closing my eyes, yanked the page free. I felt a tremendous shudder go through the covers of the book. Dr. Hechenbach shuddered too. The torn page thrashed in my hand and almost got away before I was able to shove it into my mouth.

The page very nearly broke my teeth, and it tasted like blood and scabs. I choked it down and stared at the doctor. He had become pale, but I noted a stirring in the crotch of his pants. I began again.

"At house number 5300 on South East Maple in Boston, Massachusetts, burial rites that date back to the 16th century are practiced. "

He opened his mouth. "The Maple Street dead are anointed with honey and- and- "

When the entry materialized under "Burial," I flipped to the page and yanked it out before the words resolved. The page managed to wiggle free from my fingers. It flew through the air, caroming off of walls, tapestries and casements. I struggled to my feet and chased it, making great swooping grabs.

" —and powdered teas," Dr. Hechenbach said. "The dead are then placed under sunlamps where they are—" I had never been so hungry, Maribel. I leapt and caught the page between two fingers. It thrashed, but I managed to shove that page too into my mouth. I looked at Dr. Hechenbach's trousers. The bulge was enormous. I grinned broadly as he placed his hand, experimentally, on the bulge. I reached toward the hand and he shied away. One more.

"Under the reign of Sar Peledan of Belgium, in the year 1001, the slaughter of Romany Mail Couriers was ordered. In memory of this slaughter, mail couriers in Russia and the United States—"

I looked under "Mail," and waited for the listing to form. Nothing happened. Dr. Hechenbach began to recite.

"Dye their envelopes red in the blood of newly slaughtered oxen. The blood is then allowed to dry—"

Nothing was happening under "mail." Despairing, I flipped to "Romany." Nothing. Dr. Hechenbach continued.

"...In the open air overnight. Once the envelopes have hardened—"

I flipped to Belgium. Nothing under mail couriers. There was a listing for Sar Peledan, but it wasn't faint. I touched the letters. They didn't seem warm. Still, they were my only chance. I flipped the page. Sar Peledan had a large biography, its letters cold and hard. I sat back, breath coming in anguished heaves. But wait. Was it—yes! A dim footnote, its letters a shade grayer than the others. Within the footnote, I saw the word "Romany." I touched it. The letters were warm. I tore the bottom of the page out. Dr. Hechenbach's voice grew fainter, but still it continued:

"They are then filled with earth and tiny colored beads. Prepubescent children take the envelopes—"

The footnote was small, but it thrashed like an eel. As I brought it to my lips, a corner dug under my fingernail and drew blood. I yelped. Then it wriggled free and zoomed toward an open window. I tore after the scrap, stumbling on the great book as I did so. Dr. Hechenbach joined the pursuit. I reached out and nearly caught it. It felt slippery as it slithered between my fingers. Then Dr. Hechenbach's hand closed on the thing. He looked triumphant.

I sat down with a thump on the floor, my eyes already streaming with tears. His face glowed the way it had glowed at the lecture hall.

Then he bent toward me and gently, with calloused hands, pressed the twitching scrap between my lips.

So, my dear, dear Maribel! You can see that I too have been busy, with *les affaires du coeur*, as well as with scholarly pursuits! You cannot, cannot, cannot begin to conceive of how divinely happy I now am. But of course, being engaged, you must be experiencing *exactly* the same kinds of wondrous things.

I shall be bringing my new beau to your wedding in June.

All the very, very best!

Winona

INTRODUCTION TO

THE HEROIC DEATH OF LIEUTENANT MICHKOV

CARRIE VAUGHN

Carrie Vaughn grew up living the nomadic existence of an Air Force brat. She has since managed to put down roots in Colorado. She completed an M.A. in English Literature at the University of Colorado and attended the Odyssey Writing Workshop in 1998. She has a penchant for such aristocratic hobbies as fencing and horseback riding when her budget is better suited to chucking rocks at tin cans. Carrie's stories have appeared in *Talebones* and *Weird Tales* and will soon appear in *Realms of Fantasy*.

THE HEROIC DEATH OF LIEUTENANT MICHKOV

CARRIE VAUGHN

In the cavernous reception hall, the sorting of paper rustled like bats' wings.

Dispatches and more dispatches. Every morning, Lieutenants Michkov and Romey sorted through dispatches sent from across the Empire, from generals at the front lines, ministers in the Capital and wardens in the gulags. The two undersecretaries arranged the dispatches in order of importance, condensed the content, and organized the features into easily digestible reports for the Emperor.

Troop movements, supply schedules, projected deployments, morale reports. Dissatisfaction, unrest, starvation, defeat. Every day, the story of the Empire told by the dispatches grew more dismal.

"I wish—" Michkov said, then sighed. The shuffle of paper at the other desk stopped, and Romey—a small, thick, badger-like man—glared at him from under a creased brow.

Long used to Romey's expressions, Michkov hardly noticed. "It's the same every day," he continued. "The line at Kajin has fallen back again. Casualties mount. A plague has decimated the Fifth Regiment. I wish there were better news. A victory. Or at the very least some tale of courage. We need more heroes. I can't think of the last time His Majesty awarded a

Meritorious Service Medal for field duty." Chin propped on hand, elbow propped on desk, his eyes gazed unfocused at the mass of papers spread over his desktop. "We need more heroes. I wish—I wish I could be there. At the lines."

Romey snorted. "You'd be the first one in the pits they dig for graves there."

Michkov didn't feel like arguing the point that morning. Just because he hadn't proven himself in battle didn't mean he couldn't. He'd most likely never get the chance. He discovered recently that his father, a Sub-Minister of the Interior, in return for some arcane favors had convinced the Dispatch Office to refuse all Michkov's requests for a transfer to the front. The elder Michkov had secured this undersecretary post for him instead—a very fine post, with great opportunity for advancement in the government, as well as money and favor. Far better than being forgotten on the war-torn frontier, eh?

It was much spoken of in the family that Michkov did not quite resemble his father.

Between the courtyard and the military detachment offices ran a long corridor lined with cracked and darkened portraits of old Emperors, fathers of fathers of the one who currently reigned. The corridor ended at a double doorway, made from slabs of oak cut from a single immense tree and carved by northern craftsmen with depictions of battles from old epic songs. The door opened into a round chamber where petitioners of the regional director gathered. Another, much smaller door led to the reception hall— with walls and floor of polished rose granite, tall windows covered with dusty curtains, a ceiling with faded allegorical paintings, and numerous glowing lamps—where Michkov worked with Lieutenant Romey.

Every day at noon, the Emperor and his entourage marched down this corridor, passed through the round chamber and a crowd of bowing petitioners, through the smaller door, to the reception hall where the Emperor received oral summaries of the daily reports. His Majesty always asked his young undersecretaries about the state of affairs, a personal attention amidst the cold stone bureaucracy. A young lieutenant in this position could easily gain the notice of the Emperor and advance to a stunning position, if he were worthy and able. If he could fashion his reports to gain the Emperor's notice.

Michkov and Romey heard the great double doors open on their ancient hinges, giving them time to stand at attention before the entourage crossed the round chamber and entered the reception hall.

The Emperor, stiff as though propped up by the gold braid and medals on his uniform, stood between the desks, looking at them each in turn. "Report, lieutenants."

Romey stared suggestively, so Michkov cleared his throat to speak first. The most urgent dispatch related a defeat of Battalion Nineteen at the eastern frontier. The troops had fought to nearly the last man, and Michkov endeavored to paint a veneer of heroism on the tragedy, which cost the Empire a valley's worth of villages. With so much sadness, Michkov longed for some spark of hope.

His enthusiasm carried him, despite the weakness of his argument. "I am sorry, your Majesty, to report the loss of a portion of territory. But you will be pleased to hear of the bravery and loyalty of the men who fought and died in your name. I have a list of commendations from General Tanov, who speaks highly of—"

The Emperor drew a tired-sounding breath. "How many men died, Lieutenant Michkov?"

Too many. That was always the answer on Michkov's tongue. But he had numbers. He could give the Emperor numbers, when his enthusiasm failed him, as it always did when he saw the Emperor's weary face. "Battalion Nineteen, your Majesty."

"The entire battalion?" Michkov nodded, and the Emperor's gaze fell, like a farmer who learned that yet another crop was blighted and was unable to raise his ire against the hand of a God who allowed such hardship. He turned to Romey. "Lieutenant Romey?"

Where Michkov longed to see the heroic, and perhaps crafted his reports to reflect his longing, Romey saw insecurity and conspiracy.

"The Empire is beset, I fear I must report. Revolts have been uncovered at these villages." He listed. "These garrisons inform they are undersupplied and cut-off." He listed. "Because of thieves, the roads are nearly impassable at these junctions." Again, he listed, until the Emperor raised his hand, commanding him to stop.

"Enough. I will read the reports."

At this stage, Michkov and Romey handed their neatly-written reports to the Emperor's aide.

Today, breaking the routine, the Emperor paused before continuing with his entourage to his study beyond the reception hall. He said, in a voice soft with defeat, "When I was a boy, there were heroes to carry the day. Great men. What have we now? Dispatches."

All the portraits in the long corridor had stories to accompany them, great men who built the Empire from scraps of feuding lands. With them served more great men, subjects of a hundred tales of generals fighting off barbarian hordes, discovering new lands to farm and mine, falling in love and rescuing fair ladies from evil marriages.

As a child, Michkov loved the stories of heroes—of a single man changing the world for the better, wielding a saber at the front lines of the eastern frontier, inspiring his whole division to push on, to rally for the Emperor—

As a child, Michkov had such dreams for himself.

After the entourage left, closing the door behind it, Romey said, reprimanding, "You'd do well to remember that His Majesty wants facts, not stories."

Flushing, Michkov muttered as he returned to his seat, "Stories never hurt anything."

...the Hero ducked bullets, flares, cannonballs, all pouring over the battlefield in an unearthly hail. A young lieutenant, he was leading his first patrol into battle. Against battle. He'd been ordered to flank the enemy's position, disable the spur of artillery that had pinned the division in this bottleneck of a valley. He had twenty men who could not move without the threat of being shot. Impossible odds, a fool's mission. So be it.

"What now?" his sergeant asked as he slid into the turf beside him. "We'll run out of ammunition before they do."

Staring down the rocky hillside, the Hero considered. A ravine, where snowmelt ran off in the spring, cut a narrow gash along the edge of the hill. Only large enough for a single man, the enemy had neglected to cover that position, rightly assuming the Imperial forces would not even consider sending forward troops numbering less than a patrol, at least. The Empire's strength had always lain in numbers and persistence. Neither had saved them on this treacherous frontier, with its windswept mountains so unlike the ancient forests and meadows of home.

But the ravine led directly to the first row of cannon currently slaughtering his countrymen. One man with a pistol might inflict damage.

"What do we do?" the sergeant repeated, as if the Hero had not heard him over the noise of the shelling.

Before beginning the trek down the hill, the Hero reloaded his pistol. "We crawl on our bellies like worms, Sergeant."

Michkov had been daydreaming again. He remembered running in the streets of the capital with his brothers and their friends, playing soldier, pretending they were brave officers fighting for glory on the front. His daydreams had changed over time, as he completed his schooling, graduated with his commission, and learned that military service had more to do with standing at attention than showing bravery. Now, if he could have one wish, it would be to make his daydreams for the Empire come true, somehow.

Another battle had taken place on the Eastern Front, and wondrously, this had not ended in so sound a defeat. So the report was not quite as dire as it had been the day before. Perhaps, perhaps...

He gave this report to the Emperor: "The battle in the east continues. Again, I regret to report that the losses are great, your Majesty. But there is a small story of wonder. A young lieutenant showed great bravery when he crawled behind enemy lines armed only with a pistol. With stunning marksmanship, he shot down a whole line of cannoneers. Against all odds, this man returned to camp, ragged, bruised, but whole and inquiring about the safety of the men under his command. The crippling of the enemy artillery saved the lives of countless soldiers who otherwise would not have reached camp safely."

Michkov's voice, normally only just greater than a whisper, grew vibrant with the telling. He felt as though he had seen his Hero's actions with his own eyes and wanted to shout the deed to the world. When he finished, Michkov became aware of his voice echoing in the granite hall. Suddenly self-conscious, he lowered his gaze, afraid he had overstepped his bounds before the Emperor.

After a pause that lasted long enough to be awkward, he looked and saw an amazing thing. For the first time in memory, the Emperor smiled.

His eyes shown with an emotion that was not exhaustion but—pride. For a moment, the Emperor seemed to hold up his uniform, instead of being held by it.

"How…heroic," the Emperor said.

Then the Emperor shocked them by not asking for Romey's report at all.

"Lieutenant Michkov. Write to General Tanov. I would hear more of this young officer of his." And he led his entourage away, his stride a bit longer than usual.

Michkov had done it, made the Emperor smile. Such an easy thing, when he put his mind to it.

Romey crossed the space between their desks and rummaged through the piles of dispatches. Michkov, wearing a pleased and almost giddy smile, was still watching after the Emperor and almost didn't notice. When he did, it was with a sense of curiosity rather than anger.

"What are you doing, Romey?"

"Looking—ah, here it is." He retrieved a document and read it quickly, eyes darting. His look darkened. Scowling so that his jaw trembled, he glared at Michkov with bullet-dark eyes. "That lieutenant didn't crawl into enemy range. This says he was trapped there while looting bodies and was forced to shoot his way free."

Michkov blushed. "Yes, well—the end result was the same. He did disable the entire line of artillery. And—did you see him?" Michkov gestured at the closed door where the Emperor had gone. "Did you see how pleased he looked?"

Romey slapped the dispatch against the desk. "No more of your stories, Michkov. I'm warning you."

Michkov, declining to be intimidated by Romey's theatrics, raised a brow. "We'll go on as we always have, I expect. You continue to tell your stories, Romey. I will continue to tell mine."

From then on, the Hero performed only the most daring of exploits. He assassinated enemy generals, rallied his men in the face of defeat and led them to stunning victories. He raided a den of highwaymen, making safe once more a road that was essential to the resupply of the army. He refused promotions, preferring instead to remain with the infantry, fighting in the dirt, smoke, and blood with the rest, where he felt he could do the most good.

The medals which he was awarded remained in a box, kept by a provincial gentleman's beautiful daughter, to whom the Hero was betrothed.

"Well, Michkov—do you have any new reports of our young lieutenant?" the Emperor asked his undersecretary with startling familiarity.

Over the course of several months, Michkov produced everything the Emperor had hoped for in his great army, everything Michkov had dreamed, a respite from the dirge of dispatches they faced each morning, simply by painting the young lieutenant—his Hero—into his reports.

"Ah—he has a young lady he wishes to marry when the war ends, your Majesty."

"Of course, of course. But the end is near, I think. I'm pleased I promoted General Yurivno. The new blood may turn the tide yet. Dear General Tanov was long due for retirement. Then again, those new supply lines may make all the difference."

Michkov's stories had done more than cheer the Emperor. They had revitalized him. No more a tired old man resigned to the wounds fate dealt him and his Empire, he reassessed his army and his frontier war, found them lacking, and went about repairing them. His inspired enthusiasm traveled down the chain of command. A battle won here, a new road there, made a difference.

"Perhaps—Lieutenant Michkov, do you think I should award our hero a medal? A Meritorious Service Medal." His eyes lit with the thought. "I could summon him to the capital. We could have a ceremony."

A little too quickly Michkov said, "Your Majesty—I am sure he is needed on the front, he may not be able to leave his duties—"

"Ah, yes, you're right of course. Well. When the war ends, yes?"

"Yes, Your Majesty," Michkov said, sighing as he bowed.

When the door closed and the undersecretaries were alone in the reception hall, Romey trained his ferret gaze on Michkov.

"I don't believe your reports. I don't believe your dispatches hold anything but catastrophe. There are no heroes."

In a bright mood, Michkov laughed. "A sad life you must lead, Romey.

Can't you consider for one moment that some good might exist?"

"I have never seen it."

"You've never seen a whale, either, but I assure you they're real."

Romey could not know what Michkov did or did not fabricate, how much his reports shaded the line between fact and interpretation. Each morning, half the dispatches were placed on his desk and half on Romey's. Romey could have no idea what information lay in Michkov's dispatches, what he may or may not have been inventing.

At last the day came when Michkov arrived at the great reception hall and found Romey already there, all the dispatches sitting in a pile before him.

"I've read them all," he said. "I see nothing here about our great Hero of the eastern front."

"Perhaps you're not looking closely enough," Michkov said, frowning.

"Find your Hero there, if you can." Romey handed him a carefully sorted stack of dispatches.

None of them involved the war on the eastern front—they all told tales of plague laying the troops low, unrest in the capital, uprisings in the mines. Many people had died, none of them heroically.

So a day passed when the Emperor received no news of the young lieutenant. Then another. And another. Every morning now, no matter how early Michkov arrived, no matter that he awoke with the milk maids and street sweepers to win these battles, Romey was already there, had already read and sorted all the dispatches.

"I do hope he is well," the Emperor said after a week of this, his face creasing with worry. Michkov's stomach churned. He wanted to give the Emperor good news, to continue the Hero's story to a glorious conclusion.

The door closed behind the entourage. "Yes," Romey said, grinning carnivorously. "I do hope nothing has gone wrong."

Perhaps if Michkov had remained silent, had never mentioned the Hero again, Romey would have been satisfied, content to merely stifle Michkov's hopes. But the Emperor always looked so pleased to hear of the Hero, and seemed sad when there was no news.

"We have not heard about him in so long because the Lieutenant is recovering from a bout of the eastern flu. The company doctor is frankly surprised he's gone so long without catching it. But the Lieutenant is in good spirits. The doctor jokes that this is probably the only way they'd get him to rest after these last hard months."

The Emperor chuckled at this, for indeed the Hero had been extraordinarily busy all along the eastern front. "Shall I write him a note, do you think?"

"I think it would cheer him immensely," Michkov said, his stomach knotting. The Emperor was smiling again, yes.

But so was Romey.

The Hero was not the best patient. So much remained to be done. The tide of the war was turning. He could not pause now. A raid on an enemy stronghold was planned for the next week. They'd at last retake the valley that had been lost months before. He assured the doctors he was well, begged them to let him rise, take his horse, and return to the front lines where he belonged, where he could lead his men. He wondered how the sergeant was handling the new recruits. Such young boys they sent him these days...

But the doctors kept him to bed, fed him medicines, told him he must rest until the fever stopped burning. Fever, ha! It was his blood, longing to strike the blow that would end this war.

Until then, he had his love's letter, scented with her perfume, and in the stupor of a sleeping draught he read and reread her words of devotion.

Michkov feared the worst from Romey's animosity. The next day, Romey's report came directly to the point.

"Your Majesty, I have a most dire report of treason, committed in your very presence, by one of your own undersecretaries."

"What?"

"There is no heroic lieutenant fighting on the eastern frontier. I have letters here from Generals Tanov and Yurivno, and they know nothing of this man. He is purely the invention of Lieutenant Michkov, who has been deluding us all for months with his flights of fancy."

The Emperor's expression fell. He aged years, all the sadness that had been kept at bay the last few months crashing on him at once. If his uniform had been any less starched, he would have sunk to the floor.

All the disappointment he turned on Michkov in an expression of betrayal. "Lieutenant Michkov, what do you have to say to this? Is it true?"

"Your Majesty, if I may explain—"

"Please do."

"Your Majesty. The stories haven't hurt anything. Look at the reports..." He swallowed. He could plead innocence or ignorance. He could, in effect, lie. He'd all but admitted his guilt. He could defend himself without lying. *Try* to defend himself. "Look at the reports... Your Majesty, you are winning the war! You weren't, six months ago. Who is to say there isn't a Hero behind this?"

His brow furrowed, the Emperor lowered his gaze as he considered.

"You think this change is because of your *stories*?" Romey, harsh and indignant, interrupted the pause. Michkov stood accused, and he would accuse him, before the Emperor could ponder. "You believe that in telling fables you have succeeded where the vigilance of the Empire has failed?"

In fact, Michkov could, because the Empire's vigilance *had* failed. But to say so here and now *would* be treason.

Michkov stood rock-still beside his desk, hands tucked regimentally behind him. "Morale, good or bad, is a powerful thing. But I claim nothing more than the offer of a spark of hope."

Romey pitted his vision of the Empire against Michkov's. The paranoia of one who saw only impending disaster against the idealism of one who still indulged in his childhood daydreams. The one who could make the Emperor and his train of glazed-eyed advisors believe his own vision would triumph.

Michkov waited for the Emperor's answer to his plea, but once again Romey filled the silence.

"Your Majesty, Michkov has done this only to flatter your fine sensibilities, a deceit to win your favor and his preferment."

Ah, here was a familiar tale of greed and fraud that the Emperor could well believe. And if Michkov claimed that such a plan had never entered his mind—*that* would be most unbelievable to the men of court.

With his eyes clouding as doubt left them the old Emperor stared at Michkov, frowned, and gestured to the soldiers at the door. "Arrest him."

Michkov held the Emperor's gaze. It was the least he could do. Perhaps he should have apologized, but he did not think he was really sorry.

And so Michkov was officially charged with fabricating reports during wartime, a treasonous offense punishable by death. And so, come spring, he was convicted and sentenced to hang.

Perhaps he deserved this. To the letter of the law, perhaps he had committed treason. Perhaps he had been naïve to expect the Emperor's forgiveness. Perhaps Romey was right, and the age of heroes had passed forever. If only Michkov had been able to prove him wrong.

Stories *did* have power over life and death. Michkov had always believed that.

The dreams always ended badly. Standing on the scaffold, rope around his neck, Michkov dreamed the Hero's death, not in battle, cutlass slicing the air, shouting in defiance at the enemy that overwhelmed him, but in his sickbed. He was so strong, everyone had been so sure he would recover. But the illness consumed him. He died clutching his sweet lady's letter.

The following week, a new undersecretary, a Lieutenant Orfiev, who looked even younger than Michkov had, occupied Michkov's desk. Here was a whelp Romey could bully. Part of what had been frightening about Michkov was the sense that nothing Romey did affected him. He had those bright eyes that always seemed to look elsewhere.

By chance, Romey received that morning's oddest dispatch, postmarked the day of Michkov's execution.

"What is it?" Orfiev asked when Romey's face turned white and his hand with the sheet of paper began shaking. When Romey didn't answer, Orfiev was so bold as to take the sheet from him. He had heard rumors of what went on in the reception hall, what dire news was buried and what lies were told the Emperor, who was too old to know better. He wondered what could be so terrible that not even the Emperor could know.

He read aloud, "'Dispatch. Message from General Yurivno. The Lieutenant has surprised us again and climbed from his deathbed. Last rites had been given, but the next day the fever broke. Heaven be praised we have our Hero back with us! Already he is calling for his horse, but the doctors say he must move slowly. Me, I think it was a new letter from his dear lady that called him back from the dead.

"'Your Majesty, I do hope your undersecretaries put this at the top of their report: our Hero, Lieutenant Michkov, lives!'"

THE DOCTOR

CAROL EMSHWILLER

From her website, Carol in her own words,

"I was born in Ann Arbor, Michigan. My dad was a professor, at first in the English Department, and then he founded the linguistic department. My mother was a housewife. She was the life of the family with a terrific sense of humor. Where she was, there was the action and the fun. I have three brothers. We adore each other. People keep calling me a feminist. Well sort of, I suppose, but I'm nuts about men!

"Through my husband, Ed, I got to know (and love) the SF world and wanted to join it. I began to sell stories almost right away. Later on I took classes with Anatole Broyard and Kay Boyle, but I learned the most from the class with the poet Kenneth Koch. No wait, I learned the most from the Milford science fiction workshops. I attended the very first one and most of them from then on.

"I didn't begin writing until I was over thirty and had had my first child. (I had three, so I had to struggle to get any writing time at all.)

"Ed started out as an science fiction illustrator, but then went into abstract expressionist painting and experimental film making. We influenced each other. I went into more experimental writing and became part of what others called the new wave in science fiction.

"About my writing, a lot of people don't seem to understand how planned and plotted even the most experimental of my stories are. I'm not interested in stories where anything can happen at any time. I set up clues to foreshadow what will happen and what is foreshadowed does happen. I try to have all, or most of the elements in the stories, linked to each other. Ed, used to call it, referring to his experimental films, structuring strategies. He taught a film course he named that.

"How I write is by linking and by structures, and by, I hope, not ever losing sight of the meaning of the story. My favorite writer is Kafka. He kept everything linked and together and full of meaning!

THE DOCTOR

CAROL EMSHWILLER

He dates his third wife often but she'll not come back to live with him. Even before it got this bad she said he'd have to clean this place out first. Have to get new couches not so clawed and peed-on. Use a lot of spray for the smell. But there's no way to clean it up now without burning it down.

She left him five years ago. She had good reasons, lots more than just this mess. One was, he was a partying person and she wasn't. (Of course if she came back now there couldn't be any parties anyway, at least not for a long while of cleaning up.) And of course you never can know people's reasons for leaving — nor for coming back.

The doctor has rugged sexy good looks. He's still attractive even though in his seventies and even though he broke his back which left him with a crunched down look. He used to be six feet three but now he's only six feet. As a young man he had dislocated and broken his fingers so often they look terrible now, crooked and with swollen joints. One wonders how he can be a surgeon, thread his needles, and tie the fancy little knots anymore.

The house is a huge Victorian with a front stairway and a back stairway, five bedrooms not counting the maid's room, two upstairs bathrooms and one downstairs (only one toilet still works, but the doctor is alone, he doesn't need more than one). The front parlor is all bay windows and the back parlor is all wood paneling.

There's an empty field behind the house and little patches of forest on each side. Sometimes deer come into the doctor's back yard.

The third wife said if he'd clean the place up even a little bit she'd think about coming back, but he's like those old men who've never thrown away a *Life* magazine or a piece of string. With him it's mostly medical journals. He's not thrown one away since he's been in medical school, nor any books either. Lots of other junk around, too, parts of old motors, rusty tools... Two dead cars are in the garage. He has to park his diesel sedan in the driveway.

When the doctor and his third wife bought this house, the wife kept things more or less cleaned up. If she was still with him things wouldn't have gotten quite so out of hand. She never did like having all this stuff, but it was in some control and mostly out of sight. Actually the house was full of junk from the moment they moved in.

The doctor loves a big house like this. When his wife was still with him they could invite guests to stay over. He likes to play the pater familias. Of course he can't do that anymore. Now he does it in a smaller way. Whenever he goes to a party he always brings big chunks of cheeses and special black bread. Sometimes a ham. Sometimes a five-pound bag of pistachios. Always more food than anybody can use in a week.

His dog died shortly after his wife left him. He buried it in the back yard. That dog... Twelve years before he had taken home a sick mangy puppy, slept with it on his chest and got mange himself. It was a type of mange that human beings are not supposed to get. The puppy grew up to be the dog that died.

But on the other hand, the doctor taught heart surgery by having the students operate on dogs.

The house badly needs painting, but the doctor doesn't notice. If he did, and though it's a huge job, he'd probably plan to paint it himself. He'd buy the paint and keep it in the garage or the basement and now and then think about doing it.

The cats started more recently when the doctor discovered a family of feral cats in his garage and began feeding them. One was pregnant. It was getting colder so the doctor made a little cat door into his basement. It gave them the run of the house.

He's not sure how many cats are in there now. And he thinks he saw a possum.

The cats are mostly tabbies, some gingers, a calico or two… Only one is white. That's his favorite. White cats always have a hard time hunting. They're so easily seen. And she's smaller. She's the underdog cat. He has always loved underdogs best. Besides, she's so luminous. She seems to glow in the dark. He named her Nimbus. He wonders about her fur. He looked at it under the microscope to see if he could see what caused the sheen. Too bad he doesn't have a normal white cat to compare it with, but wild white cats don't last long. He wonders how this one survived to grow up.

They're all still pretty wild. They won't let him pick them up. So far only two sit on his lap. They're nocturnal and the doctor's not home in the daytime to keep them awake. There's a lot of action through the night. They've staked out their territory and defend it with caterwauling. The doctor has learned to sleep through it.

He leaves paper grocery bags on the floors all around the house because the cats like to go into them. Also cardboard boxes here and there.

Even though he can't pick any of them up, if he sits quietly (and he makes a point of sitting quietly) one might jump into his lap.

He doesn't go on vacation anymore because he can't leave the animals. He doesn't attend medical conferences. Even going away for a weekend might be dangerous for them. Nobody could ever be persuaded to come in here to feed them. He wonders what they would do if something happened to him.

The minute he comes in, he says, "Hello" to all the cats in the kitchen. (Some of them are good at meowing back to him.) He comes in the back door, the front door is never used and wasn't even when his wife was here. There's a nice little porch out front but it's never been used either.

The doctor brings in forsythia and pussy willows to force into bloom. On hands and knees he puts in tulip bulbs, thinking all the time that, instead (if, that is, he had actually noticed the need for paint and bought it), he should be painting the house or at least starting to. He has no illusions about what a big job it is and how long it'll take but he thinks himself capable of anything regardless of his age.

The doctor brings in a large cocoon. It was hanging on a limb right over where he parks his car. He's surprised he didn't notice it before since that's exactly the kind of thing he always notices. He brings in the whole branch and nails it on the wall over the breakfast nook. High enough so the cats can't get to it.

What is born in the warmth of the kitchen is a moth of unusual beauty. The doctor can't bring himself to put it in alcohol, pin it and put it up on his wall along with the others in his collection even though it's the largest and most beautiful of any of them.

The moth won't survive these cats. He takes it upstairs and puts it in the master bedroom where there's a big bay window. (He doesn't sleep there anymore.) He shoos out the cats and shuts the door. Of course it won't last long. It doesn't have a mouth. It's purely a sex creature, alive, not to eat, but to copulate.

Fairy dust covers his hands.

The third wife never comes around to the house. It pains her to look at it. He won't let anybody in anyway. They always meet someplace else—at a nice restaurant or at a movie. Last date they had, the third wife thought the doctor looked a little odd, kind of fuzzy...greenish, mossy... And he smells odd. Not so much the damp man-smell of sweat, though that, too, but musky and marshy—a smell of growing things. It's sexy but it worries her.

The house itself is sending out waves of pheromones that bring yet more creatures to the little cat door into the basement. Nobody can guess what's in there now.

Finally the smells bring the third wife.

It's so dim in there and there's this odd strong smell. She's not sure if a good smell or bad one. At first it makes her choke. She goes back out but then she sees eyes...two huge scary black eyes peering out at her from an upper window. What might be up there looking out with such big eyes? Maybe the smell is the smell of death. (Unlike the doctor, the third wife doesn't know what death smells like.)

The third wife puts her hand over her nose and mouth and goes back into the kitchen, moving slowly. It's hot outside, but not bad in the house.

It's three stories high, and it's shaded by big trees, and the doctor has pulled all the shades to keep it cool.

At first she sees shiny eyes all around her and there's scuffling noises. She steps around boxes and stacks of magazines. She steps on a paper bag. Something yowls and tears out of it in a fury.

Then she sees Nimbus on a high kitchen shelf. The doctor has already told the third wife about her—how he looked at her fur under the microscope—how it had a glassy quality.

The third wife is wearing white. She's almost as luminous as Nimbus. One wonders how long she can be in here and keep her skirt and blouse clean.

She calls out, Are you there? It's me. It's me. Calls out, Honey? Dear?

One wonders who, or how many, out of all these creatures, might answer.

Does she dare go on, farther in? Is the doctor even home? But what about those strange big eyes in the upstairs window? The Doctor might be up there helpless, at the mercy of... Or sick...maybe sick from his own house-smells.

She heads up the narrow back stairs that go straight from the kitchen. She wonders: Is he still sleeping where he used to sleep? There are two big bedrooms, a big bed in each. He might be in either. Though what if those rooms have gotten filled up with junk? He might have had to move to a smaller one.

Then she thinks maybe she should have called the hospital first, to see if he was there. You never know when he might be operating. He's called out at all hours. (She always thought it odd that he never seemed to mind. She remembers one Christmas dinner, all the family there, the turkey just brought out...) But she's come too far now, she might as well take a look.

The upstairs hallway is narrow and dark by the back stairs but broadens out for the fancier bedrooms. It's daytime, but it's awfully dim back in the narrow part of the hall. Cats have followed her. The white cat, in its catty way, circling her feet, first one side and then the other. She has to be careful not to step on her.

At the far end, where the hall broadens out, there's a window with a dirty lace curtain. The window sends out dusty beams of light. The third wife can see…or she thinks she sees, tiny creatures in the dust, flying in the light. But how would you know the difference, dust or bugs?

But where *is* the doctor? She calls, "Honey? Are you there?"

She'll go on. She has to see if the doctor is all right.

The white cat still circles her legs, purring now.

"Honey?"

She was right about the first big bedroom. Nobody could sleep in there. There isn't room. The shades are drawn against the heat and the third wife sees the gleam of a few sets of eyes. She backs out and shuts the door.

It's from the window of the second big room that she had seen the huge eyes staring at her while she was still outside. She doesn't want to look in there, she's scared to, but it might be important.

As she opens the door, something flutters out from behind the curtain. That's what the eyes were. Big wings with huge eyes on them. And it seems as if it's looking at her but of course that can't be. Those eyes are phony—meant only to scare, but they work. She can't help but step back and huddle into herself.

The big, big-eyed moth follows her out of the room and back down the hall, always just a few yards behind. It seems to be growing. The third wife wonders if that's really happening or if she's just scared. And she wonders if it's true about moths not having mouths. Maybe *some* do.

She finally gets to the little maid's room. As she opens the door somebody says, "Come in. I've been waiting for you. Waiting and waiting." The voice is deep, resonant. Growly. Is it really her husband's? Perhaps he's sick. He sounds sick. But it's a voice full of love. The third wife wonders how she ever could have brought herself to leave him.

The white cat goes in first. She lights the room with her glow. But the third wife's white blouse glows, too. The moth comes in last. The third wife thinks it's grown to the size of a blanket.

There's something long, lumpy, and greenish lying on the maid's little bed.

Nobody knows exactly what happened with the white cat and the moth and the doctor and his third wife, but, after all those pheromones, one can imagine the sexuality of it. There's the handsome sexy older guy, and the third wife is still pretty and is a lot younger than the Doctor. And then there's the beauty of all the creatures: The softness of the luminous cat fur, the large black eyes on the wings of the moth that must have seemed to watch as they made…some sort of love.

He once asked his older sister—she was eighty and wondered if she should still go up into the altitude. So he asked her, "How *do* you want to die?" After he asked that, his sister went back up, into the mountains and climbed higher and harder. One hopes this is a way of death the doctor would have chosen.

That very same day the house burned down. Also there was a sudden, violent thunderstorm. Water from the attic came down on to the fire. There'd have been sparks, as what was left of the electrical wires shorted out. Imagine the creatures running for their lives. One hopes there were more ways to escape than through the little cat door in the basement.

INTRODUCTION TO

THE SEA MONKEY CONSPIRACY

DOUGLAS LAIN

Douglas Lain was born at Graceland, in Memphis, Tennessee in 1970. His parents moved to Colorado Springs shortly after this event. They took Douglas with them.

In 1977 Elvis died and in 1980 the world lost John Lennon. Later Jim Henson died and then John Denver. Lain has nothing much in common with any of them.

Lain has been writing since he was eighteen, longer if you include book reports on Anne Frank and papers on the reality of Extrasensory Perception.

Douglas Lain currently lives in Portland, Oregon with his wife, son, and daughter. His short stories have appeared in *Amazing Stories* and *The Third Alternative* among other places.

THE SEA MONKEY CONSPIRACY

DOUGLAS LAIN

I was eighteen years old, a freshman at Eckerd College, but rather than undergoing dream analysis or guided regression, I was instructed to play. The graduate student pulled out a trunk of therapeutic toys: wooden horses, flexible plastic people, a toy house with green shutters and a doorbell that would ring if you pressed the button vigorously.

I made the Papa doll watch television while the Mama doll did the dishes and the boy doll slowly and deliberately took apart the moorings of the house. The frame collapsed, folding in on itself, and I stepped back and pondered.

"Why did that happen?" the graduate assistant asked. She wrote something on her clipboard and pulled a lock of hair back behind her ear. "Why did the boy do that?"

"He doesn't believe in the house," I said.

"Why doesn't he believe in the house?"

"Because it isn't real. Look, it's just a toy. See? I can take it apart here, and there's this corner that moves out like this, and that's not supposed to happen in a real house," I said. I moved over to the Colorform set. "Do you have anything else I can break?"

The graduate student smiled and then handed me a remote control. I was left alone to watch television and doodle.

I watched CNN and CSPAN and the network news shows on video tape, and I wrote down my responses, my feelings, just like they asked.

Smart bombs don't take good pictures, I wrote.

Next there were clips from Mr. Roger's Neighborhood, Sesame Street, and 3,2,1 Contact.

I'm special, I wrote.

X is for X-ray.

Fish can only live underwater.

The road trip to Eckerd College felt more like a family vacation than a goodbye. Despite the physical fact of the three of us jammed in with my steamer trunk, my desktop computer, and a few dozen books, we weren't really together.

We stayed at Holiday Inns and Best Westerns. Each room smelled of air freshener and every room had a balcony and was near the swimming pool or the ice machine. We took turns in the bathroom, took turns at the gift shops, took turns reading bestsellers or watching golf tournaments on cable TV.

"You understand that this will be tougher than the Army?" my father asked. He twisted to look at me in the back seat and took his eyes off the road, surprised me with his attention.

"What?"

"You'll have to really apply yourself. If you'd joined the Army it would have been easier, but now you'll have to apply yourself, make your own way," Dad said.

He'd never told me that he wanted me to join the Army. My father was a psychiatrist with a private practice in Denver, not a military man.

"I should have joined the Army?" I asked.

"It was an option," Dad said.

"Not one that I ever considered."

"Well, it's too late now."

I bought some postcards and a *Writer's Digest* magazine at a 7-11 in Nevada. All of the postcards were the same. There was a faked photograph of a rabbit with antlers on the front, and a description of the species "Jackalope" on the back. I filled out each card, with the same message.

This is me.   I'm an exotic species rarely seen except by drunks and small children.

I tried to think about creative writing, about the degree I'd be working for once I arrived. I read my *Writer's Digest* and was assured that I could find the right agent, informed that I could sell my magazine articles, and admonished to protect my intellectual property rights.

"Hey Dad, did you know that every story has to have characters?" I asked the front seat.

My father didn't reply, but turned on the air. We were almost there, had already crossed the Florida State line, and the humidity was oppressive.

"You could have joined the Army," Dad said. "I told you that. I know I told you that."

"Mom, what is he talking about?"

"You know very well what your father is saying."

"Yes, but I don't know why," I said.

And they, both of them, relaxed. I'd said the right thing, for once. Dad turned on the radio, spun the dial until he found something upbeat and bouncy. Dad blasted Salsa music out the back speakers, keeping me from asking him what he'd meant, keeping me from asking anything.

When I signed up for the study I didn't think it had anything to do with me. The psychology department was offering a hundred dollars a week if I'd tell them what I thought of the situation in the Persian Gulf and attend some therapy sessions.   That sounded easy enough. I was against the coming war, against wars in general, but I didn't feel strongly about it. I just liked the idea of studying for exams during the day and then stopping off at the psychology department to fill out forms and look at inkblots.

I signed up, agreed that the College was not responsible for any physical or psychological injuries I might sustain during my participation in the study, and it wasn't until the package with the Sea Monkeys and John Philip Sousa LP arrived in my mailbox, wasn't until the cartoon missiles flew across maps of the Middle East on television, that I knew I'd made a mistake.

I opened the official Sea Monkey Handbook, skipped past the explanation of their origins, and followed the instructions.

The first step was to add the water purifier, the package of dust that would neutralize the poisonous metal oxides from the plumbing. I tore the packet open with my teeth, dumped the contents, and then stirred with the plastic feeding spoon that came with the tank.

Sousa's "Stars and Stripes" played on my old turntable; majestic trumpets sounded as I read aloud from the Sea-Monkey Handbook:

Now that you've completed the first step, your MAGICAL MOMENT is about to begin. You will now bring the Sea-Monkeys to life!

I poured the contents of packet number two, the dehydrated Sea-Monkey eggs, into the miniature tank and waited for instant life.

And waited.

I looked down at the manual again.

You must let the water purify in stillness for thirty hours before proceeding to step 2.

"Stars and Stripes" reached a crescendo and I blushed.

I'd killed the Sea-Monkeys.

Frannie was skeptical as she lay down on my cot, pulled off her short-haired blond wig, and ran her fingers through her own spiky copper colored hair. She was an art student working on an MFA in photography and she lived upstairs.

We'd spent a lot of time together in the first few weeks. Having both arrived a day ahead of schedule, the only students on campus that first day, we'd strolled along the inlets and docks near campus, explored the concrete bunkers that made up the college itself, and ended up in a sort of romance.

There were no ivy-covered halls at Eckerd, no hundred-year-old brick buildings with famous quotations etched along the lattice work; instead there were concrete boxes with metal stairs up the sides. Eckerd was a generic place, an anonymous institution. Only the palm trees and the tough tall grass made it tolerable.

"It's not an appealing place," Frannie said.

"You don't think so?"

"How did we end up here?"

"Did you go to high school?" I asked back.

"Yes."

"Me too...I think that was our mistake."

We went to pick up our mail, not that we expected there'd be any. The mailboxes were by the front gate; one whole wall of the student center was taken up with mailboxes, rows and rows all the way to the ground.

"How will people with the lower boxes open their mail during the winter?" I asked Frannie.

"What?"

"How will people get their mail when it snows?"

"When it snows?"

I was out of my element in Florida, and by January I was sunburned and nauseous. I was sunburned, nauseous, and paranoid.

"Why would the Psychology department send you Sea Monkeys?" Frannie asked as she lay across my cot and pulled off her wig.

"Why would they send John Hinkley a copy of *Catcher in the Rye*? Why would they flash subliminal pictures of skeletons during the *Late Show*?"

"Are you really telling me this, or is this one of your story ideas?" Frannie asked.

"I don't know. Can this kind of thing really happen?"

But I knew it could happen, had happened. At the University library there were hundreds of documented examples, case histories of CIA and psychiatric experiments that utilized exactly the kinds of technologies and techniques I'd experienced. Tape loops, psychedelics, electric shock, isolation, and so on...

The real question was whether this could be happening to me.

Was my mind not my own? Was my life, despite its mediocrity, directed by others?

I was working on a word puzzle, searching for "aspirate" and "phosphorous" in the jumble of letters that the new graduate student provided me. This one was older than the others, in his late twenties he looked more like a professor than a student, but once the session started it became clear that he was just working for his degree like all the rest. He was following orders, reading from the prepared script.

I clicked my pen, tapped my teeth with the inky end, and listened to him read from his clipboard.

"Since World War II the United States has been the primary global power. This, in itself, is an explanation of its role as a source of global terrorism," he said.

"Annihilate," I said as I found the word.

"Despite a national ideology that includes protection of human rights, equality, and freedom, the United States has employed censorship, murder and torture to protect the national interest."

"Contagious," I said.

The letters were clearing a path for me. The words emerged one by one as I listened to the grad student. It was remarkably easy.

"Jingoism."

"What the neocolonial project relies on, what must be delicately maintained at home and brutally enforced abroad, is a complacent public. What must be suppressed, if our democracy is to survive, are demands for participation in the decision-making process." The student paused, took a sip of diet cola, and looked up at me, noticing my progress.

"Invertebrate."

"Good," he said. "You can stop searching now. Just listen. 'There is no contradiction between the national ideology of freedom and the practical reality of U. S. aggression.   Rather, these discrepancies merely reflect the complexity of true democracy, the ambiguity of freedom.'"

"Ambiguity of freedom."

"When you go back to your dorm you are to take notes. Please watch the evening news on channel four and take notes," the student said, and then flipped the page on his clipboard. "Now, think about the Sea Monkeys and be very quiet."

I did as he asked. I pictured the Monkeys twirling around in their tank, bouncing to the music of the graduate student's voice. Sea Monkeys danced to U. S. atrocities.

"Take my picture." Frannie handed me her 35mm camera.

We were standing outside the Federal building, mingling with the street protesters and banners. We were in the thick of the dissent, mingling with the "No Blood for Oil" signs, but only so Frannie could get her homework done. The protest was just another assignment.

"Take my picture," Frannie demanded.

I aimed, looked through the lens. Frannie was dressed like a secretary from a Hitchcock film, like a Norma Jean or an Audrey Hepburn, and somehow the giant puppets and magic marker signs in the background complimented her pose.

She stared up into the sky and I zoomed in, framing her skeptical but frightened face with skyscrapers.

"Now you should dress up like a French Maid," I tell her.

"Okay."

"No, wait. Put on the bikini and smoke a cigarette."

She stripped mechanically and in full view, right out of her underwear, and then stepped into the yellow bikini bottom and pulled the top across her chest. She grabbed her purse and fished out a package of Virginia Slims. The anti-war people closest to us, a couple of post-hippie kids in Birkenstocks and tattoos, seemed to forget their militant rage as they stopped chanting and gawked.

"Do I look like an advertisement?" Frannie asked.

"You do, only you should spread your legs and take a strap off your shoulder."

"Okay. Now take my picture."

The hypnagogic images were not my own:

Vietnamese refugees pounded by U. S. bombs, hundreds of Panamanians summarily executed, Nicaraguan children blown to bits by a U. S. sponsored attack on an elementary school, all of it runs through my mind as an abstract. Without persistent guidance from the graduate student, without her narration, I wouldn't be able to tell one atrocity from another.

I woke up at the airport, found myself sitting in an orange plastic seat, watching 747s land and take off. I had a gun in my hand. It wasn't concealed. It was sitting in my lap and I fingered the safety, flipping it on and off.

To my left the student—this one was an attractive blonde in a denim skirt—was talking to a man in a black suit, a fat officious man who looked uncomfortable in his clothes.

He listened to the student's questions, shrugged, and then glanced over at me. He pointed me out to the blonde student, told her that I was awake again.

"What are you doing up?" the girl asked me.

"Hmmmm?"

"The Sea Monkeys — ," she started.

"I'm tired of the Sea Monkeys."

"The Sea Monkeys are swimming," she said.

More men in black suits clustered around me, about five or six of them, all of them pointing at me and reaching for their pockets.

"I'll play with the Sea Monkeys," I said.

"Good," the student said.   She made a hash mark on her clipboard. "Good."

"I'll play," I said.

Sousa's "Liberty Bell" was the theme song for *Monty Python's Flying Circus*, and I couldn't listen to it without laughing, without imagining a giant foot falling from the sky and squashing the orchestra.

 I filled the tank again, dumped in the water purifying powder, and waited. I put the miniature tank on the windowsill and waited for the oxides to be defeated, for the impurities to dissolve.

 I loaded my .32 caliber pistol as *The Liberty Bell* came to an end. The next number was *The Star Spangled Banner*.

I like Sea Monkeys. I've always liked them.

When I was a little kid I thought the Sea Monkeys represented the perfect family — smiling, smooth, and royal. When I was eleven what I noticed was the strangeness of their bodies; the way their cartoon arms had no joints and how the red freckles, the spots, decorated their bodies. Later on, when I was twelve or thirteen, the fact of their neutered nakedness was what fascinated me most. But all along there was the King Monkey, the Queen Monkey, and the Prince floating on the back of my *Captain America* and *X-Men* comic books. They were always perfect, perfectly smooth.

I fantasized about them; wanted to be a Sea Monkey, thought I secretly was a Sea Monkey. My father, I convinced myself, was actually the King or President of Atlantis. My mother, of course, was the Queen. We were hiding in the United States, in disguise, but one day our fins would reemerge, our tails would sprout, and we would dive back into the Atlantic Ocean. We would return to our depths.

Or, I was the son of the King of Atlantis, but my family didn't know it. I was somehow switched at birth, abandoned with this terrestrial family, but would one day be reclaimed by the Monkeys.

Frannie and I were in bed, crammed together in my small cot, wrapped in bed sheets. Sweating, uncomfortably rearranging ourselves, tangling and untangling, we were both fully dressed. Both of us shy and unyielding.

"They say I'm making progress," Frannie said.

But, this disclosure came late.

We'd been wrapped together for hours, and I was tired; tired of listening to her questions and answers about the war, tired of our guilt. Each time she put her mouth against my ear I'd start, grow erect, and then she'd whispered words like "Napalm," or "Hiroshima," and I'd close my eyes again, feigning sleep.

"I'm getting rid of my exterior in order to make room for the facts. My therapist said it's normal, healthy even, to feel flat and false and to work on getting rid of your masks. She talks about masks a lot," Frannie said.

"She's not a therapist. She's just a student," I said. I kicked off my shoes, pulled at my collar, and then sat up to adjust the pillow.

Here's what Frannie said as she, finally, started to take off her clothes. Here's what Frannie said before she let me touch her that night, before we both gave in to each other.

"It's not enough to know the truth of our guilt. We have to be destroyed by it. They're going to make us into clean slates. We have to be clean slates."

I nodded as I pulled off my blue jeans.

"I'm making progress," Frannie said.

On August 2nd, 1991, Iraq invaded Kuwait.
John Philip Sousa was born on November 6, 1854.
The Sea-Monkeys are a gift from modern science.

My creative writing professor read these sentences slowly and then turned my paper over, pretending to hunt for the rest. "Is that it?" he asked.

"Should there be more?"

"I would think there would be more."

"I tried to make every word count."

My instructor pulled on the sleeves of his tweed jacket and put the paper down. He looked around the room for a raised hand, and when he didn't find one he cleared his throat and looked at me expectantly.

I didn't say anything.

"It's very factual, I guess," he said.

"Except for the last sentence," I said.

"What?"

"The Sea-Monkeys aren't necessarily a gift from science. That's opinion," I said. "That's just my opinion."

"How are you feeling?" the female graduate student asked.

"Captured."

"Sorry, but it's necessary."

The straightjacket was uncomfortable, but ·the student did press a button next to the glove compartment and my seat belt slackened and I leaned forward. I opened the glove compartment with my mouth and a pile of tapes, unmarked black cassettes, fell into my lap.

"What are these?" I asked.

"We've been monitoring you while you write your reports about television," the student said. "Would you like to hear what you've been saying?"

She popped in one of the cassettes. "That's the CBS eye," a voice said. It was my voice. "That's Bugs Bunny in a dress."

"Listen, I'm going to untie you and then I'll be giving you a gun."

"Okay."

"Your target is coming in on flight 231."

"Is that where we're going now?" I asked. "The airport?"

"Yes."

"Why?"

"This is part of your therapy. This is going to help you feel better."

"Matlock is winning his case," my voice, preserved on magnetic tape, squeaked out from the van's speakers.

Frannie and I were at a coffee shop, a *Starbucks* where some friends of hers worked and we could get mochas for free. She was dressed like a seventies porn star, with a rainbow colored halter-top and hip hugging jeans.

"I'm thinking of dropping out of the photography department, out of school entirely," Frannie said.

"Why?"

"It's too humiliating," Frannie said. And then she told me about her dream.

It started with a toy, a talking robot with an eight-track voice that asked her personal questions and then rejected Frannie's answers.

"Is it true that you feel no guilt? Press the red button for yes, blue for no, green for maybe, and yellow if you don't understand the question," the robot instructed.

She was alone in the playroom; she was about three or four years old, and alone with the Legos and action figures and the little eight-track robot. She felt she'd been left alone with this robot every day for weeks, and every day she would press the wrong buttons and get a mild electric shock.

"Do you feel guilty when you're alone? Press the red button for yes, blue for no..."

After weeks with the eight-track robot, weeks of interrogation in the guise of play, the machine was finally taken away.

"You're not making any progress this way," the man in the lab coat told her. "We're going to try something a little more extreme."

"Is it going to hurt?" she asked. A lot of what the man in the lab coat did to her hurt.

"That's up to you, Frannie. I'm going to let you play with any of these toys that you like. We're not going to test you any more, and you can just play. But, we are going to leave this box in here with you, okay?" he asked, and then turned away before Frannie could answer. He walked towards the door and started stroking his beard and staring at his charts.

"What's in the box," she asked him.

"You're not to touch the box. Understand? Don't go near the box and you won't be punished," he said.

"Okay, but what's in it? Is it a present?"

"It's not for you," he said, and then he was out the door.

Somehow she knew that some kids leave the box alone at first. In the dream she imagined a kid coming to that little playroom for weeks and minding his own business for a long time. But she also knew that no kid could avoid the box forever.

She went for it right away.

It was a square box, just big enough to hold a coffee cup or a snow globe, and it was wrapped in paper with little fish symbols all over it. It didn't make any noise if you shook it, but the wrapping paper wasn't taped on and she thought she could probably unfold the outer layer and open the box without causing any damage. She could make her crime undetectable.

Inside there was nothing but darkness. She held the box up to the light, turned it upside down, but somehow it was impossible to see inside.

It occurred to her to put the box back, to refold the paper into place, and put the box back on its shelf and try to put the whole thing out of her mind. It was probably empty. It was obviously a trap.

But she reached inside, put a clenched fist down inside the cardboard, and then spread out her fingers.

"What's inside, Frannie? What did you find?" I asked.

"It's a trap. A rat trap. I spread out my fingers and hear a metallic snap, and then feel the pain and see the blood. After the trap goes off I can see into the box with ease. My small hand is stuck in a big mouse trap. My index and middle fingers are cut and bleeding and held fast," Frannie said.

I was always on the outside of my family. I was always at the periphery trying to figure out what was going on at the center.

When I was fourteen I went to Vail, Colorado with my family. It was a business trip disguised as a vacation.

"I wonder who designed this resort," my father said to his colleague as we unloaded the station wagon, tightened our ski boots, and clomped off, heel to toe, for the gondola. "It's like something out of *Brave New World*," my dad said.

I dropped my skis in the snow and looked up at the wires and gondola cars as I struggled to get my equipment realigned and propped on my shoulder.

"You talk too much," my father's friend said. He was dressed in a black, skin tight, snowsuit; he looked like Jacques Cousteau or like some sort of high-tech soldier. His goggles were mirrored and his skis were thin and flexible, not downhill skis but cross-country. "You people in research talk too goddamned much."

"It's just an observation," my father said. His ski suit was the opposite of his colleagues with lots of padding and made of bright red fabric. "Ski resorts are, in themselves, interesting experiments in manipulation."

Dad's friend quickened his pace, causing both of us to gallop clumsily behind him, stumbling and tilting back and forth as we tried to catch up.

"I come here every winter," Dad's friend said, "and I come here of my own free will."

We reached the line for the gondola and Dad fell silent. We made our way to the front, through the maze of people, the system of lines and checkpoints, and I watched the red and yellow gondola cars swing over our heads; watched the people step into each box, watched them spin off into empty air.

I stepped forward — heel to toe, heel to toe — and put my skis in place at the back of the gondola car. I turned to speak to my father, but he was still in line, watching me. He'd let me get ahead of them, let me go up on my own.

"I'll meet you at the top," my father said and shrugged. "Mr. Jenkins wants to talk."

"What?" I asked, pretending I couldn't hear his instructions over the din of the machinery.

"Go on!" Dad yelled. "Go on!"

I opened the door to the gondola, stepped inside, and sat down on the metal bench to my right. I was alone inside a metal box, and I shuddered as one of the lift attendants stepped forward and closed the door.

I closed my eyes as the car was shifted onto the wire, as I was moved along and then jerked forward, into empty space.

Frannie was dressed up as a college student. She had a knapsack over her shoulder, a Yale University sweatshirt tied around her midriff, and a pair of torn jeans and a half t-shirt on. She wore a pair of Lennon-specs and bright red lipstick.

"My roommate is going out for the night," she said.

"Yeah?"

"I'm all alone," she said.

I took her picture, a shot of her perched at her desk, leaning on her desktop computer, and then watched as she started to undress. I put down the camera and went to her, put my arms around her waist and my lips on her neck.

"What are you doing?"

I didn't answer, but put my hand between her legs, underneath her unzipped jeans.

Frannie didn't say anything as I shoved her onto the cot, as I kissed her mouth and face. She didn't respond at all as I unbuttoned my own jeans and pulled off my own college sweatshirt.

I embraced her, took her breasts in my hands, and pressed up close.

Her skin was cold, covered in goose bumps. Her body was stiff, unyielding.

"What are you doing?" she asked.

And it dawned on me, finally. Frannie had been dressed up like a college student and I'd taken her picture. She'd started to undress but only so she could change into something else, into somebody else. It was just a part she was playing, the sexy coed, but I'd taken her seriously.

"Frannie?" I asked.

She didn't say anything, but got up and went to her dresser. She put on a terry cloth robe and unzipped her knapsack.

"I'm sorry," I said. "My timing is bad."

Frannie didn't reply but began to take off her make-up. She tore open a wetnap and ran the pad over her lips and cheeks. She took off her black-haired wig.

Finally, when her make-up was gone, when her lips were clean and nearly invisible, she looked in my direction.

"We're finished for today," she said. "I'm done."

"Frannie?"

She didn't even look at me.

The flight attendants unlocked the doors to the walkway and people ambled in from the landed plane. I watched them, tourists blankly staring past each other as they deplaned, husbands and wives returning from business trips who were surprised to discover that their families weren't there to greet them, and then the men in black suits behind them.

"Who should I shoot?" I asked.

"Do you think you're supposed to shoot somebody?" the student asked me.

And then he stepped out from the gangway. He was just like the others, just a man in a black suit, but I knew that he was the one I was supposed to hit. It was my dad getting off the plane. I aimed my handgun at my father's head, and contemplated filling him with holes.

"Son," Dad says, "what have you gotten yourself mixed up in?"

"Are you my target? What's going on, Dad?"

"The Sea Monkeys are swimming," the student reminded me.

"How do you plan on setting up a control?" my father asked the student. "Are you going to find somebody else from the agency, enroll their kid, give them a gun, but not condition them?"

"You'll have to bring up your concerns with the department head," the student read from her clipboard. "We have a signed release absolving us of any responsibility," she said. And then she turned to me. "Shoot the target."

I raised the gun again, this time not aiming too carefully but pointing it in her direction, and pulled the trigger. The student flinched as the gun clicked away. There were no bullets.

"I can't believe the university funded this," Dad said. "Didn't we learn anything in the seventies?"

"You'll have to take up your concerns with the department head," the student repeated, but her heart wasn't in it. She was rubbing her forehead, examining the spot where the bullets would have penetrated her skull if there had been any bullets.

"Is this going to be discussed at the conference?" my father asked.

"We have a signed release absolving us of any responsibility."

Dad kneeled beside me, shook me hard, and tried to get me to hold his gaze. "What's the trigger phrase?" he asked.

"Sea Monkeys."

"Son, listen close. I'm going to tell you something about the Sea Monkeys that you need to understand," he said.

"I'm tired of Sea Monkeys."

"When you get back to your dorm the Sea Monkeys are going to tell you to call me. When you get back to the dorm you are to call me on my cell phone," Dad said.

"I almost shot you," I say.

"Never mind that. Just think about the Sea Monkeys."

Frannie was packed and waiting for traffic. She'd dressed in a plaid skirt and white blouse and in a long light blonde wig. She stood at the curve in the highway, with her hands behind her back and a duffel bag at her feet, and I was reminded of the Beatles song *She's Leaving Home*. I was reminded of Natalie Wood in *Rebel Without a Cause*. She was going to hitch without using her thumbs, going to catch a ride based on a stereotype.

"You're not only leaving the College," I told her. "You're also leaving me."

"You'll take care of my plants?" she asked.

"I can't promise that."

"I have to leave. This is getting to be too much for me. I can't go on with this, with the program."

I took her hand in mine, and then grabbed her and pulled her close, but she was stiff in my arms. Unmoved.

"What was that about?" she asked.

"I don't want you to go. I don't want you to leave me."

"Do you really think this is about us? Can you even remember what our relationship was like before the project?"

I couldn't. All I knew was that Frannie was my girlfriend and she was in the art department and I was supposed to help her with her thesis. I was supposed to take the pictures.

"I'm in love with you," I said.

"That's very nice, but I have to leave now. I'm going to get away and you're not going to stop me."

I had no intention of stopping her.

Frannie stood at the curve in the highway, with her hands behind her back and a duffel bag at her feet. I aimed my pocket camera at her back and pressed the button.

I watched CNN, CSPAN, and the Disney Channel and took notes in my green spiral notebook, just like I was instructed.

The victory parade makes me sick. Yellow ribbon, tanks, healthy white people eating hot dogs and waving flags, I watch this on television and wonder what it has to do with bombers, metal death, bulldozers.

Even Sousa is better than this.

Something was wrong with me. I wanted to tell the other students in the lounge—the kid with the neon-orange hair and Buddy Holly glasses or the one with the briefcase, about the U. S. Ambassador who gave Hussein the green light to invade Kuwait, or the Russian peace proposal, or about how we bombed the water supplies. In Baghdad oxides are the least of the problems. But I couldn't say anything.

Instead I listened to *Stars and Stripes Forever* and wondered if it was coming from the TV or from inside my skull.

Back in my dorm room I called my dad.

"Son, you need to quit school now."

With every round of mortar and every Stealth attack on the TV, it became clearer. The images on the screen were merely reflections of my inner state, my own hidden motives and impulses. I 'd done something, or would do something, that made all the killing on the television screen justifiable. There was something about me that made all of the atrocities inevitable.

"The Sea Monkeys want you to go home for a while," Dad said.

I was one of the victors. I was one of the people who dropped the bomb on Hiroshima, napalmed Vietnam, supported the Shah and Marcos and Pinochet.

But none of it could touch me.

"I'll be wiring you the tickets, the airline tickets, tomorrow morning."

Aspirate. Annihilate. Contagious. Jingoism.

There wasn't any me to touch. I was not I.

"Son? Are you there?"

No.

"What did you do?" I asked.

"What was that? What did I do about what?"

"What did you do...during the war?"

Looking at her pictures, the photographs that she left behind, I realized that even though Frannie could make herself glamorous she was never beautiful or even pretty. She was just ordinary. In most of the photos she looked terrible. She looked confused and tired and sort of frumpy.

I missed her terribly.

How had she done it? How had she gotten away? She'd been eliminating herself, following the instructions, but somehow she still managed to escape. She'd gotten away from the project, from me, from the flash and the click of the shutter.

How?

I put her photographs aside and opened my green spiral notebook:

On March 2nd the 24th Infantry Division attacked the Hammurabi Division as the Iraqis fled. Our boys destroyed six hundred vehicles in this attack, and there were reports that the bodies of the Iraqi soldiers were buried in the trenches. There were reports of people buried alive, attacked from behind, bulldozed into the earth.

Looking at the photographs, listening to John Philip Sousa, reading my notes in the green spiral notebook, I thought, again, of the Sea Monkeys.

The Sea Monkeys in their tank, the Sea Monkeys and the instruction manual, were all I had left. They were my last hope.

I turned on the Sousa music, marched back and forth in my dorm room, and conjured up my own version of a Sea Monkey, watched as this cartoon version, with his crown and his freckled fins, bobbed up and down to the martial beat.

I shut my eyes tight, sat down on the cot, and asked the Monkey what to do. Asked for my instructions.

"Open packet two. When the Sea Monkeys are born you will experience instant life," the shrimp said. "When the Sea Monkeys are born you will not go back to the psychology department, you will not call your father, you will not watch CNN or CSPAN, and you will throw your notebook away."

"How can I do it? Where will I go?" I asked.

I opened my eyes and picked up the Sea Monkey manual. I hurriedly flipped to the back of the booklet and read the Emergency Instructions:

When born your Sea Monkey has but ONE eye, right in the middle of his "forehead." As he grows older, he grows two more eyes on each side of the middle one, making him a three eyed "freak" of nature.

Your failure to SEE them is one of the most common reasons for thinking they did not hatch.

They will NOT hatch ON TIME if you fail to WAIT long enough.

Put the container in a light, warm area and let it stand undisturbed. You will have your Sea Monkeys soon.

INTRODUCTION TO

THE ROOM ON THE ROOF

VANDANA SINGH

Vandana Singh was born and raised in India. She grew up hearing stories, legends and village lore from her mother and paternal grandmother, which profoundly affected her view of reality. Later she obtained a Ph. D. in Physics and had a brief career as a researcher – all of which confirmed her suspicion that the universe is a very strange place.

Presently she lives in the United States and devotes all of her free time (which is to say, not much time at all) to writing science fiction and fantasy. She likes to draw from her experience as an Indian, a woman, and a scientist to address such questions as identity, gender, culture, science and society, exile, and otherness. Vandana also volunteers with a South Asian women's group that assists Asian victims of domestic violence, and works with a collective of Indian, Pakistani and Bangladeshi women striving for peace in the subcontinent. Her other passions include Indian classical music, protecting the environment, teaching science to young children, and spoiling her family. This is Vandana Singh's first published story.

THE ROOM ON THE ROOF

VANDANA SINGH

The old women, the grandmothers and widows in white saris, say that the monsoons awaken longings in all beings. The rain calls, they say, to hidden things, to seeds sleeping in the earth, to desire in the desiccated branches of trees and in the hearts of the young. As they tend the stove in the houses of their grown sons or daughters, as they sit on the balcony to sort rice or shell peas, as they look unseeingly at the grimy skyline of the city of their exile, they recount these myths and village lore, embroidered by their own imaginings and unfulfilled longings. Nobody listens but the young ones; the grown-ups, busy with jobs, chores and bank-balances, have no time to draw from wells of wonder. News of a story-telling grandmother goes from house to house, and soon the audience swells to accommodate the children of neighbors.

The girl who watched from the window was one of these; not having grandparents of her own living with her (the two surviving ones lived in a remote village in Bengal), she had grown up with stories told by the grandmother of a friend on the next street. So her mind was open to the notion that behind the dreary ordinariness of the world were wonderfully strange impossibilities. Her name was Urmila and she had just turned thirteen.

It was the first rain of the monsoons. It had started with dark falling in the middle of the afternoon; then a mad wind had come down from the sky, banging doors and windows, making the washing flap crazily on clotheslines, driving before it the litter on the streets, blowing summer dust in clouds everywhere. When the rain came down in great, roaring, shining columns, there was a dash for shelter amid laughter and rejoicing, and dusty umbrellas blossomed. The children pulled free of scolding mothers and ran into the street to dance and shout. Only the girl Urmila and her nine-year-old brother, Somnath, stayed indoors, in the upstairs room they shared.

In past years Urmila, too, had celebrated the advent of the monsoons by dancing on the street with her friends; this year she felt a reluctance to do so. She waved at the yelling, gesticulating, laughing children below, and she smiled and shook her head, although there was a wistfulness about the way she perched on the damp sill, the way she cupped her chin in her dark, slender hand. Leaning on the metal grillwork of the window, she looked back at her brother, who was sprawled on his stomach on the other bed, his crutches flung carelessly on the floor. He was absorbed in a game of chess. The girl shivered suddenly and looked out again at the sky, the rain.

Over the steady, friendly sound of the rain Urmila was aware of other sounds: the movements of chess players over the board, her brother muttering, negotiating with an enemy knight, taking an enemy pawn by surprise. There was a beetle clattering about on the cold, bare floor of the room. Urmila's mathematics homework lay neglected and slightly damp on the desk near the window: a page full of carefully drawn Venn diagrams, circles intersecting circles, like so many overlapping universes. She had recently come to the conclusion that the world she lived in was not a separate, self-contained thing, but actually an intersection of many worlds. There was the world of the beetle, the world of her mother pounding spices in the kitchen downstairs, the chess-world, where her brother battled the evil enemy king, and who knows how many hidden worlds outside her awareness?

She was given to fanciful thoughts such as these, most of which she kept to herself out of embarrassment or shyness; but as she sat musing, looking out at the slowly drowning world, something extraordinary appeared at the end of the street.

It was a woman. She was walking down the street without an umbrella or a sense of urgency, looking about her, shading her eyes from the rain with one hand. Her bright green salwaar-kameez clung wetly to her skin as she splashed slowly through the water-logged street. The girl saw all this and a thought came into her mind: This is the woman who will change everything.

The woman paused at the girl's front gate, opened it and walked the few steps to the front door. The next moment a bell jangled in the house.

Later, when Urmila remembered the events of that rainy season, she wondered why she hadn't felt more surprised that the woman upon whom she had laid such a great responsibility—that of changing everything, or at least that one thing that had been worrying her—should have chosen, of all streets in Delhi, her particular street, and of all houses, this one house. Of course they had the room on the roof to rent, and an advertisement in the local paper, and they weren't more than a twenty-minute bus-ride from the Vishwakarma Institute of Fine Arts, so you could explain the whole thing quite logically. But it was still quite extraordinary how it turned out...

At first, nothing much changed after the woman moved into the room on the roof. Her name was Aparna Bhuvan, and she was a sculptress; she brought with her just one suitcase, several lumps of clay and a faint fragrance of wet earth. She went every morning to the Institute and returned in the evening with clockwork regularity. Urmila's mother approved of her because she was polite and decent, ate all her meals out and never brought anyone home. She was only a small ripple in the melancholy orderliness, the dull routine of the household, but to Urmila, she was a presence redolent with significance. The room on the roof was another world that had nothing to do with the rest of the house: the drawing room with its decades-old furniture, its display shelves crowded with bric-a-brac, the mute sitar propped in the corner; the neat parental bedroom with the mauve and brown sheets, the venerable sewing machine and gargantuan steel cupboards that smelled of mothballs and old dreams when they were opened. No, Aparna Bhuvan lived in a different world, Urmila imagined, one with earth-smells and rain-smells, colors and carefree untidiness. The woman herself was quiet and unobtrusive, but her brown eyes were alight with laughter and secrets, and her hair was always loose, resting on her shoulders like a cloud on a mountaintop. Her clothes were colored like rainbows, in swirls of red and ochre, or green and mustard-yellow. Every evening she would pass the children's room as she went light-footed up the stairs, and when she saw one of them looking out at her she would smile.

It rained without respite on most days, and dark fell early. In the evenings Urmila stayed in her room, reading and watching over her brother as he played his interminable games of chess with an invisible enemy. It had long ceased to be merely a game; last year, Som had cut a giant chessboard out of a piece of cardboard, marked the squares and then proceeded to put in the other features: the fort walls, the river, secret passages. The board was alive with mysterious symbols in black ink. The rules, too, had changed: the movements of the chessmen (each of whom had a name) were governed as much by intrigues, secret loyalties and betrayals, past histories, future aspirations—as by the traditional rules of chess. Urmila remembered how voluble and eager he had been last year, describing it all to her, building his world brick by brick. In this world the boy who could not play cricket or even walk without his crutches became a tall, turbaned warrior, fearless and compassionate. In her mind's eye she had seen him walk the passageways of the fort, inspecting the defenses, encouraging the men at the narrow slit-windows on the ramparts. His short brown fingers had lingered over a knight or pawn, his eyes seeing not the chessboard but the hills and valleys and townships of his embattled country.

But now he had shut her out with his silence. For months he had been reticent about his made-world, responding to Urmila's questions with a mulish sticking-out of his lower lip, or a shrug or a grunt, not meeting her eye, turning away from her as he had not done in all the years of his life. He had always been quiet, wary with strangers, set apart from his schoolmates by disability and temperament, but he had never been distant from her before. She was haunted by the growing certainty that one day he would disappear completely into the chess world, leaving nothing behind but a pair of crutches—and that this silence between them was the first phase of his retreat. There was nobody she could confide in; her one close friend was out of town for the holidays. Her parents constantly fretted about Som's future prospects—who would marry a cripple? How would he manage after they were gone? But now, as long as he did well in school and was healthy, they saw no reason to worry about him. Once Urmila had talked to her mother about Som, and her mother had said, "He will be a chess champion one day, like Kartik Krishnan." And she had wiped her eye with the corner of her sari and sighed.

When the sculptress had wrought no magic in her first week of tenantship, Urmila began to lose hope. One evening, after the dinner dishes had been cleared away, and her father had established himself on the sofa with the newspaper, Urmila went up to him.

"Papa?"

She had rehearsed it all in her head: Som's retreat into the chess-world, his silence, his turning away from her. But her father said, in his soft, deep voice:

"Turn on the TV, child. It's time for the news."

The words died on her tongue. She did as she was told and stood leaning against the doorway. The TV man's prophet-of-doom voice filled the room: the gross national product had fallen again and the North-East crisis had taken a turn for the worse. Urmila's mother came in and sat down on the sofa, stirring isabgol into a glass of water with a spoon, a nightly ritual to ward off constipation. The sofa dipped and creaked with her weight. Her husband glanced at her in irritation and she stopped stirring and began to drink, talking between gulps in her tentative, Bengali-accented Hindi about her day, the rise in the price of flour, the servant-maid's tardiness. "Quiet!" snapped Urmila's father, leaning forward into the TV's glare. "This is important..."

If Aparna Bhuvan had truly possessed magic, Urmila thought, the TV would have blinked out with a wave of the hand. And then the sitar in the corner, the sitar her father had studied and given up when his father died, would have spoken; the strings would stir, softly at first, and then the music would fill the room. As her parents looked around in wonder (she imagined) the souvenirs on the shelves (gifted by globetrotting friends and relatives) would come alive: the little dancing girl from the mountains of Assam would begin to smile and sway, the windmill from the Netherlands would start turning its great wheel... Urmila let out a deep breath and left the room.

Now even her room, which had been a refuge of sorts from the rest of the house, began to oppress her, with the moist patch on the ceiling and the square window framing incessantly falling rain. "This terrible rain,"

Urmila's mother would say, oiling Urmila's hair, combing it out in long, slow strokes. "Your red kurta took three days to dry on the verandah — three days! I told Dhanu to iron it for you but she has left early again, the lazy girl..."

Every week Urmila braved the murky weather to go to Charu's house on the next street, where Charu's grandmother held court. From the open windows came the endless pattering of rain and odorous gusts of wind from the swollen river. The children waited restlessly for the stories, munching crisp, spicy hot pakoras, wiping oily hands unconsciously on their clothes. The grandmother's stories matched the mood of the season: they were delightfully scary tales of ghosts in banyan trees and things that came out of wells. "Dead things," the grandmother would say, "rocks and dust and bones, all desire life. Their hunger is so great that it brings the monsoons to us, so that they may, at least for a while, know what it is to be alive. And the fire-fiend comes out of the marshes, and disturbs the village girls..."

But nothing ever happens here, thought Urmila.

One evening after dinner, after her brother had retreated upstairs, Urmila went to help in the kitchen — the servant-maid had been unable to come. When her parents were huddled together before the TV, listening to the news with the blind innocence of grown-ups, she made her way slowly up the dark stairway. Light spilled from the open door of her room, and the bass cackle of the TV retreated with every step. Her eyes filled suddenly with tears.

But her room was empty. She looked up the stairs to the light from another doorway, from which she heard the soft murmur of conversation punctuated with laughter. She stood on the landing for a long time, caught between the two worlds, above and below. Then she went into her room, found a book and gazed unseeingly at it until her brother returned. She did not look at him. When he turned out the light a little later, she heard the familiar creak of his bed and a small sigh against the wall.

After that Som went up to see the sculptress nearly every evening. Once Urmila crept up the stairs and crouched on the fifth step from the top. Her brother was standing leaning against the part-open door, silhouetted against the light from within, his crutch held idly under one arm. She could just see Aparna Bhuvan's brown, skilled hands shaping a moist lump of clay on the table with sinuous, graceful movements. Every once in a while her face would come into view, with the humorous, mobile mouth, the eyes agleam in the light, a strand of black hair falling across her clay-streaked cheek. The window in the room must have been open because the air smelled cool and moist, and the clamor of the rain filled the ears of the watching, listening girl.

They were talking about the chess world.

"A good strategist concentrates on what he can change." The sculptress's hands paused at their work while she spoke as seriously as if she were talking about events in the real world. The sound of the rain rose to a crescendo and then faded. "The king, now, he cannot change everything. Of course," now a smile crept into her voice, "he has to find out first what it is he can change, and what he can't."

The boy said something inaudible and they both laughed.

The next afternoon, when the sculptress passed the children's room on her way upstairs, she smiled at them both as usual but her eyes lingered in a kindly way on Urmila. So Urmila knew that Aparna Bhuvan had been aware of her watching and listening the night before. After that she stayed in her room in the evenings.

Then one day she noticed a small clay soldier on her brother's desk. It was unpainted, an earthy orange-red, so real that it startled her. The end of the soldier's turban flapped behind him in a permanent breeze; one hand shaded his eyes from the sun, and in the other he held a spear. When (in her brother's absence) she touched the figure with a tentative finger, it felt almost warm, as though it had only lately emerged from the kiln.

After that she began to notice a difference in her brother. Som still didn't talk to her—he would lie on his bed, staring at the giant chessboard, glancing up to look at the soldier on his desk, swinging his crippled leg rhythmically over the edge of the bed as he planned the next move—but there was a lightness about him now, as though his center of gravity had mysteriously shifted. He seemed to lean more easily on his crutches; his shoulders no longer hunched defensively against the world. Urmila began to sense that the mysterious and troubling barrier between them was dissolving, and that she was being forgiven for some lapse, some insensitivity of word or deed that she had been trying to remember for a year.

But what finally turned hope to certainty was the object that she discovered on her desk one evening. It was a terracotta figurine of a young woman standing with her arms outstretched before her, in a gesture of greeting or release. Her long skirt swirled about her in a gust of intangible wind, and her hair streamed out behind like a banner.

Urmila stared; she picked up the little figure and turned it slowly in her hands.

"It's for you, Didi," her brother said. He looked hopefully at her. She took a deep breath, feeling light-headed with relief and delight. They smiled tentatively at each other.

"Aparna-di made it. She says will you come up and see her in the evenings?"

So Urmila came to understand that there was magic in the world, even if it worked at its own pace, in its own way. Certainly there was something magical about the room on the roof: here the rain was no longer dismal—it sang to them, sometimes loud and wild, sometimes a lullaby. A fine spray often blew into the room from the open window, but no mold grew on the walls as it did in the other rooms. The light in here was warm and yellow, the air smelled earthy and wonderful, and the sagging bed was the most comfortable thing to sprawl on while the children watched the clay take shape under Aparna's hands. They would try to guess what each lump was destined to become and laugh at each other's guesses. The sculptress would laugh at them both.

"I never know what shape the clay will take," she'd say. "Clay has dreams too. When I mix earth with water, I feel the clay move under my hands; all I do is guide it."

"You must be the best sculptress in the world," Som said, once, eyes wide. She shook her head, smiling.

"I'm only a junior instructor at the Institute. You should see some of the really good people at work."

She showed them the Institute's yearbook; they leafed through glossy photos of paintings, sculptures in clay, stone and metal, vast studios filled with sunlight. So this was her other world. Here was a picture of her, in one of those sunny rooms, bending over a student's work. Now a full-page photograph of a man caught their attention: tall, slender, with round fanatical eyes under shaggy black eyebrows, his longish graying hair combed back like one of the more flamboyant movie stars. "Ah, the genius," Aparna said, glancing up from her work. Her tone was curiously flat. The nationally recognized artist, Vardhaman Mitra, the article said, in his beautiful home, surrounded by his work. His sculptures were abstract, fluid, suggestive.

"That's his wife, Renuka." Aparna pointed with a grimy finger at the picture of a smiling, statuesque woman in a glittering sari standing at the top of a marble staircase. "My friend. She used to be a sculptress too, a good one."

"Why doesn't she sculpt anymore?" Som lifted curious eyes from the page.

"Because she's forgotten who she is," the sculptress said harshly, turning away, slapping water on to the clay with unnecessary violence. "Now she is content to inspire him, or so she tells me."

"What's he like?"

She was quiet for a second or two.

"Vardhaman? Difficult," she said. "Ambitious. Arrogant."

It was some time before she smiled again.

The children finished looking through the yearbook and as Urmila closed it and set it on the bed beside them, she had the disturbing realization that the sculptress inhabited, for the better part of the day, a world completely unfamiliar to them, centered around Vardhaman Mitra and his glittering wife—a world of mysterious adult tensions, with no place for Urmila or her brother.

Their collection of her work grew. On Urmila's desk was an eagle, a dolphin and a creature that was half-bird, half-woman. For Som there was a long boat complete with tiny men bearing oars, a rectangular vase for his pencils and, incongruously, a life-size pair of clay shoes. They were amusing, those shoes, with their floppy laces, the frayed cuffs, the well-worn shape. For a boy who had to use crutches and wear special shoes this would have been a cruel gift from anyone else, mocking his deformity, but from Aparna Bhuvan it was a happy, amusing present.

About this time Urmila began to have vivid dreams that were sometimes disturbing in their intensity. In these dreams she knelt in pools of wet clay, her hands cupped, pouring the silken, liquid mud on to her legs and arms. Snakes rose from the clay pools and slid into the undergrowth with sinuous grace, and once a bird emerged, wet and earth-colored, and took flight. Always, the sculptress was a subtle presence in her dreams, no more tangible than a shape in the distance, an awareness behind the trees. Sometimes she dreamed of her brother; lately it had been the same dream: the rain had stopped and moonlight came through the window, falling on the bare floor in a wash of silver light. Som was dancing in the middle of the room without his crutches, his clay shoes making a comical, hollow sound as he turned and dipped and whirled. When she woke and sat up in bed after one of these dreams, the moonlight was real, but her brother was fast asleep in his bed, in the dark shadows at the far end of the room. In the rainless stillness his breathing seemed to fill the space between them. She lay back, lulled to sleep by the rise and fall of his breath.

The next evening, as she watched Aparna at work, Urmila found herself wondering about her. The sculptress liked to talk as she worked but she never spoke about herself, the way ordinary people did.

"Tell us about yourself," Urmila said abruptly. She wished she could be more graceful in her speech, but lately her words emerged without warning in awkward, staccato bursts. The sculptress looked startled for a moment. "Tell us—tell us about your home—where you come from. How you came here."

"I come from rather far away—a place where nothing ever happens. The kind of place you leave to see the world…"

"Is it as far away as Bengal?" Som said. "My nana and nani live there, in a village by the sea. We've only been once."

Urmila looked at him, surprised. He had been so little on that visit— was it possible he remembered?

"My mother never goes back home," he continued. "She's Bengali, you know, but my father isn't. They married… for love," he said shyly.

"We saw the sea only once," Urmila said. "But my father couldn't speak Bengali. He didn't like it. And he doesn't like fish. And my mother was supposed to marry someone else who still lives there. So we don't go there any more."

She paused, thinking about the trip. Som said, "We're talking about ourselves again. Tell us about your family, Aparna-di. And how you came to Delhi."

Her strong hands worked vigorously for a second or two. She picked up a round-tipped wooden tool and began to shape the clay. She looked at them through the hair falling over her face.

"Nothing much to tell. I grew up with Renuka, the lady you saw in the yearbook. We were closer than sisters. Then almost exactly two years ago she got the fever to see the world. She came here, joined the Art Institute. Never came back, only kept entreating me to join her. I've seen some of her early work—she could make the clay sing! But by the time I got here she was married and no longer working. I stayed with them for a while, then I wanted my own place. And here I am..."

She was speaking lightly, but her eyes were careful. Behind them lurked some unidentifiable emotion, Urmila thought, feeling her own eyes fill unexpectedly with tears, feeling shut out, stupid, ashamed.

"You'll stay here now, won't you?" Som said.

Aparna smiled ruefully.

"I'll go home some day, maybe sooner than I thought at first," she said. Urmila gripped the edge of the bed. "One must always go home, you know. It's like music. You start with a theme. You wander from it, using a raga or mode as your guide and constraint. You play around, but at the end you come back to the beginning. The beginning is the end."

"If you never go home," the sculptress said, bending over the clay, her hair a monsoon cloud on her shoulders, "you are like a kite whose string has been severed..."

Urmila thought of the sitar in the drawing room, and the village by the sea. Perhaps there was no magic, she thought with a pang. If the sculptress also knew pain in her life, if there were things she could not fix, why, she too was as human and helpless as any of them. There was nothing anyone could do. Then the rain started up again; Aparna began to sing as she worked, and Urmila's sudden gloom lifted as quickly as it had come.

As the rain-filled days passed Urmila was aware of a subtle change in herself. She had always thought of herself as quiet and steady, the kind of person people rely on to be responsible and stable, but now she was aware that there was a wildness in her, as though something inside was responding to the rain. She was filled with a desire to run out into the street, to fly up in the clouds. The world itself seemed more interesting and mysterious than it ever had before; it was rife with secrets, a place where so many other worlds intersected, and she wanted to discover and explore everything. In the circle of children that attended the grandmother's storytelling sessions every week she was gregarious, happy and not at all shy. But sometimes a hopeless melancholy possessed her, and she thought the rain would never end, and that she and her brother and parents would never be happy or free, that beyond one wall there were others, an infinite concentricity of walls. Up in Aparna's room every evening, she felt joy and yearning like a fever, and underneath it the fear that all she had gained was temporary, that one day the sculptress would leave them and the magic would go out of their lives. Sometimes she caught herself holding her breath, waiting for the change.

But the change that came was not the tender, sorrowful parting she had been dreading. One evening Urmila was waiting for Aparna on the landing. It seemed to her that the sculptress was later than usual, and her brother too got to his feet on one crutch and limped over to join her. As they stood together, leaning against the banister in the semi-darkness, with the TV going on below them, they saw Aparna coming in at last. Her hair was more disheveled than usual and her face was terrible and grim. Her eyes were like hot coals, furious, red-rimmed, bleak. She did not look at them. She ran past them up to her sanctum; they heard the door slam. The air around them still quivered with the swiftness of her passing, and there was the faint, familiar smell of moist clay.

Urmila put out an arm to steady Som, whose frightened breathing filled the darkness. She led him into the room and sat with him on his bed, putting an arm around him as she used to when he was younger.

She did not know how long they sat waiting, but the sculptress did not appear at their door. After a while she got up. "I'll be back," she said. She went like a ghost up the stairway. The door was shut. From within came the sounds of things breaking: baked clay statues shattering against the wall, unfinished clay thudding wetly on the floor. And guttural curses in an unfamiliar language, punctuated by howls of anguish. She imagined the sculptress whirling around the room in a dance of destruction, her hair whipping about her face, her eyes pouring forth tears of rage and loss. Urmila had never felt more a child, useless, helpless, shut out by mysterious storms in grown-up lives. She crept back down the stairs, trembling, uncertain what to tell Som, but he was standing at their door, looking up at her, listening. He had been crying. She blinked hard and took his arm, but they did not go into their room. It was all they had to offer, their silent, unacknowledged presence on the landing. They stood there until the sounds from above ceased and a dreadful silence took its place.

For three days the children stayed in their room in the evenings. They did their holiday reading, talked quietly to each other and did not speak of what had happened. But each glanced at the open door of the room when Aparna passed by on her way up.

Then one morning Urmila was sent to the milk booth, the servant maid having been taken sick. Walking away from the booth with the steel container cold and heavy in her arms, she looked towards the noisy main road. Beyond it lay the sodden cricket field and then the river, and on the other side, the specters of tall, grimy buildings, all boundaries smudged in the haze of slow rain. And there, in the park by the river, stood Aparna Bhuvan. Urmila watched, squinting in the rain. Then she trudged home.

The next evening the children heard voices at the bottom of the stairs. Urmila went to the door of their room. Downstairs her mother was holding a large fold of newsprint before her, talking to the sculptress. She pointed to something in the paper. Over the murmurs from the TV, Urmila heard Aparna say,

"Yes, that's her... Yes, from my home town."

"So very sad," said her mother.

There were more words exchanged that Urmila could not catch. Her mother's tone was curious, wistful, as though she wanted to continue the conversation, but at last she went back into the drawing room. Urmila watched Aparna come up the stairs; at the landing the sculptress looked at her with bright, sorrowing eyes, paused, and reached out one hand as though to touch Urmila's cheek. Urmila stood very still and stiff, and Aparna turned and continued up the stairs.

In the drawing room the TV was going on about unrest in the North-East. Her mother was shaking her head, muttering to her husband.

"...a fall, from a balcony. Vardhaman Mitra was away, the servants at the other end of the house... broke her neck... "

"Hmm..." said Urmila's father, leaning forward into the TV's glare.

"...imagine what a shock I got, the same Mrs. Mitra who sent us that nice reference letter. What a tragedy!"

"Shh... I am trying to listen, for God's sake..."

Urmila picked up the newspaper from its basket near the door. Up in their room they spread it out on her bed. It took them some time to find the article. It was in the obituary pages. There was a picture of the deceased, the same one they had seen in the yearbook.

The sculptress's door was open. She was working on something; she looked up at them and at the newspaper, then she sighed and smiled all at once, and made a gathering gesture with one arm. They went in and sat on the bed, glancing around as though they had never been in the room before. She had cleaned up, but there were still faint marks on the walls. It had stopped raining—a moist breeze blew in through the window, but the street below was full of watery sounds, the splash of cars passing, the plink of pebbles thrown in a ditch by anonymous children. On the table there were two new pieces: a woman dancing, holding a two-headed drum, her skirt billowing out around her legs, and a boy with a kite in his arms, looking up at an imaginary sky. "For you," Aparna said, handing the figurines to the children, her eyes bright, tender, sorrowful. They held the gifts with careful, reverent fingers. Urmila wished she had a gift for Aparna that would ease her pain, but she felt crushed by the magnitude of the loss, and her own poverty.

"We've never given you anything," she said.

"Never say that," said the sculptress. She indicated the lump of clay on which she was working. "Can you guess what this is going to be?"

They watched as the clay began to transform under her fingers.

"It's a hand!" Som said after a while. "Two hands!"

Two hands with the fingertips pointing upwards, the palms facing each other. The wrists were slender, the fingers frozen in an exquisite mudra. A dancer's hands.

"Your hands...?" Urmila said.

"This is my last piece," the sculptress muttered, as though to herself. "Everything I have made has been a gift. Thus I keep a promise, repay a debt..."

They looked uncomprehendingly at her, and after a while she looked up from her work.

"I'm going away," she said at last. The words hung in the air, and Urmila heard them echo slowly in her mind. "Home," said the sculptress, smiling sadly and tenderly at them. "I've given notice to your mother. It will be about a week I think."

They could find nothing to say. This was the moment Urmila had been waiting for, but nothing had prepared her for it. It seemed to her that everything had suddenly slowed: the sounds in the street below, the drip-drip of the rain from the roof of the house, the beating of her heart. Through a numbness that was spreading rapidly through her, she heard Som say something, and Aparna replied, shaking hair out of her face. Urmila looked quickly at him; he was quite composed, but she thought he would cry later, his face turned to the wall by his bed. A lump formed in her throat then, and she felt a great stirring of blind emotion, hot as lava, surging inside her.

She knew without asking that when the sculptress left there would be no forwarding address, no letters exchanged. The room would be empty, as it had been before. But the world would have changed. She wasn't sure how she would live in it.

Aparna began to clear out her room. She took her last sculpture to the dessicator and kiln at the Institute, as usual, but she did not bring back the finished work. She packed her few clothes and sundry belongings away in her suitcase. For Urmila time seemed to pass quickly and confusingly; she could not keep up with it. Her chest felt full of butterflies.

Two days before Aparna left, the news came. It was in newspapers, on TV, in glossy magazines: the terrible, violent demise of Vardhaman Mitra. He had been found in his marble bedroom by the servants, strangled to death by an unknown assailant. The guard at the gate had heard nothing, nor had the servant polishing the banisters a few feet from the bedroom door. There had been no visitors, suspicious or otherwise. The newspaper had a picture of the great artist after his wife's death, looking shrunken, with desperate, hungry eyes. "I cannot work," he had said then. "She gifted me her dreams. I gave them shape in clay..." Now he too was dead, and his murderer had left no clues apart from the indentation of fingers around the neck of the corpse. There was no sign of a struggle, but for a clay sculpture that lay smashed beyond recognition on the floor.

Aparna did not comment on the tragedy. She answered Urmila's mother's questions willingly enough, shaking her head sorrowfully, nodding at all the right places. She went out to the dhobi's stand on the next street with the bedclothes and curtains and had them washed and ironed. It seemed as though she had already washed her hands of the affairs of the Institute, that her mind was on the journey home.

Finally there came the evening of the last day. The sculptress had sent her suitcase on already. The table was clean and unfamiliar, the sheets on the bed smelled like the coal iron of the dhobi. It was raining again in a slow, sulky way, perhaps the last rain of the monsoon. Aparna Bhuvan was wearing her red-and-ochre salwaar-kameez, defying the grayness outside. Around her neck was a silver necklace Urmila had given her (a gift from some forgotten relative when Urmila had been small), and in her hand she held Som's Queen from the chess set. She thanked them with bright eyes.

Urmila said, "Are you taking the train?" and did not understand when Som and Aparna both laughed gently at her. Of course, she would take the bus first, Urmila thought. Her mind felt thick. Aparna embraced first Urmila, then Som, enveloping them briefly in the fragrance of moist earth. Now she was making her way down the stairs, Som following, thumping on his crutches. The boy and the sculptress said something to each other at the landing, then he went into the room and she continued down the stairs, getting smaller and smaller, like a bucket being let down into a well. She paused at the door to the drawing room, limned for a moment in the garish light from the TV, and said something to Urmila's parents. Then she was gone.

The sound of the front door shutting woke Urmila from her stupor; she began to run down the stairs, two at a time. Som called out to her but she didn't stop. The streetlight outside the house was out but she saw Aparna several paces ahead, walking quickly and gracefully through puddles and over potholes. The narrow street was lined with cars, and the rain cascaded gently off them. Urmila followed quickly, not knowing what compelled her, or what she would tell Aparna when she caught up with her. On the main road, with the crowds, the cacophony of car horns and the glare of headlights, she lost her quarry for a moment and stood looking frantically about, soaked to the skin, her hand shading her eyes from the rain. A man nudged up against her, leering, and she gave him a fierce, indignant look and joined a group of people with umbrellas crossing the street to the bus stop on the other side. But Aparna was not there. Urmila looked behind the bus stop at the soggy cricket field, and the dark river beyond it, and the wavering city lights on the other side. There she was, standing on the riverbank, staring away at something. What was she doing there? There was a bus coming now, it would go most of the way to the railway station. People dropped off the bus as it lurched, belching, to a stop; now the crowd surged towards it in a body. Urmila slipped away into the darkness behind the bus stop and plunged ankle-deep into the mud of the cricket field.

The sculptress was standing, stretching her arms before her, bending her body as if in obeisance to the rain. She lifted her face and let the rain fall on it. Only a faint wash of light from the street fell on her; she was a dark silhouette against the murky, glimmering river. Urmila stumbled towards her, dragging one foot, then another in the mud. Aparna must surely have seen her by now; she paused in her stretching and swaying, and perhaps she smiled. Urmila stopped. Aparna knelt, rain falling on her in thick shawls. Now Urmila saw that she was naked, except for the gleam of the silver necklace around her neck; somehow her clothes had rolled off her, or had been dissolved in the rain. She was holding something—the chess queen?—in one hand. Rain fell on her bare shoulders, formed a thick rivulet between her breasts, cascaded over the dimple in her belly, pooled in the hollow below, flowed smoothly over her thighs. Her hands dug into the mud; she bent her head, her hair falling in a wet, tangled mass over her face. Now a forest of hands rose from the mud, clay hands, loving hands, drawing the woman down into the earth. Her body seemed to become molten; a ripple ran over her. Before she sank completely, before her shape had altogether lost form, she raised her head and looked at the girl standing in the rain. Then there was nothing there but trampled mud, and the rain falling on it, smoothing it.

Urmila felt it then: a lightness spreading inside her, not joy, not pain, but something more complex, a kind of effervescence. She began to walk home in the rain. On her street the house lights shone warmly; open windows let out the sounds of conversation, laughter, plates in the sink. In Charu's house the grandmother would be tucking the smallest ones into bed, telling them a story about the monsoons. Urmila understood at last that what the monsoons brought was nothing less than the possibility of dissolving barriers between worlds.

Inside her gate she paused. She could hear the babbling of the TV; the blue light flickered in the window. She stood in the rain, feeling reluctant to go in. It fell on her like a benediction. Over the sound of the rain, the cackle of the TV, she heard it, so soft and tentative that she must have imagined it: the hollow clunk of clay shoes on the floor of the room upstairs, dancing, dancing to the rain.

INTRODUCTION TO

DO GOOD

JAMES VAN PELT

James Van Pelt writes and teaches in western Colorado. During the school year he teaches English at both Fruita Monument High School and Mesa State College. His fiction has appeared in several publications, including Analog Science Fiction and Fact, Asimov's, Realms of Fantasy, and Weird Tales. His non-fiction work has appeared in Tangent magazine.

In 1999 James was a finalist for the John W. Campbell Award for Best New Writer. Several of his stories have received Nebula and Stoker recommendations including two pieces that made the preliminary Nebula ballot.

His stories have been listed on the honorable mention lists in both Datlow and Windlings *The Year's Best Fantasy* and Horror and Dozois' *The Year's Best Science Fiction*.

His first collection, *Strangers and Beggars*, is now available from Fairwood Press.

He has a science fiction novel that has cruised much of the English speaking publishing world without finding a home. Currently he is working on a new novel that he hopes to complete some time soon.

Most importantly to him, his wife Tammy, and three children, Dylan, Samuel and Joshua, think he tells a pretty good bed-time story.

Scott Nicholson at *The Haunted Computer* web site asked James what his long term writing goals were. He said, "I feel a little like that guy in the old Tales From the Crypt comic who was trying to blow the ultimate jazz riff on his saxophone. He kept trying and trying and trying, until one day he finally did it. I don't remember what happened to him, but it was cosmic. I'm like that with my writing. I'm trying to write the ultimate string of sentences that will result in something cosmic. I know, it's an unreachable goal, but maybe along the way I'll write some decent riffs."

Do Good

James Van Pelt

Dedicated to Richard Vernon, Marshall Strickland and Edward Rooney

Vice Principal Welch studied the empty hallway for an hour, waiting for ghosts. He leaned loosely against a wall, arms crossed on his chest, as if watching the Homecoming dance from an out-of-the-way corner. An empty school is a quiet thing, but it is not silent. He felt as if he'd put his ear to a seashell, except the seashell had swallowed him, and the waves rolled, almost forty years of them.

He'd unlocked the front door at 4:30 in the morning, turned off the alarms and slipped in. The lockers echoed his footsteps, while a security light at the end of the hall provided illumination, reflecting a thick, moon-white stripe from the middle of the waxed floor and a bright star on every locker handle. The hallway smelled of books and old paint. Out of habit, he looked at his pocket planner. Nothing scheduled until 7:30. He sighed, then put it away.

Years ago, when Welch took the vice principal job, Principal Robinson, who retired and died the year after, had taken him to a bar on the far side of town where Lincoln High parents seldom gathered. He told him after their third beer, "That school's been there since 1902, Welch, and it started with greatness. We'd have been the state football champs in our first year, but the wingback broke his leg in the last game. Think of its tradition. What are you going to add, Welch? How are you going to make a difference? What are they going to say about you when you're gone?"

"I don't know," said Welch, his voice sudden and unexpected in the hallway's quiet.

At 5:30, the heating system kicked on overhead, and a series of sharp pops ran down the ducts. Lilly, the head custodian, would be coming in soon, tuning on lights, unlocking doors, opening the school to the Monday parade. He reached into his wallet for a ten dollar bill, smoothed it against the wall and wrote, DO GOOD. He thought for a second, then added, KILROY. From his coat pocket he took a roll of tape, put an inch-long piece on one end of the bill, then walked down the hall. He closed his eyes, spun around a few times, and then stopped, his hand holding the bill in front of him, finger pointed. Locker 457. His master key opened the door. Books covered the bottom: A.P. ENGLISH, CALCULUS, MODERN U.S. HISTORY, a senior's locker, a senior who evidently didn't have homework over the weekend. Magazine photographs of body builders were stuck to the door's inside along with a valentine neatly inked, TO KIKI FROM HER BUDS. He taped the ten dollar bill next to the valentine before closing the door.

Down the hall, a row of lights flickered on. Lilly had started her rounds.

Welch sighed and headed toward his second-floor office. No ghosts this morning. Not a one, but that didn't mean the school wasn't haunted. As he walked up the stairs he could feel the crush of students coming down, all those faces across the years streaming around him and through him.

"Good morning, Mr. Welch," said Pamela Howel, the Principal's secretary, as she paused outside his door at 6:00, early as always. He glanced up from the bi-monthly incidents summary. She carried a briefcase in one hand and a cell phone in the other. Perfectly coifed black hair. Wire-rimmed glasses. Narrow, thirtyish face. Metabolism and personality of a hummingbird. She'd taken the job in September and had already remade the office in her image.

"Hello, Pamela. Good weekend?"

"Nope. Visiting in-laws. Don't forget I need your intention sheet for next year on my desk by Friday."

Welch checked his planner. Written next to Friday's date was the reminder about the retirement intention form.

"Are you going to hang it up?"

Welch shrugged.

"Not that we want you to go," she said before dashing to her office.

Fifteen weapon violations since March 1. Eleven knives, a ninja throwing star, a broken bottle, a BB gun and a sawed-off pool stick. Twenty-three fights. Vandalism in the football weight room. Six car burglaries. A fire in the girl's bathroom next to the cafeteria. An attempted suicide. Four incidents of senior hazing, each involving duct tape. And then the folder filled with complaints about Beau Reece, a mouthy second-year freshman who weighed maybe eighty pounds. Welch sighed and pushed it to the side. All in all, a pretty calm two months. He raised his pen to sign the report.

A movement caught his eye. A student in the chair next to the desk crossed his legs.

Welch looked up. No one sat in the chair. He blinked. The skin on his arm prickled as if all the tiny hairs had been tugged. Was it someone he knew? That was the problem: after so many years, it seemed he knew everyone he met. They could be former students or retired teachers or parents he'd met years before. Every face sparked a vague familiarity.

Welch put his head down to look at his papers again, trying to achieve the same state of mind he'd had the moment before, but the chair remained stubbornly empty.

He'd started seeing students who weren't there the week before Christmas break. At first they were a motion in the corner of his eye, but now he saw them straight on. He thought of them as ghosts, but they were more like remnants of the absent. He saw last year's graduates and kids from his first years of teaching, and, occasionally—he shivered to think of it—the dead too.

Twenty minutes later, a pair of noisy baseball players on their way to the gym for before-school throwing practice passed his door. Phones rang. Voices murmured. Doors opened and closed. An unbroken succession of students streamed by. He locked his door behind him, did hall duty until the final bell emptied the passage, hurried a handful of the tardy to class, then slipped into the only empty desk in Miss Knapp's room for a quick evaluation. Thirty-three students filled the rest of the room. A few glanced at him when he sat down. A slender, shiny-cheeked girl who didn't look a day over twelve years old moved her backpack so Welch had room for his feet.

At the blackboard, red-haired Miss Knapp smiled nervously in his direction. She was fifty or so years old, come late to teaching after decades in the private sector. This was her third year in the building, her tenure year. If her evaluations were good, her job would be much more secure in September. He nodded and opened his notebook.

When Welch was a young teacher, he noticed students stopped talking when he passed. Not all the time, but often enough that when he heard a hushed, "Shh! It's a teacher," he longed to step up to them and ask them to share the secret. He wanted to tell him that five years ago he'd been like them. He was still seventeen in his heart.

It grew worse when he became vice principal. It spread to the teachers. Now he'd been vice principal for so long, he no longer recalled what teachers stopped talking about when an administrator came near. He'd asked his sole friend, Coach Qualls, who taught mythology and the humanities, about it once. "You're the troll, Welch. No one loves the troll."

Miss Knapp trembled slightly as she copied an assignment on the board.

Her fear annoyed him. I'm just a regular guy, he thought. I'm the fellow across the street. He waited until she looked at him, then he frowned and wrote in his notebook, PICK UP GROCERIES TONIGHT. She paled and asked the class for their attention. Welch wrote, BROCCOLI, RYE BREAD and MUSTARD, as if he'd just noticed a critical deficiency in her technique.

He stayed ten minutes until she handed out a worksheet. He had four other teachers to evaluate before first hour ended, so he noted in his planner that he'd observed her class, then rose to leave. Miss Knapp put her book on her desk. "Mr. Welch?"

They talked in the hallway outside the room.

"Can I do anything for you, Mr. Welch? Is this about Beau Reece?" Miss Knapp hid her mouth with her fingertips while holding her wrist. "I didn't see him today, but Friday he provoked the seniors again."

"No. Just a drop-in visit." Welch thought she might be an attractive woman if she didn't suck her cheeks in. He wondered if she was scheduled to supervise the dance this weekend. They might have a chance to talk more casually there.

"My methods, do you think they're sound?"

Suddenly, he felt guilty and mean. He shouldn't have written in his notebook like that. "Yes, of course. You're doing fine." He searched for a more specific observation. "I'm impressed with how you hold the attention of such a full class."

Her eyes darted to his notebook. He could tell she didn't believe him, not for a second. "Oh," she said hopelessly, "my next class is much larger."

"Really? Where would they fit?" He leaned around the corner and looked into her room. Half the desks were empty. The students slouched over their worksheets, their pens a litany of scratching in the silence. The desk where the shiny-cheeked girl had sat was unoccupied, no backpack on the floor. His face felt cold.

"Are you OK, Mr. Welch?"

Welch squinted his eyes shut and rubbed his forehead. "Yes. Have a good day." But as he moved away from her room, he knew she wouldn't. She'd worry all morning about what he'd seen in her room. She'd complain to her friends at lunch, and when she taught in the afternoon, she wouldn't be quite as effective as she would have been if he had never visited. Maybe it would be better if she wasn't coming to the dance. He envisioned two hours of polite conversation filled with bitter subtext.

In Mr. Mendez's Algebra I class, Welch watched the students' backs bent over their work. He'd come in quietly, and only a pimply-faced boy whose purple-penned notes were unreadable noticed when Welch took a seat. Mendez continued sketching a long equation on the board. "The formulas never lie," said Mendez. "Even imaginary numbers tell the truth."

Welch sat for several minutes, his record book unopened. Mendez taught in Lincoln High's original wing. The ceilings rose ten-feet, and rather than the anonymous white tiles and fluorescent lighting that marked the new wings, a dozen light fixtures hung down, each bright bulb surrounded by a green reflective collar, like a bed of metal and glass daisies growing from the ceiling. A hundred-year old math room, thought Welch. Over and over, the same lessons: Balance the equation. Seek the lowest common denominator. Chart the axis. Solve for X.

Were any of the students here the least bit . . . nebulous? Welch leaned forward, stretching his trembling fingers toward the pimply student's arm. Mendez kept lecturing. Welch realized the man hadn't faced the students the entire time. The class could sneak out, and Mendez would never know. Welch's hand approached the boy's arm, close enough to touch his sleeve.

Will my fingers slip through?

Welch could see the pores in the boy's hand, the tendons in his wrist.

The boy looked up, his eyes wide, watery and brown. "Yes, sir?"

"Nothing, son. Keep up the good work."

Welch grabbed his notebook, and his pen clattered to the floor.

"Ah, Mr. Welch has joined us," Mendez faced him, chalk in one hand. "Perhaps we could show him the magic of the quadratic."

All heads turned to look at him. Welch backed out of the room. "No, no. I'm just leaving." He fled to the safety of the empty hall, breathing hard. He realized he hadn't touched the student. Now he'd never know.

Coach Qualls, grading papers in the teachers' lounge, smiled when Welch walked in. His bulk swallowed the kid-sized plastic chair. "You all right?" he asked. His jowls were huge and covered with a perpetual five-o'clock dusting of white stubble. At sixty-four years, he was as the last staff member who'd been in the building longer than Welch.

Welch sank into a seat of his own. "Yes, of course."

They sat for some time. Qualls moved from paper to paper, check-marking mistakes. Welch looked out the lounge's window, but it faced the side of the school across the open quad below. Sun washed the bricks. No trees or birds or open sky. Just a white wall from top to bottom. Dim sounds from the band room drifted up, throbbing bass notes and the drums. They started and stopped a dozen times, the same thirty seconds of music.

"I turned in my intention form for next year. Time for me to check out," said Qualls. "Are you going to be the old man?"

Welch opened his planner. He hadn't written down anything from Mendez's class, and he wondered if he could count it as an official observation. "Did you accomplish what you wanted by going into this profession?"

Qualls paused, his pen in the air. "Ah, it's one of those days."

"It's just I wonder sometimes if I've done anyone any good. What's my role in the grand scheme? You told me once in the fairy tale that is the school, I'm the troll. I've thought a lot about that." Welch pushed the heels of his hands into his eyes, lighting a thousand sparkles behind his closed lids.

"Was I drunk?" Qualls scratched his chin thoughtfully.

"No. We were between third and fourth hour on a Tuesday."

"Oh, yes. I remember. In the school's mythic landscape, you are in the troll's niche. The teachers are knights, the students are all potential heroes, and you are the dark underpinning. Loved by no one. Intimidating to all. If we just had a bridge to put you under, you'd be perfect."

"That will look damned unimpressive on my tombstone. 'Here lies Vice Principal Welch, friend to none. Troll to the end.'"

Qualls checked the clock. "Five minutes to the bell. I'm going before the halls crowd up." He stuffed the papers into a briefcase that snapped crisply.

"So, are you a knight? Do knights get to retire?"

Qualls flourished his red pen. "Not me. I'm a wizard, and I'm off to wield my spells one more time. There are kids out there ready to be charmed and bewitched."

For a second, poised at the door to the rest of the school, Welch thought Qualls did look like a wizard under his bushy, white brows.

"I'm seeing ghosts, Coach," said Welch, but Qualls was already gone.

The coffee pot hissed. Above it, on the bulletin board, a sign hung from one thumbtack. DARE TO BELIEVE IN CHILDREN. Stapled beside it, his contribution to the effort, a list of students he'd suspended and a reminder to teachers to provide them with makeup work.

At the end of the day, long after the volleyball team had departed from their spring practice in the gym, and the booster club had left the cafeteria, and the students constructing the set for the musical had put away their power tools and paint brushes, Welch roamed through the school, turning off lights as he went. He checked his pocket planner. Nothing left on the day's schedule. I'm off the planner, he thought. I'm beyond my time. He'd been in the building for the last twenty hours, but he felt restless and antsy instead of tired.

He shook the thought away. Which one would it be tonight? He jangled his keys in his pocket. To his left the lockers gave way to tall windows that looked into the business computer lab. Screen savers swirled in the lab's darkness. He turned right into the freshman hall. Lockers on both sides. Doors into classrooms topped by teacher's names and their subjects. Miss Knapp had added a big smiley face by her name. Welch grimaced when he saw it. Maybe if he dropped a note in her box tomorrow it might make up for his visit to her class.

He stopped by the locker closest to her room. His keys dangled, clinking against the metal. Inside, a cigarette-smelling jacket hung from the hook above a paperback copy of *The Odyssey*. He wrote, DO GOOD on the ten dollar bill he took from his wallet, then signed it, CYCLOPS. When he reached to stick the bill to the inside of the door, he paused. A piece of tape, brittle with age, clung to the spot he always placed the bill. How many years ago had he opened this locker, hoping his gift would make a difference?

It didn't matter. That student had long ago graduated.

Before he could move, though, an arm reached through him, seemed to extend from his own elbow, and stuck a five dollar bill to the spot. The new tape melted into the old and became one.

Blood rushed from his face, and his skin erupted into goose bumps so violently that he thought he might faint. The spectral hand closed the locker, but it was open too, both doors visible to him. Then footsteps echoed in the hallway. Welch turned to see a man walking away. It was himself, darker haired, wearing the horrible gray-and-red plaid jacket he'd given to the Salvation Army in 1978. Wrestling against his paralysis, Welch forced himself to stir so he could follow, but the man's figure faded into the shadows at the hall's end and the sound of footsteps became the pounding of his heart in his ears.

Welch blinked once, hard, then licked his lips. Of course, it made sense. Still, he was unnerved. He shuddered when he turned back to the locker. The ghost bill had disappeared, and now the locker had just one door, the open one. He put the new tape over the old, then shut the locker as softly as he could, flinching at the mechanism's loud click.

The next morning he started with the Beau Reece folder. Three teacher complaints against him in the previous week. Tardiness, insubordination and inciting a shoving match in the locker room. The two seniors swore Reece started it, but by the time the P.E. teacher arrived, Reece had vanished and the seniors were pushing each other. "I don't doubt the Reece kid had something to do with it," the P.E. teacher said.

As the halls emptied into the first period classes, Welch waited outside the band room, where Reece played the clarinet. The bell rang, and the stragglers hurried to their destinations, casting fearful glances Welch's way. He ignored them. Where was Reece? A few minutes later a student came out and put the attendance sheet in the folder on the rack by the door. The teacher had marked Reece absent.

Ditching or tardy, thought Welch. He checked his watch. Fifteen parent call slips waited on his desk. Last week's athletic eligibility reports needed to be sent to the state for validation. A dozen obligations crowded his planner. He was days behind in teacher evaluations. And, of course, the intention form for next year brooded in his "to do" box. Retire or hang on? What should he do? Welch filled a cup with coffee in the teacher's lounge, then wandered, head down, toward the auditorium. He climbed the stairs to the sound booth that overlooked the stage, taking a seat so he could see the choir practice. The sopranos held a high note, a long, trembling, wordless vowel. Welch sighed, closed his eyes, letting the cup warm his hands. The altos joined in, then the baritones and bass. Sometimes, when he felt particularly discouraged, after he'd disciplined the umpteenth student for the day, he'd go to the choir room or to the band, or he'd wander through the art classes' galleries, or he'd open the shop's storage room so he could see the shelves and chests and tables students had made. He'd run his hand over the polished joints and glassy smooth wood. The kids can do great things, he'd think. They can be marvelous. But he never worked with those kids. The ones who waited outside his office were the tardy ones, the insubordinate and combative, the criminals.

The bell rang. Welch jumped, spilling the now cool coffee down his leg. He'd fallen asleep. Could he do anything good today? Could he make a difference? He wiped his pants dry as best he could, straightened his tie and headed for the attendance office.

"Can you get me Beau Reece's phone number and his attendance folder?" he said to the secretary, a girl who'd graduated from Lincoln three or four years earlier. She handed him the papers without smiling. When she was a seventeen-year old junior, he'd suspended her for three days for smoking in the girls' locker room.

Naturally, the number was no longer in service. Welch drummed his fingers on his desk, the phone in his other hand. He looked through Reece's attendance records. Although he often skipped classes, he hadn't missed a whole day of school until yesterday. Today didn't look good for him either.

Miss Knapp knocked on his door, looking distraught.

"Have you got a minute?"

Welch nodded. He hadn't put a note in her box yet. Maybe he could just tell her he thought she did a good job.

She sat in the chair next to his desk. "I know you're working very hard to help me be a better teacher, Mr. Welch, but I don't think you get to see the best of me." She kneaded her hands in her lap without looking at him. "I'm a nervous person, Mr. Welch. I'm fine with the kids. When you're in the room, though, I get all tied up."

Welch couldn't speak. He stared at her hands, squeezing so tight the muscles in her arms quivered. He wanted to put his own hands over them and hold them gently. He'd say, "You're going to be an excellent addition to this staff. You already are."

What he said instead was, "Maybe I can arrange for someone else to observe you."

Knapp stood, keeping her hands clasped. "I don't mind you observing me. I just can't teach when you're doing it." Her expression was unreadable, somewhere between misery and confusion. She left the office like a penitent, head down. The whole encounter hadn't lasted thirty seconds. The phone in his hand began beeping, so he hung it up.

Down the hall, he used his key to enter the faculty bathroom. The intercom clicked on for the morning announcements, a litany of club meetings and graduation reminders for seniors. Above the urinal someone had written SQUELCH WELCH. It wouldn't be so bad if this was a student bathroom. He smeared the ink with his thumb.

"Hate graffiti, don't you, son?" said Principal Robinson as he passed behind Welch and let himself into a stall, closing the door behind him. Robinson's belt buckle clinked loudly in the tiled room.

"I'm having a bad day."

"It's the Reece kid, isn't it?" Robinson's voice rose over the partition. "He's the burr under the saddle. You straighten him out, and the other irritations will go away."

Welch closed his eyes and leaned forward, resting his forehead against the cool tile. "Maybe. But if I suspend him, what good will that do?"

"You've got to find him first."

The toilet flushed.

Welch looked at the partition. There were no feet visible below it.

He gasped, then leapt to the door, breaking the latch when he banged it open. No one sat there. In the bowl, the water swirled.

Welch stepped back and bumped into the wall. His legs shook and he almost fell. Then, suddenly, he laughed. The water slowed its circular path and grew still while Welch's laughs subsided to chuckles. He wiped tears off his cheeks. Now he knew a secret, not that he'd ever heard anyone ask it, but he knew. Ghosts used bathrooms.

He started to laugh again. It welled within him, but he clenched his jaw tight against it. He could see himself in three of the mirrors above the sinks, his wild eyes, his disheveled hair. "I'm hallucinating," he said. "I'm going to wake up in my bed, and I'll be twenty-two again, wondering if I should go on the motorcycle trip into Mexico with Harold." Welch remembered his brother's postcards that came every week his first year of teaching and how he put them aside while planning lessons.

"Now I'm talking to myself in the bathroom." Welch stepped to a sink, washed his face. He straightened his tie, then dabbed a paper towel at his chin where a single drop of water glistened. Maybe when I open the door, he thought, there won't be a school there at all. It could be a desert or an ocean or a blank wall. He remembered the white wall across the school's courtyard through the teacher lounge window. How many years had he spent staring at that featureless expanse?

He pushed the door open tentatively. Pamela Howel strode toward him, a clipboard under one arm. She had her "I have to deliver a hand grenade" expression.

"We have a situation, Mr. Welch."

Welch nodded, but he started making his strategy. If I visit every one of Reece's classes, I'm bound to run into him. I have a quest, a mission to turn this boy around. I don't have to be the troll. I can be Odysseus. Ten years of war. Ten years of exile, and then a just reward. He smiled as he headed toward his office, picturing Reece's schedule sitting on his desk.

Howell grabbed his arm earnestly. "Did you hear what I said?"

Surprised to see her still there, he shook his head.

"The boy who tried to commit suicide last week named you in his note. The school board put you on their schedule for tonight. You need to be there at 7:00 sharp." She pivoted on one heel and went back the way she had come.

Welch reeled; he couldn't even remember the kid. He rubbed his fingers hard into his forehead while scrinching his eyes closed. Nope. No memory at all of his connection with the boy. One thing at a time, he thought, as he wrote in his planner, SCHOOL BOARD MEETING, 7:00, SUICIDE.

First, find Beau Reece. Outside Reece's second class, Welch stood by the doorway, hands in his pockets, watching students enter. Most ignored him. Some looked at him curiously. A few kept their eyes averted. The stream slowed. The bell rang. No Reece.

Welch walked off school grounds to "skid row," where the smokers, skateboarders, Goths and dropouts went when they were ditching class. He flushed a couple out of the high jump pit by the football field, encouraged three boys sitting on their skateboards in the alley beside the track to move on, then strode behind the convenience store across the street from the high school, surprising a pack of kids smoking, mostly tobacco, but he caught a whiff of pot too. Eyes went wide as cigarettes disappeared behind backs. Most of them had been in his office at one time or another.

"Have any of you seen Beau Reece?" he asked without real hope.

No answer for a long minute.

A boy wearing black leather pants and a spiked dog collar said, "He played with the jazz band yesterday before school."

Reece didn't go to any of his classes yesterday. Welch assumed he must have been sick. "Really?"

The boy nodded. The rest of the group stood silently, little whiffs of smoke curling behind them. "He missed this morning," the boy added.

"Thanks," said Welch, then he turned toward the school.

"Umm . . ." a girl with a violet top knot but shaved close above her ears said. "Aren't you going to yell at us to get back to class?"

Welch looked up at the perfect cotton-ball clouded sky. He shrugged. "Do what you want."

Ten paces away though, he stopped and went back. The kids hadn't moved. "All of you are underage to be smoking. Throw those things away, and I'll forget I saw you." He tried to bluster, but it sounded flat and without conviction.

"Are you all right, Mr. Welch?" asked the violet top knot.

Welch sighed as if he'd been punctured. "Just get away from the store. They're business folks and you kids leave a mess back here."

When Welch reached the school, he looked back at the convenience store. None of the kids had left.

For the rest of the morning, he patrolled the building in a daze. He pulled the records of the student who'd tried to commit suicide, but Welch's encounter with him had been in December when the boy had been suspended with three others for throwing snowballs at the buses. Even when Welch looked at the boy's picture, he couldn't remember him. Why would he name me in a suicide note? wondered Welch, and why does the school board want to see me? He walked a long circuit from the agriculture building, past the swimming pool, then out to the driver's ed. course.

In all his years in education, he'd never been teacher of the year, or even teacher of the month. He'd never been recognized by the board for an "Excellence in Education" award. He'd never been asked to speak at graduation. No one ever gave him a yearbook to sign. Maybe the board would ask for his resignation, or worse, the ignominy of a forced retirement.

What did Odysseus feel like after twenty years? Cursed by the gods. All his men dead. Not even sure his wife remembered him. Hope must have dwindled within him, thought Welch. What did the troll under the bridge feel about his place in the world?

He added up all the sick days he'd never taken. If he handed in his retirement intention sheet now, he could call in sick for the rest of the year and not even go to the school board meeting. Who needed the grief?

The bell rang, sending the students to lunch. Welch walked on the left side of the hall against the flow of traffic, glad for the contact when students bumped into him, even if they did shoot him annoyed glances. At least they were real, and he was real too. A short boy passed on Welch's right. Welch grabbed the boy's shoulder.

"Beau?" he said, but it wasn't him.

School ended. The buses left. Teams practiced. Clubs met, and, gradually, the building emptied. Once again, Welch wandered the hallways. The sun, low in the sky, sent long beams of light through the windows next to the doors and down the main hall. Only one day in the spring did the windows line up with the sun on the horizon so the light reached all the way to the other end.

He felt like he walked in a tunnel of light as he fingered the ten dollar bill in his pocket. In fifteen minutes he would have to leave. His planner was very exact about it: SCHOOL BOARD MEETING, 7:00, SUICIDE.

Years and years earlier he'd started taping money to the inside of lockers, one or two bills a week. Sometimes more if there were a lot of kids through his office. DO GOOD, he wrote, but in all that time he'd never heard anyone talk about the mystery presents. He never heard what the kids did with the cash. It made him think of standing on the edge of the Grand Canyon, flicking pebbles over the edge. They vanished into the depths without a sound. How come our *good* deeds never come back to haunt us? He checked the slip in his hand. Beau Reece used locker 1209.

The doors behind him crashed open, flooding the hall with sun. The silhouetted form of a half-dozen boys filled the space, and hard-soled shoes clicked against the floor.

"What are we gonna do?" cried one. As they came closer, Welch could see they were football players carrying a boy on a stretcher. For a moment Welch was disoriented. Football in the spring? Football ended months ago.

"I think his leg is broke," said another. They rushed by Welch. Dirt and grass stains marred their thick sweaters with an "L" sewn to the front.

The boy on the stretcher moaned, his face streaked with tears. "I'm sorry, guys," he said.

"We can't be best in the state without our wingback," said a third.

"Welch could save the day," sobbed the boy on the stretcher. "He could carry the ball for us."

"What?" stammered Welch. "What did you say?"

But the team hurried down the hall, the sun glaring on their backs. They dissolved into dust motes before reaching the end.

The hallway dimmed as the doors closed. Welch looked back at the windows. The sun touched the horizon, a perfect, crimson globe beyond the glass. In minutes the hall would be dark and it would be next fall before the sun lined up once more. He glanced at his watch. Time to go.

Taking a deep breath, he found Beau Reece's locker. He flattened the bill against the metal and wrote DO GOOD. He thought for a second about signing it ODYSSEUS. He shook his head. Odysseus didn't fit. If he was anyone from that story, it would be Paris, whose bad judgments destroyed heroes, so he signed it, THE TROLL.

The key slid into the lock, but the door resisted. Welch leaned into it to take the pressure off the internal mechanisms so he could pop the latch. The door swung open. Then, slowly, a body fell out. A ghost in the locker! Welch thought, his heart fisted tight. He took it in at once. The band of duct tape around the body's torso, pinning his arms to his side. The tape around the ankles. The broad band of dull silver across the ghost's mouth. And still, it fell, until at the last second, Welch stepped forward and caught it before it hit the floor.

A solid weight in his hands, Welch sat back in surprise. No ghost. It was a real boy, a small one, unconscious or dead. Welch pressed his fingers to the boy's throat where a pulse beat firmly. He worked his fingers under one edge of the tape, and carefully pulled it away from the child's mouth.

It wasn't until the kid opened his eyes blearily and croaked, "Mr. Welch?" that he realized he held Beau Reece.

Near midnight, while sitting in the hospital's waiting room, it occurred to Welch he'd missed the school board meeting. It didn't matter. He couldn't help smiling. The doctor told him Beau was dehydrated but would be fine. "Don't you have rules against hazing?"

The glass pneumatic doors from the parking lot wheezed open. Coach Qualls and two other teachers came in.

"What are you doing here?" said Welch. Qualls looked so misplaced. Welch realized in three decades he'd only seen him at school.

"The night nurse is the superintendent's wife, and she called him. His cell phone went off right in the middle of his closing comments. We came straight over. Good work, man." Qualls slapped him on the shoulder.

Welch shrugged. "Just luck, really."

Qualls sat next to him. "That's not what I heard. The secretaries told me you'd been looking for Reece since yesterday. Good instincts, I'd say."

Welch sighed and let himself sink deeper into the chair. The day had been a long one. Another teacher walked in, and before the doors closed, Miss Knapp followed, rubbing her coat sleeves against the cold of the spring evening.

"You were all at the meeting?" asked Welch. Through the doors he could see other teachers in the parking lot heading toward them.

"Sure," said Qualls. "Weren't you supposed to be there too? That kid who tried to commit suicide named twenty-four of us in his note. Typical school board over-reaction. They wanted to talk to us about sensitivity. Did you hear how he tried to do himself?"

Welch shook his head. The room filled with teachers.

"Four bottles of antacid pills." Qualls laughed. "He thought an overdose of anything would kill him."

The superintendent of schools joined the crowd, spotted Welch. "It's caring educators like yourself who make us proud to be teachers." He squeezed Welch's hand. "Forty years in education, and you're still making a difference. You saved that boy's life. "

A news truck pulled up to the doors.

Welch stood next to Qualls. Teachers filled the room. Qualls raised his hand and waved, then slowly dropped it, turning toward Welch.

"What?" said Welch.

"It's the darnedest thing."

"What?"

"I thought I saw Principal Robinson. For a second I thought it was Robinson over there."

Welch sighed. "It happens to me all the time."

"Where's this Welch fellow?" said a man with a television camera tucked under his arm.

"Must be a slow news night," said Welch, suddenly so embarrassed that he looked for a door to duck into, but the teachers surrounded him.

Afterwards, when the television crew departed, and most of the teachers had trickled away, Miss Knapp approached him, still wearing her coat.

"This was marvelous." She looked around the room. "So many of us came."

Welch didn't know what to say. Outside of the school, he had no words for her. But he wanted them, words that wouldn't make her nervous. Surely he could talk to her about subjects other than attendance and discipline and teaching strategies.

Something in her expression seemed strained, then a realization dawned on him. "Qualls did this, didn't he?"

Miss Knapp blushed. "No . . . oh, no. We really were glad to come, really. Well . . . he said you'd been a little down. You're not angry, are you?"

Welch shook his head. They stood without speaking for a few seconds, then she put out her hand, "I have to get going. Congratulations, though. You did a good thing. Will you be at the dance Friday?" Her delicate and cool fingers rested against his palm.

Dances featured ear-crushing music by groups he didn't recognize, gate-crashers from other schools who had to be tossed out, kids who came to the school drunk or who snuck into their cars for a beer or a joint before trying to get past him, and afterwards there would be torn confetti and crushed paper cups and decorations to be taken down. That's the way it always was. But he also knew the dance floor would be full of students and ghosts. He could live with the ghosts. And for the real kids? Warm hands on bare backs during the slow songs. Shy smiles. Genuine laughter. He would stand to the side, arms crossed on his chest, watching, like a knight on a castle wall.

"Save a dance for me," he said.

It was his place.

INTRODUCTION TO

LAIKA COMES BACK SAFE

MAUREEN MCHUGH

Maureen F. McHugh lives in Northern Ohio in a subdivision on the edge of a dairy farm. She lives a pleasantly boring suburban life with her husband and teenaged son, golden retriever and miniature dachshund. Her mother is from Barboursville, Kentucky, where she still has cousins. Her first novel, *China Mountain Zhang*, won the *Tiptree*, and she won a Hugo for her short story, "The Lincoln Train." Her latest novel is *Nekropolis*.

LAIKA COMES BACK SAFE

MAUREEN MCHUGH

There was a special program when I was in fourth grade where this photographer came and taught us. It was called the Appalachian Art Project and it was supposed to expose us to art. We all got these little plastic cameras called Dianas that didn't have a flash or anything, and black and white film. The first week we took pictures of our family and then we developed them and picked one for our autobiography. Then the next week we took pictures of each other. Then the third week we took pictures of important things in our lives. The fourth week we took pictures of dreams.

Not hopes and dreams—we were supposed to take a picture of something that was like something we would dream about. I had a book from the school library about exploration in space. It was old, from the seventies, twenty years before, and it talked about the history of space exploration. It was really more of a boy's book. My favorite books were horse books. All I remember from it was the part about Laika the dog. They trained this dog and they sent her up in space and they used her to see if people could survive in space and then because they couldn't bring her back down they left her to die up there.

That really bothered me because I had a German Shepherd named Lacey and I kept thinking about Laika up there all by herself and then just her bones going around and around. I had a bad dream about Lacey being taken to go to space. So when it was time to do the photograph of a dream, I took string and tape and I taped Lacey up with spots of tape on her chest and her head and I took her picture sitting there in the backyard. I had a parachute from one of those plastic soldiers you get that you wrap up in the parachute and throw in the air and hope the parachute opens and I taped that on Lacey, too, and had my mom hold the parachute—you can see her hand and a little of her arm in the picture—and then while mom kept Lacey from pawing all the tape and the string off, I took her picture. It's a good picture. She's looking at me and she has her ears up. I titled it "Laika Comes Back Safe".

We put all the pictures on the chalk rail. I remember somebody took a picture of their steps down to their cellar. Nobody seemed to think anything of "Laika Comes Back Safe", maybe because you could see my mom's hand and the parachute was really too little.

Tye Petrie stood behind me in the lunch line. "Brittany, is that your dog?" he asked.

"Yeah," I said.

"She looks like a neat dog."

That was more than Tye Petrie had ever said to me in my life. Even though he was my second cousin, we didn't have picnics and family reunions or anything with the Petries. "Her name is Lacey," I said, and then I said, "I love her more than anyone else on Earth."

I thought it sounded like a stupid thing to say, but Tye Petrie just said, "Really?" in this way that made it sound like he thought that was good thing.

"Do you have a dog?" I asked.

"No," he said. "I'm not allowed."

"You can come and pet Lacey," I said.

We had a little white house on cinder block—my dad had built most of it himself. I was doing my homework and my dad was getting ready to leave for second swing, the shift he was working at the plant before he got messed up, and my dad looked out the window and said, "What's that briar doing hanging on the fence?"

My dad didn't mean anything by it, he called everybody a briar, but Tye Petrie had a real light head of hair and real pale eyes in a tan face and he did look a bit like white trash. He was waiting around by our gate. "He's come to see Lacey," I said, and went out.

By that time Lacey was barking her fool head off. I untied her—Dad said she had to stay tied up even though we had a chain link fence because she crapped all over the front yard—and she went bounding over towards Tye. She stopped when she got close to him, looking back at me with one paw raised like she wasn't sure of something. Then she lowered her head the way she did when she was being introduced to another dog, tail sort of neither up or down and wagging just a little.

She was acting that way because Tye was a werewolf, although he wasn't really, not yet. I didn't know Tye was a werewolf because he didn't tell me for years and years. In movies, dogs are afraid of werewolves, but that's not true. They just think they're other dogs and if your dog hates other dogs, then they'll hate a werewolf, too. I'm like an expert on werewolves, after knowing Tye all these years, but it's not something that will ever do me any good. I thought about calling the *X-Files* people and seeing if they could use all that stuff for a movie, but I really can't tell, and besides, I wouldn't know how to get the phone number for a television show.

Tye and Lacey liked each other fine and we took her for a walk down the street. We hung out and he took me to the place where he'd made a fort in the woods. He came over pretty often after that and I think he went roller skating with my mom and me once. We never talked at school because I was always hanging out with Rachel and Melissa and Lindsey and he was always hanging out with Mike and Justin or somebody.

Then my dad was in the motorcycle accident and messed up his back and his leg and lost his job, and we had to go on the county until he got his Social Security pension settled. We moved into town and I transferred from the Knox County school system to Barbourville City Schools and went to Landry Middle School. We had to give up Lacey. The people down the street from our old house took her. I only saw Tye Petrie at church and we never said anything to each other.

I was in 4H then, doing sewing stuff, and I ran into Tye at the Knox County Fair. He wasn't in 4H, he was just at the fair. He wasn't hanging around with anybody and I was in the barn looking at the big draft horses. He walked up beside me like it was the school cafeteria lunch line and looked at the horse.

"Hi Tye," I said.

"I checked on Lacey last week," he said. "She's doing fine."

When we gave up Lacey I didn't get mad and scream and cry like they do on TV. I didn't say, "You can't have her!" and she didn't run away and find me, but it really hurt me deep inside and I never ever got over it. It was the worst thing that ever happened to me, even worse than when my dad got hurt. I couldn't say anything because I was afraid I was going to cry.

"I meant to tell you at church, but I never got a chance," he said. "I go check on her about once a week. They take good care of her. They don't tie her up. They let her run around their yard."

I took a deep breath and it was like a sob. "Thanks," I said. It came out a little shaky.

"So how's it going?"

I shrugged. "It sucks," I said.

"Yeah," he said. "It does."

"You want to go on the Octopus?" I said. I don't know why; the Octopus always makes me sick. But it was the only ride I could think of.

We hung around the whole day. My mom had to take my dad home because his back hurt so bad it gave him a migraine and Tye's mom and dad said they'd take me home. Tye's mom had the same coloring that Tye did, pale hair, a dark face, real pale eyes and she wore her hair up on the back of her head, kind of old-fashioned. She had an accent, Tye said, because she came from a Parish in Louisiana. She wasn't pretty or anything. She looked real plain and kind of country. She didn't say nearly anything when I was around.

Mostly, though, we were on our own and in the evening it got cool and the lights came on in the midway and the rides would take you up and back into the dark and then down and into the light.

"Brittany's got a beau," my mom said when I got home and I thought it was true.

On the Tuesday of the last week before school started I walked all the way out to Swan Pond to see him and Lacey. I got there before him. Lacey went nuts, jumping and barking, and Mrs. West came out to see what was wrong, but when she saw me she just waved and said I could come in the fence. I went inside and hugged Lacey and she licked my face. Mrs. West had a pretty garden and it had marigolds and red and white petunias.

Tye came and I said he could come in the fence. Lacey jumped all over him. Then he lay down on his back and I petted Lacey. "Do you ever wish you were a dog?" he asked.

"Yeah," I said. "A lot."

"It's not all it's cracked up to be," he said.

I thought about that. It probably wasn't. Lacey hadn't asked to have new owners, but then I hadn't asked to move into town and live on food stamps, either.

We talked about the life of a dog, and he told me about how his parents never talked to each other. They never fought, they just never talked to each other, and his father had told him once that he'd made a mistake to marry his mother. His mother took Lithium for her nerves. I told him that my mom was a bitch sometimes, which she was, and she probably should be on Lithium or something, and that since he got messed up, my dad had just given up on everything.

By the time I started home I was late for dinner, but since my dad didn't go to work anymore we just all sort of ate whenever anyway and it really didn't matter.

I told my mom that I'd gone to see Lacey. I didn't tell her about Tye because I didn't want her to tease me.

Tye and I met pretty often after that. We'd play with Lacey and then we'd walk out the gravel road to the Pope-Ball cemetery. It's just a little farm family cemetery, just a place fenced in with a wire fence and a bunch of tombstones halfway up Pope-Ball mountain. It's not any bigger than the West's yard but there are some trees all along the back fence. Some of the tombstones are pretty old, from 1890 and stuff, but most of them are my grandparents and great aunts and uncles.

Tye told me he would never have a girlfriend, never get married. There was a genetic problem in his family and he wasn't going to pass it on. He wouldn't say what it was but the way he talked I always thought it had to do with his penis or something and that's why he wouldn't say.

I still liked talking though, and I thought maybe he would change his mind about me. I thought about never having children and I didn't know if I could marry someone like that.

We met at least once a week until it got too cold, and then when it got warm I called him and told him I was going to see Lacey, slogged up through the mud and there he was and everything was pretty much the same. We started high school, and still kept it up, even when I started dating Rick. I told Tye all about Rick although I never told Rick about Tye. Tye thought Rick was a poser. Rick wore skateboarder stuff like the big pants and he really did skateboard although he didn't do stunts.

My mom was having trouble with diabetes and a lot of it was her own fault. She found out she had diabetes when she went on that liquid diet where you drink a can of stuff in the morning and a can of stuff at noon and she blacked out. Then the doctor told her to lose weight and it got worse. I never knew what we were going to eat at home—for a while she was on this Susan Powter kick. Susan Powter is that chick with the white buzz cut, and basically she says you can't eat anything good. Mom tried vegetarian for a little while until Dad said we had to have meat at dinner. Then she did the cabbage soup diet and lost some weight but then she gained it all back. Most of the time, Rick picked me up and we went down to Taco Bell or Dairy Queen and ate. A lot of times we brought stuff back for Dad.

Tye's parents filed for divorce. He said it was a relief. His mom got a job in town at Wal-Mart and his dad moved out. Since his mom was at work in the afternoon, he'd bring a six-pack of beer and stash it in the cemetery and after we saw Lacey we'd go sit and I'd drink two and he'd drink four and we'd talk about stuff.

Rick started hanging out with his friends and not coming over. He got a paintball gun and played paintball all the time and he never had any money to do anything, never wanted to come over much. He was a pain anyway because all he ever talked about was how he was going to join the Air Force and be a pilot, or the music he liked which was all Jimi Hendrix and Led Zeppelin and singing "Sweet Home Alabama", or it was Garth Brooks and Clint Black. I got sick and tired of him never having time to come over and we had a big argument and broke up and then I cried for a week.

I'd go out to see Tye almost every evening and we'd sit in the cemetery, bundled up in our winter coats, long after it got dark. I didn't think of Tye as a possible boyfriend anymore, he was more like a brother or something. He had this old plaid cloth coat and he'd sit there with his back up against my Great-aunt Ethel's red granite tombstone—it was the biggest in the cemetery even though both her and my Great-uncle Jake drank all the time and never had any money, because John, her son, and my cousin once removed, had a good job with the nuclear plant down in Knoxville and he paid for the funeral—and we'd listen to Pearl Jam or U2 or Sublime until the batteries ran out on his CD player. I was talking about being a vet. That's what I wanted to do, be a vet.

"I can't come over the next few nights," he said.

"Is your mom working days?"

"Yeah," he said. He stared at his beer. "And, um, I go kinda crazy sometimes and I'm going to do it for the next couple of days."

"You mean you like schedule it?" I said. I didn't know if I was supposed to laugh or what.

"No," he said, "I just know when it's going to happen." He was dead serious.

"Tye," I said, "what do you mean?"

He shrugged. "It's a hereditary condition. I told you I had a hereditary condition."

"It makes you crazy sometimes?"

"Sort of," he said.

"What do you mean, 'sort of?'"

He wouldn't say any more than that.

It was too cold and it was late. He promised me he'd be back out here on Tuesday unless it was raining. We had an unspoken agreement that if it was raining we just came the next time it was dry.

I rolled up our blanket and stuck it in the plastic bag we kept it in, then stashed it half under this fallen down tree and sprayed it with this pet-off stuff we used to keep the animals out. I took the beer cans and Tye took the CD player. I threw out the beer cans in the dumpster in the back of the Chinese place I passed on the way home.

We lived in an apartment complex then, and I cut across the back parking lot. I could see the light through the curtains of the sliding glass door. We had a first floor apartment because of my dad's leg.

My mom was loaded for bear when I got in. "Where have you been?"

"Shelly's," I said.

"I called Shelly's and you weren't there."

"I went for a walk."

"For four hours?"

"Yeah. I went out to see Lacey, my dog, and then I walked around."

She didn't buy it. I don't know why I didn't tell her I was with Tye except that I didn't want her coming up to the cemetery and catching me drinking beer. She was screaming about me about never being home and I just said, "Yeah, whatever," and she slapped me.

My dad said, "For God's sake, Betty, hitting her isn't going to do any good!"

"Jesus!" my mom shouted, "you want your daughter running around all night?"

Oh God, they'd been arguing. I stood there, holding my face, feeling these little sobs like hiccoughs.

"She's been out for hours without telling anyone where's she's been! Don't I have a right to know where my daughter's been?"

"You don't have any goddamn right to hit her!"

"Maybe if you acted like a father —"

"Maybe if you got off your fat ass and got a job!"

"You don't have the sense God gave a cockroach! You know something, Joseph Gaines Ball! You know something? I grew up! You never grew up! You just kept drinking and running around on a goddamn motorcycle!"

I ran to my bedroom and locked the door.

"Goddamn it!" my mother roared, "You get out here you little bitch!"

My mom started hammering on my door. My dad must have tried to grab her because I heard her slap him. Then she must have punched him because he fell out in the hall. He had trouble getting up because of his back and his leg, so she could punch him when he was down, too.

"Goddamn it!" he was yelling. "Goddamn it!"

Then I could hear my mother run down the hall sobbing.

My dad was lying out there on the floor on the mauve carpeting that didn't go with any of our furniture. "I'm going to get my gun," my dad said in a monotone, "I'm going to get it and blow my fucking head off." I could hear it clearly through the thin walls.

"Sure," my mother called from the kitchen, "lie there and pity yourself! If you think I'm going to beg you to save your sorry-ass excuse for a life, you're wrong!"

"I'm going to blow my fucking head off," my dad said again.

I laid on my bed in the dark and pulled my big stuffed dog up against my chest and pretended it was Lacey.

My mom and dad were still asleep when I got up. I was late for school the next day and missed first period General Math, which was no great loss.

When I got home, my mom was waiting for me and she started in on me again, so I said, "I'm going."

She grabbed me by the arm but I just twisted out of her grip and ran out the door. I went to see Lacey but she was in the house so I went up to the cemetery and found our blanket and wrapped up in it. I couldn't face going home yet, and I didn't know what to do. It was chilly, but not really cold. I sat leaning up against my Great-aunt's tombstone in the sun. My parents had argued until two or three in the morning and I was tired and I fell asleep there.

I woke a couple of times and then suddenly it was dark and I'd gotten cold. It wasn't completely dark because the moon was up but it was strange and creepy to be walking home in the dark. My mom was waiting for me, still mad. We had another fight, and I told her I was afraid to come home to a psycho mom. She said the school had called and said I was tardy and I said that maybe if she got up and sent me off to school like a normal mom I wouldn't be tardy.

My dad came out and said I wasn't being fair and they told me I was grounded for a week.

I didn't get to go out to the cemetery until my punishment was up. I called Tye Petrie and told him I'd been grounded. We didn't talk about it on the phone. Tye didn't like to talk on the phone. He just told me he'd see me in a week.

He was waiting in Mrs. West's yard, and Lacey was happy to see me. I did all the things she liked, rubbing my knuckles in her ears and scratching her chest to apologize for not having seen her.

"What happened?" he asked.

"My mom and dad were having an argument so I came out to the cemetery and I fell asleep and I didn't get home until about nine."

"Yeah?" Tye said. He looked tired. He'd been suddenly getting taller and he'd gone from looking like a little middle school kid to looking like one of the juniors. He even had a little bit of a moustache.

"Did you go crazy?" I asked.

"Yeah," he said.

I wanted to know what it was like to go crazy. "What did you do?"

"Just, sorta went crazy."

That's all he would say and then neither one of us knew what to talk about. "When I woke up at the cemetery," I said, "it was already dark. Scared the living shit out of me," I said.

"Brittany," he said, "you shouldn't be out alone after dark."

"I didn't expect to be out after dark," I said, irritated.

"No, really. I mean, I...um, what if something attacked you?"

"The only people that ever go to the cemetery are you and me," I said.

"What if I attacked you?" he said.

"Don't be weird, Tye," I said.

"I am weird," he said, and I grinned, but he started to cry.

I'd never seen Tye cry. "Jesus," I said, "what's wrong?"

That's when he told me he was a werewolf.

I thought that maybe he really was crazy, you know? Here he was crying and telling me that he was a werewolf, for Christsake. I patted him and said it was okay, he was okay. I wondered a lot of things about Tye, like was he gay, or was his father like, molesting him, but I never expected that he was crazy. He told me a bunch of crazy things like how he hadn't started changing into a wolf until this year because the change didn't happen until you started going through puberty. He told me about how he'd been dreading it for years, and how he couldn't really remember what had happened afterward because it was like he had experiences in a whole different way, like through smell. "So, see," he said, "I could have hurt you really bad, Brittany. Really bad!"

"You didn't hurt me," I said because I didn't know what else to say. It was really crazy. Some ways, Tye was really crazy. Sometimes he was so excited it was like he was on something and he'd be talking a mile a minute. Sometimes he would sleep all Saturday and Sunday and be real depressed.

We sat there a long time while he told me about how his mom's family in Louisiana was like this and how his mom had run away to try to get away from all that. It was crazy stuff and it was creepy listening to Tye because he really believed it but it was so strange it was really interesting. I knew if I acted like I wanted to go, Tye would think I didn't believe him.

He kept saying, "I know it sounds crazy—you probably don't believe me—but it's true," and he kept watching me in this desperate way like I was the last person in his life.

Finally I had to go home or I'd get grounded again.

The next day I half thought he wouldn't be at the Wests', but he was there, just hanging by the fence and Lacey was sitting, looking up at him as if she was trying to talk to him. I thought about how much he had changed lately and I realized for the first time how, well, sexy, he seemed suddenly.

Lacey and I said hello.

I asked Mrs. West if we could take Lacey for a walk—sometimes we did that and Tye had me so weirded out that I wanted her with me. I took her on the leash and we walked up to the cemetery. Tye got the beers and I poured some into my hand for Lacey. She liked beer.

Lacey licked my face and then stood with her front paws on my legs. She usually only did that when I was crying or something. "Lacey," I said, "what's up with you today!"

"She knows you're scared," Tye said. "She can smell your fear. She's trying to make you feel better."

I almost said, 'scared of what, you?' but it was true, I was scared. Not that Tye was going to hurt me, but that he was crazy and I didn't know what to do.

"I can smell it, too," he said.

I petted Lacey, trying to think of something to say.

"You don't believe me," he said. "I can smell that. It's okay, it's all pretty crazy. But I can smell your feelings. I can smell what you had for lunch. You had a cheeseburger."

I had a cheeseburger almost every day at lunch because it was about the only thing I could stand in the school cafeteria. I mean, probably Tye could have guessed that, I mean, we'd talked about it because we'd talked about how school lunches sucked. But the way he said it scared me even more.

"I can smell that you're worried," he said. "I can smell feelings that I don't even have names for. I can smell you better than I can see you, Brittany."

It was that I either had to believe him or I had to quit seeing him.

Things changed after that; like we were falling, out, away. I'd walk out to the cemetery and it was as if I wasn't in Barboursville anymore. Tye was taller than I remembered and the pale hair on his forearms looked so soft I wanted to touch it. I knew he had to smell that change on me, too, but he didn't say anything about it. So I studied the way his shirtsleeve was cuffed back against his skin.

He told me how when he went out at night during what we called his 'crazy times' the whole world was different because his brain was different. "I can't remember it afterwards," he said.

It started to rain. I had a jacket with a hood and the rain was hard enough that it pattered on it like a roof. All around me I heard the rain on the dead leaves and the cemetery was deep in maple and oak leaves.

"I watched a place last night," Tye said. His eyes were dark looking underneath like he hadn't had much sleep. "When I got there the light was on and I could see it through the curtains, so I lay there next to the door with my nose pressed up against the crack. I smelled macaroni and cheese."

I felt the hair lift on the back of my neck because I knew whose place he had watched.

"I wasn't thinking 'macaroni and cheese'," he said. "But today I can remember the smell, and the smell of people inside, a man and two women."

He told me all the things we'd done, watched TV and stuff. I thought about how when I was doing my Spanish homework there he was, not five foot away, smelling me. I had a funny image of Tye lying there in the dark on the patio: a person, not a wolf. It was creepy.

He told me how the lights had gone out and how he had heard the television still on. My dad often sat in the dark and watched tv.

Tye coughed. He had a cold.

I wanted to touch his arm, but I sat on the tombstone and felt the rain on my chilly hands. "I went to the next window," he said, "and I smelled that smell almost as familiar as my own."

I started to cry. I lifted my face to the November rain. Everything was spinning so fast. We were on the spinning earth whirling along. The cold rain was wet on my upturned face and Tye leaned over and kissed me and we fell out into the sky, like Laika, whirling away.

His lips were cold from the rain and so very soft.

"I'll hurt you, Brittany," he said. "I won't mean to. I'll follow your smell."

"No you won't," I said. I was crying so hard that the words came out all muddled. "You'd never hurt me!"

But he got up and walked out of the cemetery and down the mountain.

The next afternoon I went out to see Lacey and Tye never showed up. I went every day for a week and he still didn't show up. So I called his house — something I almost never did — and he came to the phone.

"Hey, Tye," I said, "it's Brittany."

"Hi," he said. The silence hung there. "I'm going to get a part-time job."

"You can't get a job," I said, "you're only fifteen."

"I can get a work permit for hardship because my mom's divorced, and there's this guy that's going to hire me to work in his bait shop. I won't be able to come up to see Lacey anymore."

"You can't," I whispered.

"Brit, I gotta go." And then he hung up.

I didn't see him for over a year after that but then he got a job at the Pick n' Pay as a stock boy and I'd see him when I went in sometimes. He'd say hello to me and act friendly, but not really personal. More like polite. And by that time I was dating Kevin and I had a job at Dairy Queen so I didn't have a lot of time. I was saving money to move out, but the radiator and the water pump went out on the old Accord and we had to have a car so I had to fix it because my mom didn't have the money. Things just kept coming up.

It was Jack Pope who first told us the news. I was sitting at the kitchen table after school watching my tape of *General Hospital* and my mom was eating some of those fat-free cookies, even though I'd told her they didn't do her sugar any good; they had more sugar in them than the regular kind.

Jack doesn't drive and he and his wife live out on the mountain near the Pope-Ball cemetery, so he walks miles and miles, and when he comes by our house sometimes he stops in for a glass of water. I didn't think anything about it when he poked his head in. He said to my mom, "Betty, did you hear about Tye Petrie? He done killed himself."

Normally I wouldn't believe him. Jack doesn't lie but his two kids are in special education and they come by it honestly, so I'd have figured that he got something mixed up, but when he said it I just knew it.

My mom said, "Tye Petrie? Roger Petrie's oldest boy? You knew him, didn't you Brit." And then she called to my dad, "Joe? Joe? Jack Pope's here and he says Roger Petrie's oldest boy killed himself!"

My dad was in the bedroom like usual, but he limped out into the kitchen even though he probably didn't know or care about Roger Petrie or Tye Petrie. He didn't say nothing, just stood there looking at Mom and Jack.

Mom asked Jack Pope what happened, but I didn't want to listen. There was a ring of water on the kitchen table where my glass of diet coke had been sitting and I drew lines across the ring with my finger, drawing out the water.

My dad was standing there in the kitchen, and my mom was talking to Jack Pope. I just sat there and died and no one noticed.

My mom's been having more and more trouble with her sugar, and now she has trouble seeing. The way she keeps eating I figure she's going to go blind and I don't know how my dad is going to take care of everything. Lacey died the year Tye did. Her hips got bad with hip dysplasia and she had to be put to sleep. I hadn't seen her since Tye stopped going to the cemetery. Sometimes, when I was remembering Tye and everything that had happened, I thought she was me.

Kevin, my boyfriend, has a job at a machine shop and he's talking about getting married. He wants a little land so we can raise a couple of beef cows, like his dad does. I don't know any reason not to get married and Kevin says a dog would be great. I'm going to have a bunch of dogs, German shepherds and huskies and stuff. I'm going to be a veterinarian assistant, but I can't yet because we need more money than that so I've got a cashier job at the Pick n' Pay.

Sometimes we go down to Corbin to a bar down there that plays country and teaches line dancing, and we go out the interstate. Jack Pope told us they found his car parked on the interstate on one of the bridges. As we cross the bridges I find myself thinking. Could I do it? Is it hard? Did he have to work up the nerve?

They say when you jump there's no feeling of falling. Maybe he just leaned forward and fell into the smoky blue-green air.

INTRODUCTION TO

THE MAIN DESIGN THAT SHINES THROUGH SKY AND EARTH

BRUCE HOLLAND ROGERS

Bruce Holland Rogers lives in Eugene, Oregon, and writes genre fiction and literary fiction. His recent short story collections are *Wind Over Heaven* (Wildside Press) and *Flaming Arrows* (IFD Publications). He is the author of a book on meeting the psychological challenges of the literary life, *Word Work: Surviving and Thriving as a Writer*.

This story is a symmetrina, a fixed form of prose or poetry consisting of shorter stories or poems that share a theme or topic. The sections must fit a word count and increase in size by any mathematical progression of whole numbers. The base count (n) of this story is 250 words and the progression ratio is the first few Fibonacci numbers: $1n$, $1n$, $2n$, $3n$, $5n$, $8n$. After the center story, the sequence counts back down. More complete information on the form is posted at `http://www.sff.net/people/bruce/odds`.

THE MAIN DESIGN THAT SHINES THROUGH SKY AND EARTH

BRUCE HOLLAND ROGERS

1. FOR THE GIRLS WHO HAVE EVERYTHING

During the drive, Heather says, "Aunt Sylvie, what's for lunch?" She asks it just before we pass the last burger place, before the roads change from asphalt to gravel. She was along when I shopped for groceries: Oatmeal. Spaghetti. Rice.

I say, "Apples and cheese. Maybe a tomato. Want to split a tomato?"

"Okay." She watches the burger place go by.

I could afford to buy her a burger. By myself, I eat them whenever I want.

Another few miles of dirt road and sagebrush, and we're home. My house sits on ten acres of flat scrub. I have a bedroom, a sitting room, and a kitchen. I could have a bigger house somewhere else. But this is where Aunt Sylvie lives.

My sister has an enormous house with fourteen rooms, green lawns, and stables out back for the girls' horses. The girls take music classes, and gymnastics. They play soccer and softball. They have everything. *Everything.*

Heather helps me cut apples so thin that before we eat each slice we can hold it up to see the light shine through. When I share the tomato with her, she cuts her half into small bites to make it last. She knows that a weekend with me is a long time. Aunt Sylvie is boring. On these weekends, the only way to not go crazy is to do one thing at a time. Cut the tomato. Smell it. Taste this bite.

After lunch, there's nothing to do but watch the clouds.

2. FIRST DAY

It's your first day as a teacher, and all day, you're remembering. You show them the coat room. Today, no one has a coat to hang up. It's hot out. But you remember the red and blue reversible jacket you had and how you could stretch the tails out like a sail and lean into the wind. You believed you could fly, that you were always about to lift off.

The number one pencils haven't changed. You pass out the paper with solid and dotted lines for practicing letters. At the chalk board, you demonstrate writing the big O and the little o with a piece of chalk from a box that has never been opened before. Once, the smell of chalk dust was new.

As you go from pupil to pupil, correcting how each holds the pencil, you remember the smell of Mrs. Wolff, your teacher back then. She smelled like strawberry Kool-Aid. You think of those colors and flavors, the green green of lime, the red red of cherry, purple color that you never saw on a real grape any more than you ever tasted that flavor in anything but grape Kool-Aid and Jell-O and lollipops.

When your boys and girls say "One and one make two, one and two make three," you remember that you once knew the personalities of numerals: the aggressive 2, the mysterious 5, the happy 8. You remember that the child who made these memories — why should this be so startling? — was you.

3. MS. AMANTE

Biology One is being team taught this year. One teacher is Mr. Tott. The other is Ms. Amante. Ms. Amante has long legs and wears boots that grip her calves. Her lipstick is the color of blood. Sometimes when she pauses and thinks of what to say next, she bites her lip. Her full, red lip.

During the unit on perception, Ms. Amante says that Helen Keller could tell one person from another by scent, and never mind perfumes. That's not what Ms. Amante is talking about. She means the clean scent of skin, and the students can smell it, too, if they try. She says that a man may fixate on the way a particular woman smells, may pine for her as he holds a sweater that retains her scent. That day, she's wearing a sweater.

There's something like spice and earth in the air on the days when it is Ms. Amante's turn to teach.

Ms. Amante says, during the unit on arthropods, that the male preying mantis doesn't know if he's going to get lucky, get eaten, or both. She says this with a smile that makes the boys wonder if Ms. Amante can read their minds.

Males compete. Red-winged blackbirds hurry north in the spring to scout locations the females will like. Big horn sheep make the mountains echo with the clash of horns. Deer lock antlers. Stallions rear and kick and bite. Some seagulls feed the females in courtship. Dinner first, then mating, says Ms. Amante. She says that humans like to pretend that biology somehow doesn't apply to them.

Her fingernails are as red as her lipstick. Her hips are wide.

All that effort to bond, and what's the result? Thirty percent of the chicks in a given nest are the offspring of another male, and it's not just mama birds that are stepping out. Rabbit, elk, and ground squirrel females slip away for something on the side, and maybe on the other side, too.

Ms. Amante is married. She never talks about her husband.

A certain hormone called oxytocin inspires the urge to cuddle. And other things. An ovulating mouse that gets an extra dose of oxytocin will work twice as hard to get males to mount her. As she reports this, Ms. Amante enunciates. Her mouth makes an O when she says *mount*.

The unit on vascular plants seems to be mostly about flowers. A male wasp sees the female of his dreams and copulates with her. Then he sees her sister—even better!—and has another go. But really, it's two orchids. The flowers have duped him twice. He's been taken advantage of, used up, and dropped off to walk the rest of the way home. And the students wonder, *Does he mind?* Such speculation is not officially part of the lesson plan. Ms. Amante won't answer the question.

Powdery anther. Sticky pistil. When Ms. Amante describes them, all the students, boys and girls alike, want to hear more, more, *more.*

4. GURU

Sam could have taken the number 15 bus. The stop was closer to his house, the route more direct. Walking two blocks out of his way for the 64 guaranteed that he'd be late, and being late could be one more thing that was wrong. One more thing in a long list. His house was a mess—dishes piled in the sink, floors that hadn't been swept in recent memory and probably had never been scrubbed since he and Cheryl had bought the place. The diaper pail stank. Cheryl's old cat had started peeing on the rug. Somebody ought to be taking care of all this, but Cheryl's hands were already full as she juggled all the things that had piled up during her maternity leave. Sam and Cheryl didn't have the money for a housekeeper on top of day care, not with the mortgage. On top of that, Sam worked for idiots. He didn't know anyone who didn't work for idiots, but his particular idiots were worse than most.

When the 64 arrived, the driver was some woman. Sam stood on the bottom step and said, "Albert working today?"

"Yep," she said, "but he's got the other 64."

Sam said, "I'll wait."

It would cost him the fare of $2.50 plus another half an hour of waiting to ride Albert's bus, but as soon as Sam saw the driver's face, he knew it was going to be worth it. Albert was smiling at something a passenger had said as the bus doors opened. "Well, good morning!" Albert said.

"Hey, good morning," Sam said, paying the fare. The greeting was so warm and personal, but Sam doubted that Albert really remembered him. Sam had ridden with Albert only twice before.

"How are you?" the driver asked.

"Not so good," Sam told him. "Life's a mess."

"What kind of mess?" Albert said, still smiling. "What could life get to be, that you'd go calling it a mess?"

Sam told him: the house, the new baby, the idiot bosses.

"Well, sure!" Albert said. "But life is good. That baby, I bet he's beautiful."

"She."

"Aw, yes. Looks like her mother, don't she?"

"As a matter of fact, she does."

"Now," said Albert, "you tell me, sir. Did you marry an ugly woman or a pretty one? Did you love her on first sight, or did you have to force yourself?"

Sam laughed. "Sort of in between. I mean, I noticed Cheryl gradually. She's beautiful."

"I see. Beautiful wife, beautiful daughter. Nice house, too, I bet. A job that makes all this possible. What am I forgetting?"

Sam was smiling. He could have told himself all this, but coming from Albert, it had power.

"Oh, I know," Albert said. "You ever try washing a dish for pleasure? You make the sudsy water hot, and the rinse water cold. Makes your hands tingle."

"Can't say I ever tried that."

"Sounds like you've got a whole house full of pleasure waiting for you every day," Albert said.

Other passengers, Albert's regular riders, nodded their heads.

In spite of arriving late, Sam had what passed for a pretty good day at work. He rode the 15 home and got dinner started. He played with his beautiful baby while Cheryl finished dinner. After dinner, he loaded the dishwasher and then scrubbed the kitchen floor with warm water. It didn't exactly make his hands tingle, but he found that if he was really paying attention to it, even scrubbing the floor could yield a sort of pleasure.

Cheryl had put the baby to bed, and then she had fallen asleep on the couch. Sam lay down next to her and stroked her hair. That Albert, he thought, knew things. The man was a guru of simple truths.

Albert, at the end of his shift, returned home weary. He had a beer to help him unwind. His face ached. It took something out of a man, being so damned sociable all day.

At the supper table, his boys were in high spirits, cracking wise. His wife told them gently to settle down. They didn't.

"You two cut it out," he warned.

They were quiet, but then one showed a mouthful of chewed peas to the other. They both laughed.

"Damn it!" Albert shouted. "Is a little peace and quiet in my own home too much to ask for? Go to your room! Both of you!" Then he threw down his napkin. It was already too late to enjoy his supper.

5. THE GREAT POEM OF LATVIA

Foul weather began the misadventure which was to terminate in verse in a difficult tongue. The captain had hunted seals off the English and Spanish Maloons before, and he knew the islands thereabout, but in a heavy fall of snow and a swirling wind the island profiles were changed in their aspect. What seemed familiar was not, and the familiar lay hidden. Thus the captain, seeking safety on Swan Island, mistook some other rocks for a point that he must round for Chatham Harbor. He was confident of deep water, but the ship struck with great violence a ledge that was under the surface.

Under the American captain were four sailors: a free Negro from New York called Henry Dodge, two young Englishmen of excellent character called Joseph Matison and Richard Kenney, and the Spaniard Tomaso Limero who had signed articles in Montevideo when the ship needed to replace an American crewman who had to be put ashore there for reasons of severe ill health. It was this particular composition of crew that doomed the ship, for as the captain perceived how he might save his vessel, badly stove as she was, so did Tomaso Limero have his own contradictory notions. Limero had always claimed to know these waters better than the captain himself, and in this moment of extremity he asserted his knowledge and insisted that he knew how to bring the ship at least to a place where she might be grounded and her stores salvaged for the survival of the crew.

For every order the captain gave, Limero interfered and gave a contradictory one. Matison took the captain's part and argued for discipline, whereupon Limero argued that the captain's orders were very foolish and should end in the extinction of all aboard. While these two nearly came to blows, Dodge and Kenney were thrown into a great confusion, obeying first this order and then the contradictory one. Either the captain or Limero might have prevailed as the ship's savior, but neither set of orders was carried to completion, and the ship soon took on so much water that she had to be abandoned in haste.

They rowed the ship's boat through a growing storm, and for some time they followed an iron-bound shore where even if they succeeded in landing beneath the cliffs they could not haul the boat up and prevent her being dashed to pieces in the night. At last they espied a shelf that suited them, and they spent a wretched night soaked through, with the boat whelmed over on the rocks as their only shelter.

In the morning they sought the ship, but she had utterly foundered without trace. The men despaired of their continued existence. However, for their physical continuation they had tools that might serve even through winter if the men did not lose their wits. They had the boat for going among the islands, which the captain now recognized in clear weather. They had knives, some iron tools, and a quantity of cut saplings carried aboard the ship for the making of seal clubs. They had steel and flints for fire.

They at first killed sea-elephants only for their blubber, which served as fuel. In time, as they exhausted their hard tack, they began to eat the lean of those creatures. They also hunted seal and wild fowl. The birds of the Maloons were so unaccustomed to man that they might be killed rather easily by stoning, and foxes that made bold to raid the larder also made easy prey.

The shipwrecked crew built a shelter of stones. They dried the skins of fur seals, rubbed them soft, and sewed them with a sail needle and thread ravelled from the boat's sail. They roofed their shelter with fur seal skins, and fashioned Mockasins from the tougher skin of hair seals. When Macaroni penguins arrived and made a rookery among the albatross, the men feasted on eggs.

All of this bespeaks their efforts to remain strong of body, but the greatest danger was to their minds. For the short season when they might eat fresh penguin eggs, the men had brief respite from ordinary fare so vile it could be swallowed only with the sauce of immense hunger. The fox, rook, and seal flesh were often only half cooked over the spitting fires of blubber. The smoke of those fires made the skin of the five men all of one sooty color. When there was no blubber, fires made of dried Tushook grass were even smokier, more bitter, and less effective for roasting. Every day made the men more wretched.

The captain thought the circumstances of the wreck best forgotten as the matter now was of survival. Limero and Matison, however, regarded one another in enmity, and either one might erupt at any moment in insults for the other. By the light of a smoky fire one night, Matison beat Limero about the legs with a seal club and said that he would kill him for a mutineer. The captain intervened, but later Matison and Limero each sought out Kenney and Dodge to propose a murderous alliance. The captain ordered a truce but did not know what else he could do.

The next night, Henry Dodge began to mutter in rhyme. The words, as far as the others could tell, were nonsense, but when questioned, Dodge averred that they were a poem in the Latvian tongue. The poem was an epic of that nation, taught to Dodge by a sailor with whom the Negro had once shipped. And as he muttered, the other men grew restless to know the story of the poem. Dodge allowed as he could remember the story only in the Latvian tongue, but he would teach the words and their meaning to the men a few lines at a time, if they were agreeable.

Winter followed on with snows so heavy and deep that betimes there was nothing for the men to do but remain in their pinched shelter, chewing on the roots of Tushook grass and repeating lines of the heroic poem that Dodge taught. Now when disputes broke out, they were mild and about the poem, about how a particular line went. Dodge was a poor teacher as he often remembered a line in complete contradiction to how he had taught it only the day before. The men often remarked that Latvian was a queer tongue and took Dodge to task for his poor recollection of it. But through the winter, the poem grew more intelligible and satisfying to teacher and students alike, and the men took turns reciting it. Spring returned at long last, and a Nantucket whaler one day was seen and signaled with smoke, and the men were saved. Henry Dodge signed articles aboard that ship, and the other men were put ashore at such ports as suited them. None of them ever saw any of the others again.

The captain returned at length to sealing, taking pains to teach the men under his command a most strict obedience in nautical matters, and teaching them also the poem which gave him and many sailors under him a curious comfort in stormy seas. He learned only in his retirement and upon meeting a scholar from the city of Riga that the epic was only the most absolute nonsense in Latvian or any other language, which made the captain cease to teach it, but also to take all the more comfort and amusement in reciting it.

6. Legacy

Starting in her sophomore year, Karen tried three times to register for Dr. Laurel Black's section of EDU 455, Methods of Secondary Instruction. The closest she got was the seventh spot on the waiting list, and that wasn't close at all. The few, the lucky few, who managed to get enrolled in Dr. Black's section were unlikely to drop and make room. So Karen had to take Methods from Dr. Ryerson instead.

Dr. Black's fans—and they were numerous among the education majors—insisted that ending up with Ryerson was just short of disaster. The man wasn't a bad teacher. But in Black's section, students got the skinny on how to thrive as a high school teacher.

"Like what?" Karen asked.

"Philosophy of teaching stuff," said one friend. "Questioning assumptions. Working the class, not the front office. Putting the student first. The real student, not the student you imagine."

Another friend told her, "You get all these great tricks from Black, like 'Don't commit to teaching for more than a year at a time.'"

"That's a great trick?"

"Yeah, because you don't want to get dragged under by things that haven't happened yet. Or won't happen. She says you've got to teach like an athlete. You've got to be ready to return the ball."

"What does that mean?"

"You'd have to take the class. A lot of what she says sounds weird out of context. Besides, she says that we have to process things for ourselves. Teach the student, not the subject."

The closest Karen ever got to Dr. Black was passing her in the hall. She wanted to stop her and say, "Give it to me in a sentence. What do I need to know?" But she didn't. In Ryerson's section, she got some good practice in teaching by lecture, demonstration, dialogue, and group discussion. She did not learn how to be ready to return the ball.

In her first year as a new teacher, Karen went to the principal. She said, "I don't like the memo."

"Which memo is that?"

"This business about submitting lesson plans two weeks in advance is a waste of my time and yours."

He considered her. His frown was a bit like one of her father's frowns. "Miss Garry, you're a first year teacher."

"Exactly. What will do me more good than writing out formal lesson plans is to have you observe my teaching more often. I'd appreciate the feedback."

His eyebrows went up. "I don't have time for extra observations."

"You can use the time that you would have spent reviewing my lesson plans."

"Everyone got the same memo. If you don't submit your lesson plans, I'll have to write a letter for your permanent file."

She thought, *That's okay. I'm only committed to one year of teaching anyway.* She said, "I have to do what's best for my students, and that means using my time well."

During her first term, she was observed once by a senior administrator, once by the principal, and once by a master teacher.

The senior administrator saw her give a demonstration. At the start of the class, she discharged ammonia gas in a beaker of phenolphthalein solution. The solution turned pink. Then she inflated a red toy balloon with ammonia gas and put the balloon in another beaker of the same solution. At first, the solution remained clear. Karen lectured on the states of matter. By the end of the hour, that solution in the second beaker had also turned pink. "We won't get to kinetic theory for two more weeks," she said, "but in the meantime I want you to come up with at least three possible explanations for why this solution turned pink and a method for testing each explanation."

Her written evaluation from the senior administrator noted that two weeks was too long for students to remain in suspense about a demonstration. He noted that a red balloon might serve to confuse some students and said that she should have used, say, a blue one. He also observed that state-wide exams stressed factual knowledge and that demonstrations took up valuable time.

Later, the master teacher observed a session where Karen opened with a dialogue about what happens to sugar in a glass of water, led the students in an experiment at their lab tables, then demonstrated Brownian motion with a beaker of water and a drop of food coloring. Karen closed with another dialogue to confirm what the students had learned. The master teacher offered a few concrete tips, but wrote that Karen "clearly knew what she was doing."

The principal's only written comment was that Miss Garry was not submitting her lesson plans in advance, as required.

Karen took all of this to mean that she was doing as Dr. Black would have advised, teaching the class and not the front office.

Karen corrected the lab books for spelling and grammar. One student complained that the class was chemistry, not English. "Do you think the world divides up the way that school does?" Karen asked him. "Do you think that the annual report of a car company can be badly written just because they aren't in the publishing business?" That didn't mollify him. His mother called Karen at home to complain about the unfair grading.

"All right," Karen announced to her class. "Anyone who brings a note from home excusing you from learning job skills in this class will be graded strictly according to test scores."

Two notes came in. One referred to her as the "teecher." The other was typed, grammatical, and spelled correctly. She honored them both, and supposed that this constituted returning the ball.

No one had ever told Karen that Dr. Black used dynamic equilibrium as a metaphor for the classroom, but Karen thought of it as the sort of thing that Dr. Black would have taught. It fit. Like the chemistry of a living cell, the classroom was always shifting.

Walking was another good metaphor for teaching. A person walking on two legs is never perfectly balanced. The body is making constant adjustments. It's not balance that keeps us on our feet, but constant motion.

In Karen's second year, a student that she'd taught in the fall committed suicide late in the spring. He shot himself in the head on a Saturday night. Monday morning, the first period class wanted something that Karen wasn't trained to give them. So she gave them what she had. She invited them to talk about the boy who had shot himself. They asked questions she couldn't answer.

Near the end of the hour, she went to the blackboard and wrote:

$$\mathrm{KNO_3} \quad \mathrm{C} \quad \mathrm{S}$$

"Gunpowder," she said. She explained that potassium nitrate's role was to provide oxygen for rapid combustion of the carbon and sulfur. Gunpowder didn't need air to burn. In a confined space, combustion would result in a very fast build up of pressure.

One girl said, "Why are you telling us this?"

"I don't know," Karen said. "It's the place where what happened touches on chemistry. And also, I think, because sometimes the best way to think through something that weighs on you is to really look at it, to see it from every angle."

Later, she wasn't sure if it had been the right thing to do. But it was what she had done. She had kept moving.

After that, she did her best to notice the students more, to really see each one every day. *I like the new haircut. What's the T-shirt logo? Is that a band? Pink really is your color.* It made a difference, she thought, though she couldn't be sure of exactly what the difference was. And two years later, there was another suicide. Like the first one, he was a boy who had been in her class before, but was not a current student.

She dreamed about this boy. She dreamed that she opened her front door, and there he was, soaking wet, standing in the rain. He said, "It's okay." She tried to speak. She couldn't. She could barely breathe. He said, "It's not okay, is it? It's not okay." She woke from the dream struggling for breath. At the end of the term, she committed herself to teaching for just one more year.

Because she committed herself to just one year at a time, she always knew how many years she had been teaching. In her eleventh year, one of her students would come to her morning class with alcohol on his breath or his pupils dilated. She told him he had a problem and that he should talk to her when he was ready to get treatment. Soon after that, he disappeared from school for three weeks, then called her at home. "I've screwed up everything," he said. "I don't know what to do." When she called his mother, the woman was drunk. Hell, no, her son didn't need rehab. He needed a kick in the ass now and then, but he was *fine*, and fuck you, anyway.

Karen drove the boy to a treatment center and got him admitted. Days later, she was in the principal's office answering the mother's charge that Karen was having sex with her son. "I don't care how necessary it was for you to drive him," the principal said. "You should have been smart enough to have someone else along. I don't believe her, but you've opened us up to a nuisance suit. You've got to think these things through!"

The boy wrote her a long grateful letter. She saved it. For one thing, she might need it for evidence in case the mother sobered up and still wanted to sue.

She won no awards for her teaching. Some students adored her. Some didn't. Every year, she decided again that teaching was important and that she wasn't bad at it, so committed herself to another two semesters.

In the midst of her twentieth year, one of her college classmates phoned her. "Have you heard that Laurel Black died? You were one of her students, weren't you?"

Karen was not technically entitled to a bereavement leave to attend the funeral of a favorite college professor, but the new principal was younger than she was. She persuaded him.

Dr. Black had retired to her childhood hometown in Iowa. Karen rented a car at the Des Moines airport and drove for two hours along fields of stubble. Trees had lost their leaves. The sky was gray.

At the funeral home, she met Dr. Black's daughter, Elizabeth, who told Karen what a great, encouraging mother Laurel had been. Karen told Elizabeth that Dr. Black had been a superb teacher as well. For the first two hours, Karen was the only visitor who was not family.

In death, Dr. Black looked smaller than Karen remembered her.

At the memorial service the next day, the minister recounted Laurel Black's great contributions to generation after generation of student teachers. There weren't many of those former students in attendance. The chapel was small, and half of the pews were empty. The minister invited friends and family to stand and offer remembrances.

Karen stood. She said, "There may be days where I don't think of Dr. Black in my classroom. But there aren't weeks. She shaped what I do. I hope I'm a good teacher. I think I am. That after twenty years I still care whether or not I'm good at what I do, that's something I owe to Dr. Black."

Afterwards, there was a reception where Karen offered her sympathies to the family. A man Karen's age approached and said, "I had her for Methods."

"You're a teacher?"

"Was. I got out after six years. But what she taught me touched on everything else I've done. Thank you for saying what you said. You spoke for a lot of us."

"I never got to thank her."

"When were you her student?"

Karen said, "I've never stopped being her student."

7. CURRICULUM VITAE

It was, from some perspectives, a brilliant career. When Lance Reed first joined the humanities faculty, the theater program was like the theater program at any other tiny, struggling liberal arts college. Each year they staged two productions with cheap costumes, unimaginative acting, and uninspired direction. A year after Reed had been teaching, the students were acting convincingly in four plays a year on well-designed inexpensive sets. Where before the audiences had always consisted of students, parents, and a few idealistic faculty, now word began to spread in town that the college's productions might be worth seeing.

Reed brought a kind of energy that his mid-western students had never encountered before. He talked about their bodies as their *instruments*. As he coached them in breath, posture, familiarity with the muscles of their bodies, he would touch them, men and women alike. He would stand close to shape and arrange them with his hands. "Breathe in so that your belly pushes against my palm. Yes, like that! Now tighten your buns. Good."

The first student he slept with was the young woman playing the title role in *Hedda Gabler*. Teresa kept the affair secret, but suffered for living two lives. Suffering, Reed told his students, was good for any actor, but especially young ones who had little experience with it. "Boleslavsky said that acting is the soul receiving its birth through art. Birth is painful. It is a struggle!"

Teresa's soul was born on that stage as she played Hedda. "Now I am burning your child, Thea! Burning it! Curly locks." Lance had all the power in their relationship. Teresa knew a lot about Hedda Gabler. The affair didn't last, but Teresa was the first of Reed's students to go on to a successful stage career.

Reed's romance with Alice added little to the staging of *Oedipus Rex*. The production was done in masks and relied on technique rather than method acting. That was Reed's downfall; he was attracted to Alice, who played Jocasta, without ever having seen her act from her own core. But the time he discovered how little she had to draw from, she was pregnant. He married her knowing that such a marriage was doomed. But he lived what he taught: that the artist suffers.

The Dean of Faculty was appalled by the marriage, but by then Reed was attracting serious grant money to the school, along with students who came specifically to study with him. Reed was warned, and then tenured.

A few years later, the junior who played Helena in *Uncle Vanya* was indiscrete. Jordan pledged her best friend to absolute secrecy, then told her about liaisons with Reed. In a week, almost everyone in the production knew. A freshman who disapproved of adultery on principle thus kept a prim, tight lid on her performance as Sonia. In the title role was a young man who had a crush on Jordan, and his speeches to Helen sometimes veered close to things he really did feel for the actress. Serebrakoff was played by a student who somehow missed the rumors, but who detected and responded to the tensions in the rest of the cast. In short, the entire ensemble was perfectly motivated. A reviewer came all the way from Minneapolis to see and write about the production.

In her senior year, Jordan played Lady Macbeth, Roxane, Katharina, and Sadie Thompson. All of these productions were emotionally charged for reasons that the audiences and the administration did not suspect. The acting and directing were consistently superb. Jordan graduated in the spring, Reed divorced his first wife in the summer, and the professor married his star pupil the following winter. Three of the students who had played opposite Jordan had some degree of success off-Broadway, and one launched a modestly successful career in Hollywood.

Jordan Reed quit acting. She bore Lance two children, kept house, and did what she could to protect his reputation with the other faculty. It wasn't easy. For one thing, most faculty continued for many years to treat her like a student. For another, her husband continued to have sex with his pupils. Sometimes he was careful, though he wasn't as effective as a teacher or director then. Intrigues and jealousies were part of what made his stage spectacular.

The year that *Hamlet* closed out the academic year, Reed was coupling with the actress who played Gertrude, sometimes in her car and sometimes behind the locked door of the prop room where her dramatic, rhythmic outcries left no doubt as to what was happening. That *Hamlet* was, according to one reviewer, better than one that had been staged the previous summer at the state university using professional actors.

The next fall found a black-haired, dark-eyed junior playing both the roles of Lady Macbeth and Reed's dark, Scorpionic lover. She liked asking him to do things to her that both excited and shamed him, and his intensity as a teacher was that year at its peak. She went on to a successful Hollywood career, though Reed often said that she'd have found her way there as easily without him. She was made for Hollywood.

He was still brilliant for a good many years after that. The college was named among the top ten undergraduate acting schools in an issue of *Stagecraft*. The alumni pledged funds for a theater building. More students made their way to New York, Los Angeles, or regional theaters.

Professor Reed's decline was gradual. His hair grayed and thinned. Though he worked to keep himself trim and limber, no man can escape the wrinkles or the loss of muscle tone that change him, in the eyes of young women, from a dangerous and exciting father figure to a pathetic, horny old man. Even if his appeal had not waned, his sexual appetite diminished year by year. His own children grew up and became parents. Eventually, he could not look at his students without thinking of his grandchildren.

His teaching became rote, routine. "Breathe in so that your belly pushes against my palm." He could give instruction he always gave, but he wasn't igniting his own passions. He wasn't making his students burn with deep emotion. Jordan had stayed with him, knowing everything, and his life at home with her became more important as his teaching became less so.

He retired early. The administration named an endowed chair after him. They were pleased to have the benefit of his reputation without the risk of, well, his reputation.

The college hired two younger professors to replace him, a woman and a man. Both came with excellent credentials as actors and teachers. The theater program continued to have the college's full support. Theater Arts was, after all, the shining star for a college that had never had much to offer beyond being small and local.

Professor Reed developed emphysema. He and his wife moved to Arizona for the sun and the air. Ten years after that, students at the college proposed a symposium in his honor.

Holding hands, Mr. and Mrs. Lance Reed sat in the darkened theater for a production of *Uncle Vanya*. The woman playing Helena could act, she could really act. More than that, she was breathtakingly beautiful. When she said to Astroff that line that could be such a disaster, "I am angry at you yet I will always remember you with pleasure," she made it true, complex, heartbreaking. *Marvelous*, Lance thought, squeezing his wife's hand. *Marvelous girl. Marvelous teacher!*

8. LITTLE MONSTERS

In the classroom, she was the grownup, the person who was supposed to have the authority, but when she told the children what to do, they often ignored her. And what could she do? She couldn't hit them. It wasn't allowed. But if she sent them to the principal's office they would come back an hour later with smug smiles.

She asked the principal about his notions of discipline, but he would say only, "Send them to me." But she wanted to know, were the children actually punished? "Send them to me." Whatever he was doing, she told him, it didn't seem to change their behavior in the classroom. "Send them to me."

That wasn't the worst of it. The worst thing was that she couldn't quit, couldn't afford to go somewhere else. She was stuck in the middle of these wheat fields, stuck in this little town that all summer baked under a cloudless sky and all winter stiffened under a glaze of ice. After school sometimes she would get in her little car and drive toward the horizon. Not far. She'd have to go such a long way for the scenery to change. A long, long way.

The kind of words she was supposed to use on the children were of no use. "Bobby, we use our indoor voices in the classroom." He'd be shrieking again in a minute, baring his teeth if he weren't getting his way. "Jessica, what have I told you about pulling hair? Stop, do you hear me?" The girl would look at her with half-closed eyes and give a slight nod. Yes, Jessica had heard, not that hearing made a bit of difference.

So the teacher gave up on the kinds of words she was supposed to use. She couldn't call the children by the first names that occurred to her, the words that children weren't supposed to know, but she thought of other things to call them. Things that struck her as funny. She thought of things to say, things the children would pay attention to. The children were as loud and unruly as ever, but she could now and then distract them with the things she told them.

The principal called her into his office. He said, "Have you really called the children in your classroom 'hatchlings'?" She admitted that she had. "And you've told them that their mommies and daddies are not real mommies and daddies?" That's what she had told them. "Why would you say such things?" Because nothing else worked. Because they really were little monsters. Because she needed to get their attention, capture their imaginations somehow. "They're children," the principal said. She told him that she was desperate. "They're children." How could she keep this up, working every day with such creatures? "They're children."

Later, she drove away from town about as far as she ever drove. She got out of her car and stood in the hot sun. If she could just keep going, there was another life out there for her. Except there wasn't, because she never did just keep going.

Back in the classroom, she didn't change what she told the children. She elaborated on it. She told them that her job was to teach them to pass for human so that when they grew up and moved to the real world, no one would be able to tell that they were monsters, little flesh-eating monsters. All the mommies and the daddies, the teacher, the principal, all the grownups in town were real people brainwashed into acting like mommies and daddies and teacher and principal. But the children weren't people at all.

The children liked this story.

The principal asked to see her again. "You have to stop this," he said, "or else measures will be taken." She wanted to know what kind of measures. "Measures will be taken." She dared him to fire her. Go ahead and try to find someone else who will teach these miserable creatures. "Measures will be taken," he said.

She got in her car and drove again, farther this time. She climbed the bumper, scrambled onto the hood and then the roof of the car. She looked toward the horizon to see if she could make out imperfections, places where the sky met the ground with the artificial perspective of a diorama painting. She didn't see any. She kept looking for a long time anyway, trying to make up her mind about which reality would be worse.

9. MR. TOTT

Biology One is being team taught this year. One teacher is Ms. Amante. The other is Mr. Tott. Mr. Tott's skin is thin and tight against his skull. His eyes are sunken. His suit coat droops and folds from his thin frame, as if there had once been more of him. When he pauses in a lesson, his breathing whistles in his chest.

For the unit on metabolism, Mr. Tott tells the class that fermentation sets its own limit on the life of yeast. Alcohol is poison. When Lord Nelson died at Trafalgar, his body was taken back to England in a barrel of rum. Mr. Tott wheezes and laughs at his own story.

Everything is food for something else. For every act of living, something else had to die if for no other reason than to get out of the way.

The classroom air is sterile, dry as a tomb on the days when it's Mr. Tott's turn to teach. His chalk strikes the blackboard with sharp taps, as if he were driving nails.

For the unit on cell division, Mr. Tott explains that there *are* immortal cells. How many students would like their cells to live forever? When some hands are raised, Mr. Tott tells the story of Henrietta Lack. She died in 1951, but her cancer cells have stayed young and healthy, thriving in the lab, even infecting other cell cultures. Yes, she's dead, but there are more living cells of Henrietta Lack today than there are of any other person in the world. He wheezes and laughs at that story, too.

It's all funny to Mr. Tott: predation, infestation, infection. He seems particularly fond of parasites. There is a worm that infests a kind of snail. The larval worms migrate into the snail's antennae, turn colors, and wriggle. The pain-maddened snail climbs to the top of a stalk of grass where it waves in the breeze and the wriggling larvae in its flesh imitate a delicious caterpillar no bird can resist. When a bird eats the snail, the larvae continue to develop inside the bird, their second host. Sometimes when he laughs, Mr. Tott coughs and can't stop.

The prettiest little octopus is the one with deadly venom. A black mamba kills with neurotoxins while the victim, wide awake, can feel it happen, can wait for the next breath that he can't quite get his lungs to breathe. Pit viper venom digests as it kills with an efficiency that Mr. Tott calls elegant.

Evolution needs death, says Mr. Tott, every bit as much as it needs sex. What's it to be? Youthful trauma? Greedy cancers? A heart that starves? Stroke? Or the tiny, progressive breakdowns of cells that just get tired of dividing? He says that humans like to pretend that biology somehow doesn't apply to them.

In a whisper that everyone can hear, Mr. Tott explains his trinity: apoptosis, oncosis, and necrosis. He's just getting started, but the students have heard enough, enough, *enough*.

10. STORIES

It's the end of your last day as a teacher. You have closed your office door and returned to your chair. Jerry Lavin, a junior, sits on the other side of your desk, alternately holding his breath to keep from sobbing, and sobbing anyway. His face is red and wet. On the last day of school, it's too warm for his letter jacket, but he has worn it anyway, as if being the star defensive back could protect him from the mess he has gotten himself into. Rosie Horne is pregnant, and Jerry tells you he has to do the right thing.

Has to. That tells you something. That hints at some possible outcomes.

You teach social studies—history—but you're also the teacher they come to with their stories, with what they think of as their happy or unhappy endings.

Jerry's a good kid. You taught his dad. You could tell Jerry a story or two about his old man, if you wanted.

For Rosie, marrying Jerry will be a step up for her. Did she know that? Calculate it?

What happens next?

There is so much that you won't miss about teaching. But these kids...which ones end up in college, dead, in jail, or working at the grocery? Now you're retiring, and you'll lose the thread of their stories. That's the thing that makes you take a deep breath, let it out.

Jerry Lavin takes a deep breath, too. He says thank you, thank you for listening.

11. SPANISH LESSON

When I put the daisies on the window sill, my father said from his bed, "Aren't the flowers supposed to come after I'm gone?" There were already two bouquets on the dresser, another on the bed table.

"Better to get them while you're here to smell them," I said.

"Can't smell anything but plastic." He motioned toward the oxygen tube under his nose. Then he said, "Teach me Spanish."

I thought, *Why?* but said, "What do you want to learn?"

"Everything."

The doctor had said, *It's a matter of weeks or days, not months.*

"Okay." I taught him the difference between the permanent *ser* and the temporary *estar*.

Yo soy. Yo estoy.

The next day, I brought him the text that I used at school. We talked adjectives.

The day after that, the nurses told me that when he wasn't sleeping, he was sounding out words in the book.

"It's backwards," he declared. "*Me lo dió.* Why isn't it *Dió lo me*?"

"Because it's Spanish."

"And who decides what's feminine, what's masculine? *La flor*, okay. But *la guerra*? War is feminine?"

"*Guer-r-r-r-a*," I said. "Trill the double r." He tried.

Three days later, I watched him sleep. He woke up, squinted. I wasn't sure, as his gaze wandered, if he knew who I was. He cleared his throat. "*Estoy rodeado por flores.*"

"*De flores*," I corrected. "*Sí, papí. Estás rodeado de flores.* Flowers all around."

"I speak Spanish!"

We laughed. And that was it, the last laugh we had together.

In memory of Damon Knight

www.ingramcontent.com/pod-product-compliance
Lightning Source LLC
Chambersburg PA
CBHW050517260626
47157CB00004B/1366